Al Arabian Novel Factory

Al Arabian Novel Factory

Benyamin

Translated by Shahnaz Habib

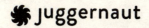

JUGGERNAUT BOOKS

KS House, 118 Shahpur Jat, New Delhi 110049, India

First published in Malayalam as *Al Arabian Novel Factory*
by DC Books in 2014
First published by Juggernaut Books 2019

10 9 8 7 6 5 4 3 2 1

P-ISBN: 978-93-5345-066-3
E-ISBN: 978-93-5345-068-7

Typeset in Adobe Caslon Pro by R. Ajith Kumar, Noida

Printed and bound at Thomson Press India Ltd

Contents

Preface

This is the story of an Arab city. It does not represent a particular city or a particular people. I have merged together many histories, characters, incidents and places to create a city that has no name. Everything in this story is real and fictional. You may find some similarities here – think of them as universalities rather than resemblances. This story is not intended to hurt anyone. It is a humble attempt to open a window into contemporary Arab life.

'Modern man likes to pretend that his thinking is wide-awake. But this wide-awake thinking has led us into the mazes of a nightmare in which the torture chambers are endlessly repeated in the mirrors of reason. When we emerge, perhaps we will realize that we have been dreaming with our eyes open, and that the dreams of reason are intolerable. And then, perhaps we will begin to dream once more, with our eyes closed.'

Octavio Paz, *The Labyrinth of Solitude and Other Writings*

Part One

Bab Al Madinah

Sunday in Toronto

Walk aimlessly or get naked. These are the best ways to communicate with your inner genius. And if both happen simultaneously, then you get twice the effect. As far as our chief editor James Hogan was concerned, this was an article of faith. And, of course, articles of faith do not exist for us to simply put our faith in them. James Hogan believed in living them.

Every day at six-thirty, he would leave the office and walk for half an hour to reach the two-room flat he had lived in for twenty-two years. After showering, he would watch television for an hour. Then he would pour 30 ml – and 30 ml meant 30 ml, not a drop more or less – of alcohol into a glass, top it off with three cubes of ice and enter his writing room. It was time to put his article of faith into practice. In his writing room, James Hogan would strip naked and start walking. And not just any old walking. It was a mad, frenzied walk, during which he would think of ideas for the next issue. Occasionally, he would pause in front of the mirror to consider his naked form, then get back to walking.

Were it not for social norms he would have walked naked in our office as well, he often told us. 'Try it out sometime when you have a big problem to solve, you will definitely find a solution,' he advised us.

During these naked marches, he often came up with some scoop idea or a controversial angle for an interview or debate. Any of the junior editors on staff could expect a call from him then. It was an unwritten rule that as long as the world had not ended, our phones should be switched on and ready to take his call between the hours of eight and ten every evening. James Hogan would call to talk about an idea that needed following up the next day. Or, if the topic was important enough, he would invite the editor to his flat right away. If an idea was not shared in the heat of its conception, James Hogan told us, it would lose its intensity.

James Hogan was single. There were no girlfriends or boyfriends in the picture either. No children, adopted or otherwise. He had zero social life and he did not visit clubs or pubs. Golf, tennis, chess – he did not play any of these. Not even card games. It was doubtful he thought of anything other than what to publish in his magazine. 'My brain space is completely dedicated to news. Like a genie trapped inside a bottle, I am trapped inside the vortex of news. Ideas. Scoops. Stories. My mind is always thirsting for them. I want to make our magazine one of the best in the world – I think about nothing else and I will go to any length for that.' This was Hogan's self-diagnosis. And perhaps this is why, under his editorship, the graph of the magazine's growth was shooting up like a rocket.

Often his calls came at that time when one had left behind the cares of work and was relaxing at home. But, of course, we were happy to abandon the evening and go running to his flat. We knew that Hogan would be waiting for us with a horizon of possibilities. If we missed the opportunity, the loss was not his, it was ours. There were many who had ascended the ladder of fame by using an idea of his. His ideas had sent many a reporter on a dizzying flight of achievement. To be assigned an idea by James Hogan was akin, within our magazine, to being offered the Pulitzer.

I received a call like that from him the other day. For a long time, I had been spared his calls because a new crop of reporters, their heads teeming with journalistic ambitions, had joined the magazine. They were ready to leap in whenever there was a new scoop. But this was something different. He wanted none but me. It was with barely contained excitement that I went to his flat.

He greeted me in his front room with a towel around his waist.

'How many children do you have?' he asked without any context.

'Two,' I replied, a little surprised.

'How many wives? How many mistresses? How many girlfriends?' came the next questions.

'Three multiplied by one equals one,' I replied in the same vein.

'What other family do you have in Toronto?'

'Very few.'

'How long can you stay away from all these people and live on your own?'

I had no idea where he was going with this. 'Only a very short time,' I replied after a pause.

'I am going to conduct an experiment on you,' he said dramatically.

'What do you mean by "experiment"?'

'You are going to leave your wife and children and friends and travel to a faraway place. Ready?'

'I don't think so,' I replied.

'You are the only person in our organization I can trust with this job. I have been thinking about this for a few days. Do you know something amazing, Pratap? There are almost two million people from your country living abroad. I don't think any other people from any other country could do this. Surely your genes must contain your people's survival skills. That's why I went over every face in our organization and finally decided on you.' Hogan took a sip of his drink.

'James, I have no idea what you are getting at. Can you please come to the point?' I said sharply.

Only once in my life had I addressed James as 'sir'. That was on the day I had joined, and on that same day, he forbade it forever. 'When one person calls another "sir", they turn into servant and master. A servant does not have a mind of his own. And without a strong, independent mind, how will he or she come up with new ideas? I don't need servants here. You can call me by my name.' Since then I have always called him James.

'We have been offered an amazing opportunity to break

new ground and do the kind of work we have never done before. An internationally acclaimed writer has picked us to do the research for his next book. As you may know, every bestselling novelist in the world works with a team. This team helps the novelist study the topic. They research the history and geography and sociology of whatever he or she wants to write about. They gather the maps and documents and old newspaper cuttings. Gone are the days when a writer sat in a closed room and imagined his or her way into a novel over the course of decades. Every novel published today is a factory product. There might be a famous name in bold on the cover of the book, but in truth, several people have worked hard to produce it. Even your own Mahabharata was written "not by one Vyasa, but many Vyasas". Now this novelist wants to outsource some of the research for his next novel because his own team is busy. It's a million-dollar offer that fell into my lap at the Frankfurt Book Fair, thanks to an agent. I cannot bear to lose it. Now tell me, will you do it?'

'Who is this novelist?' I was dying to know.

'I don't know. The agent will not reveal the name. But some day we'll know when his or her book is published.'

'And what's the topic?'

'Contemporary life in the Middle East. I know a thousand writers have written about this. And now the thousand and oneth person is going to write it again. Let him write it. That's none of our business. You are going to travel through seventeen countries, from Egypt to Iran. You are going to record what you see and experience. You are going to interview ordinary people, wealthy people, politicians. You are going to send all this information back to the writer. You have three years to do all this.'

'Yeah, right, what a great idea. Seventeen countries where terrorism is dancing a victory dance. And I on my own. James, what made you think this was a good idea? You might as well have sent me to some war zone as an embedded reporter,' I said angrily.

'You won't be alone. I am going to recruit two assistants for you. And someone from the novelist's study team will be guiding you in the beginning. You won't need to spend more than two months in each country. It will be a new experience, why not try it?'

'I need to think about this. It is difficult to decide so quickly.'

'Take two or three days to think it over. But your answer should be yes. I have already recommended you to the management as the right person for this job.'

'I am going to ignore that. There's a ninety per cent chance that my answer will be no,' I said.

'See, Pratap, all they are asking for, to begin with, is a sample study. If they like it, they will give us the contract. If not, their own team will do the job. So many people had their eye on this job, but I snatched it for us. This is now a matter of my reputation. You can choose whichever city you like for the sample study.'

'Whichever city I like?' I asked. Suddenly, a new hope sneaked its way into my heart.

'Yes. You get to choose the first country.' James Hogan took another sip of his drink.

'I will go then,' I said.

'I am not forcing this on you. Go home and talk to your family. I want you to come back and say yes to me after thinking over this fully. That's the kind of yes I like.'

'I don't need to think any more. I will go,' I said again. James looked wonderingly at me. I had changed my mind as swiftly as the backdrop in a play. He patted me on the back as I left, still looking surprised.

We all have our reasons for the places we choose to go to. I, too, had my reasons for wanting to visit this ancient port city.

Checkpost

As soon as I accepted James Hogan's offer, I searched my memory for the names of friends who lived in that city. Bijumon, who was my classmate at Mar Thoma School. My roommate at Delhi University, a Hyderabadi we called 5S Varma (Shri Satya Sai Sundara Sridhara Varma). Another Delhi classmate Daisy John. Shahjahan who used to work at the American embassy in those days – I used to regularly run into him at the three-legged bench in Chennai Manikyam's tea shop. I could count more than a dozen acquaintances and friends who had ended up in that city. But I didn't write to any of them about my arrival. I decided I would first get there, settle in and then contact them one by one. But two days before I left, I could not resist messaging Bijumon on Facebook. 'No one must know. I am coming to the city of harbours.' After all, in case there was some emergency, it was good to have at least one confirmed friend in the City. Bijumon called me that very night. We were talking to each other after many years. After high school, he joined a technical school, and not much later, migrated to the City, whereas I moved to Delhi University with my Delhi dreams. I became a journalist there and spent some time at *Indian Express* as a subeditor. Then I got married and moved to Canada with my wife Shanti, a dentist. Since the third month of my arrival in Canada, I have been with James Hogan at *Toronto Sunday*. In all this time, I have not spoken to Biju or seen him. Our vacations in Kerala have never coincided. Yet, our conversation was full of his delight at my visit. During my life in Canada, I had begun to forget how intense a friendship can be. Toronto is a city of formalities. Over the last ten years, I had learned that even family relationships could devolve into mere bureaucracy. Biju's call reminded me that the breezy balminess of a good friendship is still alive in a few places on earth. He insisted on coming to the airport to meet me. I said no. We had already appointed a local project administrator, Abdullah Janahi, who had offered to pick me up at the airport. Why bother Biju unnecessarily? He hung up only after I agreed to have lunch at his place on my first day in the City.

I am an acrophobiac. Even after all these years of flying, whenever the plane rises into the sky, a chill snakes up my spine. I have always avoided flying alone. I simply don't fly anywhere unless accompanied by my wife or friends or co-workers. Yet, coming here, for the first time in my life I flew all by myself. My longing to get to the City had turned into a fever by now.

From Toronto to New York City, I flew with American Airlines. My flight arrived on time. But in New York, there was a three-hour delay for the Turkish Airlines flight to Istanbul. By the time I arrived in Istanbul, I had missed the connecting flight to the City. There was a long wait for the next connection. All in all, by the time I arrived, it had been thirty hours since I left Toronto.

I knew there was no point in looking for Abdullah Janahi at the airport. Couldn't reach him by phone either. But, as my father would say, as long as you have a tongue in your mouth and an address in mind, you can get to any corner of the world. I got into a taxi and showed the driver my new address.

'That's just twenty minutes away. Get in,' said the driver.

As he hauled my luggage into the trunk, he reminded me, in perfect English, that the fare would be twice what it showed on the meter. On the window of the taxi though, there was a sticker saying, 'Insist on the meter. No meter = your trip is free. It is the law.'

'So what is this then?' I pointed to the sticker. He laughed mockingly.

'That's old stuff. If you want to ride my taxi right now, you will have to pay double the fare. I am making it clear now, so don't argue when we get there.' His voice was harsh.

I was silent for a minute.

'Decide quickly. If you don't want to pay, take your luggage out. I have other things to do.' By now he was positively rude.

I made one last attempt to argue with him. But he wouldn't yield an inch. Only after I agreed to pay double the fare did he condescend to put the car into gear.

At the exit gate of the airport, there was a giant billboard: 'Welcome. City of Joy!'

There was less traffic on the road than I expected. I noticed several concrete barricades and checkposts along the way, all intended to slow down vehicles. Like crocodiles sunning themselves on the shore, police cars were parked along the sidewalks, their blue lights flashing. The walls were stained and dirty; they looked as if they had been scrawled over with graffiti, painted over, scrawled over again, painted over again. Broken flagpoles, ragged banners, torn-down photos and ruined vehicles. There were tankers and armoured cars at the signals and masked soldiers sat atop them. Near them were more billboards like the one I had seen at the airport.

'So is it true there were attacks against tourists in the City recently?' I asked the taxi driver, without any preface.

'Who said that? It is true that we had some problems here recently. Let me assure you though, not one foreigner was harmed. This is a very safe city for tourists. You will lack nothing here.' He eyed me through the rear-view mirror.

After a bit, the car slowed down to a crawl. There was a long line of cars ahead of us at a checkpost. Soldiers were examining each car. They opened doors and trunks and pulled out people from some cars. Since we had stopped right at a curve, I could see what was happening ahead of us very well once I put my head out of the window. One car had strayed out of the line behind us and somehow elbowed its way through the traffic. A soldier yelled at its driver and made him return all the way to the back of the line.

The car in front of us was ancient. The soldier gestured at the young man driving to lower the window and peered inside. Then he asked the man to step out. The man parked the car to one side and came out. The soldier took the man's phone and started looking through it. He pointed at something and started asking questions. The man's response and the soldier thrashing him with his gun – both happened at the same time. Honestly, I think I may have felt that beating even more than he did. All the way up from my calf to my thigh, I felt the sudden sting. 'Ayyo!' I screamed in pain. My driver shushed me. The man had fallen to his knees. The soldier thrashed him two more times before asking him to stand up. The man struggled to his feet. The soldier gave him his phone. As the man started to walk away with it, the soldier stopped him and ordered him to throw the phone on the road. The man hesitated but when the soldier threatened him again, he did it. He threw his phone on the road and watched it shatter into pieces. As he turned to leave, the soldier called him back and made some new demand. The man held up his hand and started singing something loudly. I think it was the national anthem. He was made to sing three or four times before he was allowed to leave. All this while, the rest of the vehicles in the line idled patiently. We were next. My heart fluttered. What kind of questions would the soldier have in store for us? But he merely peered in. The driver said something and the soldier waved us on. There was no examination to pass. And so after that long wait, our car was finally off. Though he tried not to, the driver could not avoid driving over the ruined phone on the road.

I had seen enough to understand the situation in the City. I realized there would be no need to hunt down experiences here, as James Hogan had tasked me with. They would come in search of me.

Biju Ambalamuttam

The taxi took me to an apartment community in one of the poshest neighbourhoods in the City. With supreme indifference and without taking his eyes off of a Tom and Jerry cartoon show on his television, the security guard confirmed that an apartment had been booked for me but the keys were with Abdullah Janahi. I tried his number again but no one picked up. The least he could have done on the day I was arriving was to pick up the phone, I thought to myself. So this was the kind of irresponsibility I would have to live with during my time here.

I called Bijumon. 'Where are you?' he asked.

'Basma Residence. Opposite Ramy International Hotel. Port Road.'

'Be there in ten minutes,' he replied. I was waiting for him at the reception when someone came rushing in. It was none other than Abdullah Janahi. He had gone to the mosque for Friday prayers and that is why his phone was switched off. After seeing my missed calls he had rushed to the airport, and then having missed me there, he had come here as fast as he could, he told me as he apologized. Bijumon arrived just as we were bringing the luggage in, and he gladly joined us.

My new home was a beautiful, spacious flat on the seventh floor of a recently built twelve-storey apartment building, complete with a swimming pool, gym, health club, massage centre and a balcony facing the waterfront. The port was not far and from the balcony we could see the ships harboured there, the huge cranes rising from the shore, and the seagulls that spotted the blue sky like black kites.

'Why don't you rest now? We can talk in detail tomorrow,' Abdullah said, giving me a SIM card and some dinars before leaving. 'Call me if you need anything at all.' I revised my opinion of his sense of responsibility.

I was feeling jet-lagged but I freshened up and went out with Biju. I had promised to have lunch with him. He had a brand-new Mitsubishi Pajero. It had been twenty years since he had arrived in the City, and it had transformed him. He had moved here after his marriage to a nurse and had spent the first couple of years working as an electrician in a small company. Then, with a local as a sponsor, he started his own company. It was doing very well now, with more than a hundred employees. But what surprised me was not any of this – it was that he had become a writer and a cultural worker. The Malayali Samajam had elected him as the secretary no less than three times. Under the pseudonym Biju Ambalamuttam, he had published a collection of poetry (*The Coconut Trees of Chingavanam*) and an anthology of short stories (*When the Butterfly Chased the Elephant*). He had been awarded the Young Kerala Literary Prize and the International Malayali

Fraternity Award for Poetry. Now he had his eye on the Sahitya Akademi Award. Whenever politicians or writers visited the City from Kerala, he hosted them. All the way to his house, he talked non-stop about Malayalam literature and its new generation of writers and its latest literary movements.

This was the same Bijumon who had never, not even because he had lost his way, stepped into a library during his student days. He had never fallen in step with a political procession, not even by accident. His name had never appeared on the sign-up sheet of any cultural organization. Yet here he was, not just a writer, but a leading light of the literary culture. I felt a bit ashamed of myself. I, who had crawled over every inch of our local library, had not read a book in five years. The place you live in will remake you in its own image. I felt curious about this city that had remoulded Biju so magnificently. It would be interesting for me and my project to meet his friends and acquaintances in the City.

Biju's wife Liji had cooked a feast: boiled kappa, fried beef, chammanthi, moru and fried kozhuva. I briefly remembered the salt biscuits and tea that we served our guests at my house in Canada. In all these years, we had not even bothered to change the brand of the biscuits.

'When we didn't hear from you yesterday, I wondered if you were pulling a prank on us,' Liji said. I told her the tragic tale of my travels.

'The food is on the table. Please help yourself. I have to rush to catch the afternoon shift,' Liji said on her way out to the hospital. We opened a bottle of Jack Daniel and started playing the 'Do You Remember' game. For hours we were immersed in nostalgia. And then Biju asked, 'Do you know where she is . . . your old friend?'

Did he know? I couldn't help wonder. I shook my head as if I had absolutely no idea.

'I saw her once in Kerala at someone's funeral. But we couldn't talk. What was her name again?'

'Jasmine,' I uttered the name and turned into an adolescent again.

I had told Biju all about James Hogan and his crazy ideas to wake up one's genius. But I didn't tell Biju that Jasmine was the reason I had decided on this city, without a second thought, when James asked me to pick a place, any place.

The City

Abdullah came early the next morning and offered to take me to see a few prospective office spaces. I told him that it would be better to wait till the rest of the team arrived. Then they could have a say in it as well.

'What kind of business do you want to start?' he asked. That's when I realized he had no idea why we were in the City. As per the instructions I had been given, I told him that we were there to conduct a market study of the banking sector.

Until recently the City was a Switzerland for the nouveau riche. It was impossible to count the piles of money that had gathered in the banks here. 'It's very different now. You will see for yourself. After all, that's why you are here,' Abdullah Janahi said, half passive, half sad.

Before embarking on this journey, I had briefly chatted with the writer who had hired us. Hiding behind the profile name 'SoulofStories', he/she gave me a few instructions. We should seek 'real life' and not history. Speak to lots of ordinary people. Don't tell anyone about the novel. At the end of our conversation, SoulofStories asked me, 'So why did you pick this city?'

I wanted to reply with one word. Jasmine. Instead I said that even though the City was a conflict zone, it had been named the City of Joy. I wanted to know why. I think SoulofStories was satisfied by my answer. There were no more questions.

The first thing I did that day was rent a car with some help from Abdullah. Figuring out a way to move around freely is the first freedom to aim for in a new place. At the car rental agency, I was surprised to see many Malayalis. At the apartment building, too, the receptionist, the cleaning staff, the watchman, the pool operator – they were all Malayalis. The department stores I had visited yesterday with Bijumon were also full of Malayalis. And now a Malayali called Reji was in front of me at the car rental agency. Bijumon had mentioned that there were three lakh Malayalis in the City.

Reji was pushing me towards the big cars. The rental fees were half of what they used to be and the cars came equipped with a GPS, he pointed out, making the City much more navigable. But I didn't want to sit behind a wheel doing what a machine ordered me to do. I wanted the streets of the City for myself. I wanted to get lost. I wanted to go down the wrong street and return and wonder where to go next. That's travelling. I don't like streets with all the right answers. After all, I have been a student in James Hogan's classroom. Surely, I am obliged to be a little eccentric myself. I finally rented a cheap car of Japanese make.

It was time to turn to the task of getting to know the City and its people. Why not start now?

'So how is business?' I asked Reji.

'Very bad. No one comes here any more. You should have seen the old days. Tourists everywhere! In a single weekend, I would rent two–three hundred cars.' Reji's voice betrayed his distress. 'I don't know how much longer I can go on like this. It's been seven months since I got my salary. I forget the last time I sent any money home. Lots of debt. Haven't paid rent in a while and the landlord keeps asking for it every day. Our boss said whoever wants to leave can leave. And legally speaking, if you don't get paid for more than three months, you have no obligations to your employer. But I am hoping things will get better.'

'But why? Why not look for another job?' I asked.

'What can I say? Is money everything? I have been here for fifteen years. I was here for the golden age of the City. I enjoyed every bit of it. And now that the City has fallen on bad times, I just have to stick with it. Of course, I came here to make money. But I also made this city my home. I have friends here. I have obligations here. I feel committed to seeing the City through. What's the point of thinking only about money? What's the point of a life like that?'

I had no answer to that question. I drove into the City with that question, and other answerless questions, ringing in my head.

Shooting Star

Love is like a shooting star. It takes twelve years to complete a single orbit. In between it might disappear from view, it might get submerged in memory. But if it is true love, it will certainly return. In all the books I had read, love – whether lost or unrequited or forgotten – returned to haunt the lover in twelve years. If it didn't, the books told me, it was not true love after all. I learned soon enough that this was not just a romantic superstition. It was in the twelfth year – not the eleventh or thirteenth – that my own forgotten love returned with a vengeance.

The first sign was a message on Facebook: 'h-r-u?' I had to gaze at the profile picture for a long minute before I recognized the face behind that greeting. I hadn't realized time could redraw the contours of some faces so much. I saw a beloved face rising out of that stranger's profile picture. And my heart, like a deep-sea fish, dove into the past.

Till then I had thought of her as another woman entombed in an ordinary marriage. I never expected a resurrection. But it was as if she had rolled away the rock under which she was buried and stepped out of her tomb. Perhaps I had always known she would emerge from her tomb. Love has the power to move mountains.

How do you put twelve years into words? We talked to each other frantically. We updated each other on the new characters in our lives. We marked life events with the blandness of dates. We exchanged pictures and notes. Slowly we came back to the present. Only then did we catch our breaths. After that, we would occasionally send each other a 'hello' or 'how are you' on Facebook, greetings at festival times, a quick friendly note from time to time. What more could two people trapped in faraway cities do? I had never expected that life would bring me to her city so suddenly, so deliberately. And yet that which I did not even dare to dream of had happened.

I decided that the unexpected should not simply be unexpected, it should also be unintentional. That was the promise between Shanti and me. Though I told her, 'James Hogan insisted. Impossible to refuse,' etc., she was convinced that the reason I had agreed to take the assignment was Jasmine and nothing else. After all, she had known me several years. She also knew it would be impossible for her to change my mind. But she put forth a condition.

'Pratap, Jasmine must never know that you are coming to the City. You must wander through her city without her knowledge. You must find her through trial and error. You must not seek her help or anyone else's. Then one day you must appear in front of her suddenly. Your appearance will be so unexpected that she will faint in surprise. If you don't find her on your own, you must return to me without ever seeing her. Agreed?'

She had me there. It was as if in the middle of making

love, just as I was approaching the peak, she had stopped me and walked away. Jasmine had returned to my life like a rainbird announcing the end of a long drought. My Jasmine dream had given me a surge of energy. My pulse raced at the thought of seeing her. I felt weak with longing. Like a volcano about to explode, I yearned to tell Jasmine that I was coming to her. Three or four times I had logged into Facebook and written a message, 'I am coming to the City,' but had not sent it. Shanti had trapped me in a hole. In the name of the ten years of our marriage, I had to say yes. Of course, I could easily break this arbitrary agreement. How would Shanti know? I could make up a story about an accidental encounter. But I would be betraying myself, and what could be more humiliating. Beyond the promise I had given Shanti, this was my challenge to myself. I would find Jasmine without anyone's help.

After renting the car, I went around the streets of the City. I simply wanted to meet the City, introduce myself to it. I drove down long avenues and narrow galis. I roamed through shops and malls. I mapped the City's landmarks: Tripoli Hotel, Sana Fabrics, Baghdad Avenue, Teheran Carpets, Cairo Perfumes, Muscat Mall, Amman Tower. None of them seemed unfamiliar to me. In the last three years, I had roamed the City in my mind, holding Jasmine's hand in mine. In reality, all I knew was that she lived in some corner of the City and worked for an insurance company. But still, I kept an eye out for her, fully expecting that she would appear in front of me miraculously. From a Facebook photo of hers, I remembered the balcony in front of her flat, the peach paint on its walls, the shape of its bars, the flowerpot on one side. From an email of hers, I knew that her flat faced a mosque with tall minarets. There was an almond tree near the bus stop where she waited for her bus. Whenever I saw an apartment building with balconies, or an almond tree, wherever I saw the minarets of a mosque, I looked around eagerly.

Jasmine, I am near you. I am in the City, breathing the same air you breathe. I want to see you. That is the only reason I am here. When I remember you are somewhere here, I am filled with greed. I am tempted to tell you I am here. I could easily spoil the surprise by sending you a message. But what would be the fun in that. We may have to wait a few more days, but I want to find you on my own, without any help, even from you. That is my real task here. Wait for me, Jasmine. Our reunion is not far away now.

That night I sent her a message: 'Jasmine, do you believe in miracles? If not, start believing . . .'

Vargas Llosa

Edwin arrived three days later. I went to receive him at the airport, partly because I had nothing else to do and partly because I did not have much faith in Abdullah Janahi's welcome methods. Edwin was coming from London, where he was part of the official research team of the anonymous writer who had hired our firm. Barely twenty-five years old, he seemed to be a high-octane character. We had only exchanged a few emails and had Skype chats by then. But he greeted me as if I were an old friend.

He told me that he was a relatively new member of the research team. Prior to this, he had helped research the life of horsemen in a village called Semeru Loang, near the volcanic Mount Bramo in Indonesia, and before that, he had travelled to Rwanda to research the life of General Augustin Bizimungu, who was responsible for the 1994 genocide. 'They were both unforgettable experiences,' he said, 'experiences that taught me the meaning of life and death. I was about to head to Italy to conduct research for a new novel set in Italian churches, when this opportunity came up. I have always wanted to see the Mesopotamian desert and the Arabian peninsula, so I happily jumped ship.'

There was a woman accompanying Edwin, and as we were walking to the parking lot with the luggage he introduced her to me, 'This is Asmo Andros, from Budapest. She lives close by. We can drop her off at her villa on the way, can't we?'

'Of course,' I replied.

Asmo's villa was in an island colony called Palm Gardens, near the airport. It was clearly a wealthy community and we were subjected to a very thorough security check at the gate. As we were driving past sea-facing villas, Asmo pointed towards another island. 'That's His Majesty's holiday palace. He visits once a year or so.'

'Oh no . . . Poor His Majesty. That little hovel over there is what the Arabs call a palace?' Edwin sniggered. 'Even an ordinary billionaire in my country would live in a much better house. And we don't even have any oil; we merely steal the oil from this country. When these royal types come to our country and see our houses, they must feel very ashamed of their so-called palaces.'

I thought of some of those splendid Indian palaces. Even a zamindar in India would live in more glory than some of these Middle Eastern royals.

As she got out of the car, Asmo gave me her visiting card and told me to call her if I needed any help. I wrote down my local phone number and gave her my *Toronto Sunday* business card. Edwin got a kiss. I could sense him getting aroused as he enjoyed their prolonged farewell.

'We met on the flight,' he said on the way to our apartment. I was astonished. I thought he had come to the City with his long-time girlfriend.

'On the way here, Asmo was sitting next to me. At first she ignored me. She was reading her book very seriously as if she was a professor. When I said hello, she gave me a grim hi and went back to her book. How dare she? What is this book she is reading when she could be flirting with a blue-eyed stud like me? So I checked out her book, and it was *In Praise of the Stepmother* by Mario Vargas Llosa. I have read some of his other books but not that one, so I had no idea what it was about. I should have known something was up because after reading each sentence, the grim professor lady would give me a searching glance and laugh to herself. Then she would go back to reading. I decided it must be one of those books that make fun of men.

'At some point she fell asleep, and I picked up the book from her lap and took a look at what she was reading. I couldn't believe my eyes. She was reading about sex! It described, in full detail, a woman going wild with pleasure. Now I understood those glances, that laughter. When she woke up, I deliberately picked up the book and started reading. She began laughing. That's how we introduced ourselves to each other.

'Her family is from Lebanon. When she was thirteen and the Lebanese civil war was at its height, they moved to Budapest. But she works here now as personal assistant to the CEO of a famous bank. She was just returning from a visit to her family in Budapest.

'When I told her that I was part of the research team of an internationally renowned writer, she got very curious. And excited. After that, she would not stop talking about writers and books. Has anyone actually met Dan Brown? Have I visited Agatha Christie's Greenway House? Why did Gabriel García Márquez punch Mario Vargas Llosa? Can someone please try and recover Sylvia Plath's lost novel? Had I been to the Hay Festival? What was my theory about Edgar Allan Poe's mysterious death? Who is the most hated character in world literature: Iago or Brutus? Whom did I prefer: Roberto Bolaño or María Amparo Escandón? Was Virginia Woolf a lesbian? Is it true that J.K. Rowling was writing the new Harry Potter? Where was Salman Rushdie hiding? Had I ever had the good fortune to visit Orhan Pamuk's Museum of Innocence?

'This is what passes for small talk between book lovers. I replied as best I could. At some point, we were holding hands. It was like a meeting of souls. When you find someone of the same wavelength, it takes only moments to know, Mr Pratap. So you see, I am doubly fortunate to be stepping into this city . . .'

Fairy Tale

For Edwin the Middle East was a place of bloody legends and tales of terror. He thirsted to know what this region was really like, how it was moving forward despite its storied past.

'People on our team were scared of this project,' he said. 'That's why it had to be outsourced. I was the only one who was disappointed about that decision. So I jumped at the opportunity to come here when *Toronto Sunday* asked for someone to do some initial project guidance. Everyone in my team pestered me with questions: You turned down the trip to Italy to go where? What city have you chosen for the first study? What's so special about this city? When I showed them where the City was on the world map, Kelly John, who has a bit of a soft corner for me, fainted. With Saudi Arabia on one side and Iran on the other, I was not surprised by her reaction. But I was not scared, I was excited. I have always been curious about the City, how it rose out of dust like an enchanted land in a fairy tale.

'It was not just a journalist's interest or a European's jealousy. I, too, have an old connection to the City. My great-grandfather George Martin Lease spent a lot of his youth here. In fact, you could say he is responsible for the City's remarkable growth and its current misfortunes. You must have heard of Major Frank Holmes, who found the first oil reserves in this region and came to be known as "the father of oil". My great-grandfather was his best friend and a member of his prospecting team. They were both geologists. They met and bonded while working in the British Army's supply section during the First World War. Both of them dreamed of oil. When they came to Iraq during the war, they were both convinced that there were oil deposits in the soil. They were standing on this Middle Eastern soil when Frank Holmes turned to my great-grandfather and said, "I smell oil." After the war, they both left the army and turned to oil prospecting. Holmes had some experience looking for gold in South Africa and my great-grandfather had spent time in the coal mines of India. That was it. They wandered all over the Mesopotamian desert and the Persian peninsula sniffing for oil. They couldn't find any sponsors for their crazy ideas. They were discouraged. Mocked, in fact. Imagine, oil in this savage land. But they were not quitters. Their instinct told them there was a deep reservoir of oil somewhere underneath all that desert soil. Finally, they got some support from Eastern and General Syndicate Limited. Soon after that, they were able to find the oil and prove they were not just two crazy old men. They had started in 1925 and it was in 1931 that they found the oil. In the summer of 1932, oil started gushing out of the first oil well in the Middle East. That changed the course of this region's history. My great-grandfather returned to London, happy with his discovery. He died of cholera soon after and disappeared from the history of oil. But Holmes lived till 1947. He was honoured for his discovery. And that, my friend, is why they call him "the father of oil".

'Even four generations later, my family talks proudly of George Martin Lease and his oil days. In our living room, we still display his photos, and a photocopy of the original agreement between his company and the rulers of this land.

'The moment the children of our family could piece words together, they would start trying to read that agreement. We read it like a fairy tale. We would recite that agreement the way other kids sang "Johnny Johnny Yes Papa". Look, even now I don't have to stop to remember it.'

Sitting on the balcony of my room enjoying a beer, Edwin recited.

'Agreement between Sheikh Al Khalifah of the one part, hereafter called "the Sheikh" and Eastern and General Syndicate Limited of the other part, hereafter called "the Company". The Sheikh grants to the Company an exclusive exploration licence for a period not exceeding two years, from the date of this agreement hereby the Company shall be entitled throughout the whole of the territory under his control to explore and search the surface of such territories to a depth not exceeding twenty feet for natural gas, petroleum asphalt and ozokerite, and enjoy the privileges set out in the first schedule to this agreement; and he undertakes on behalf of himself and his successors to grant to the Company further exclusive licence and privileges, if the Company's actions meet with the Sheikh's satisfaction, as guided by the advice of the Political Resident in the Persian Gulf. Dated the Second of December 1925.'

Two Young Men

There were two more members in our team, but their arrival kept getting delayed. Their tickets had to be rebooked several times. 'Visas are not a problem for you Canadians and Europeans,' Abdullah Janahi explained. 'But the two people we are waiting for are Asians. They have to jump through hoops to get their visas.' I remembered how I walked out of the airport after five minutes of visa processing while labourers from Asian countries were being shoved into long lines as if they were cattle. Wherever it goes, the First World passport opens doors.

We could not wait for them indefinitely. It was time to start work. Edwin and I picked one of the four office spaces that Abdullah Janahi took us to. Though a bit small, it was near our apartment. It was also furnished. The rent made us hesitate, but as soon as Abdullah Janahi heard that we liked it, he went ahead and rented it, without even discussing with us. The next day, he got us phone and Internet connections.

I had no idea where to start. It's not as if we could simply waylay people on the street. How would we figure out which one of the thousands of people passing us carried interesting stories within them? Besides, would anyone we approach want to bare their souls to strangers? Could the stories we gathered from newspapers and official documents be anything other than superficial? How far could a writer go with such research? Though Edwin was supposedly there to give us guidance, I couldn't bring myself to ask a much younger man for advice. But we would often go out together to see the City. He was still enthralled at the idea of being in an Arab city. Each and every thing he saw fuelled his enchantment. The man on the cycle with birdcages strapped behind him;

the Bengali migrant roasting peanuts by the side of the road; little Arab urchins who tailed us, offering to sell us the latest cell phones at rock-bottom prices; donkey carts with oil tanks in them; women dressed from head to toe in black, posing for photos; the middle-aged man who spread out his prayer rug on the sidewalk and started praying – everything moved him to wonder.

Whenever he saw an Arab in traditional robes, he would jump out of the car and stare as if he were in a dream. He thought of Arabs as characters in some folk tale. 'I see bygone eras in their faces, Pratap.' That was his half-stupid, half-innocent explanation.

One day he went running into a random shop and asked, 'Where can I see a sheikh?'

A Malayali who happened to be at the shop said, 'Oh, we keep a pet sheikh somewhere around here in a cage. But right now he's out grazing.' Not comprehending, Edwin stood there like an idiot while laughter exploded in the shop. He would have cried if he knew why they were laughing. When he persisted, the shopkeeper pointed to a local cafe nearby, saying sheikhs often visited it. Edwin insisted that we go and sit in the cafe. Luckily no sheikhs passed that way, or I would have witnessed more of his melodrama.

Some days I would wander around the City on my own. I would visit shopping malls and galis. I was not so much searching for authentic life experiences in the City as I was hoping to run into Jasmine. I longed to see her in the street. During those wanderings, I met a couple more acquaintances from my home town. I didn't even know they lived here. They were surprised to see me as well. But the person I desired never appeared in front of me.

I was seeing the City, of course, but I was not experiencing it. Like any other city, it seemed to wake up, go through the motions of the day, and go to sleep. The usual crowds, the usual rush hour. There were no signs of the protests that had recently taken place. To think about the fear this city had evoked when I had mentioned my travel plans. 'Be careful, Pratap. It is a place where bombs go off constantly.' Shanti was crying when she bid me farewell. 'Anyone can get shot anywhere at any time of the day. If you find it difficult, don't think twice. Come back.' Some of my co-workers even offered me their condolences, 'We didn't realize James Hogan disliked you this much.' Like every other city with a curfew, this city too had certain inconveniences. That was all. Barely enough to fill a three-column newspaper article. My best bet was to meet Jasmine as soon as possible and return.

Another day when Edwin and I were driving around, he started taking photos of buildings and billboards and cars and mosques and minarets. He wanted to capture as much of the City as possible. When our car stopped at a signal, two young Arab men got out of the car in front and approached us. 'Are you taking photos of us?' they asked. They didn't believe us when we told them we were not. They asked to see the pictures. By then the signal had changed and the vehicles behind us were honking at us. The young men went running back to their car and started following us. We tried to lose them, but they were persistent. Finally we parked at a bus stop. They came running towards us again. We got ready to be beaten up, but they started pleading with us instead, 'Please delete those photos. We are innocent.' When we got out of the car, they fell at our feet and started crying loudly. At first I thought they were mocking us. But when I realized they were in earnest, I asked them why they were so scared. They were convinced that we were plain-clothes investigators and had followed them around to gather incriminating evidence. Only after we showed them every single photo on Edwin's camera did they believe us and let go of our feet.

I did not understand then why those young men were so terrified of something as simple as a photograph.

Socialism

That weekend I went to the Malayali Samajam of the City with Bijumon. It was an elegant building with huge grounds. A tennis match was being played in the court. The library was full of readers. Biju introduced me to various officials in the many offices. Some of them were anxious to hear about the possibility of migrating to Canada. I told them that there was always room for economic refugees in Canada, as long as they were ready to live in slavery. There were no more questions after that.

A seminar on 'Globalization and a Changing World' was taking place at the same time. It began with thanking His Majesty for the opportunity to organize the seminar. This was followed by fierce speeches about how globalization was taking the form of neo-colonialism, the dictatorial tendencies of world leaders and the importance of popular resistance against anti-democratic rulers. I, too, was invited to speak, but I declined. I heard someone mutter, 'What can a Canadian say about colonialism? He is probably all for globalization.' I did not respond to that. I had only pity for those who made political resistance speeches after thanking His Majesty.

By the time we left, it was almost midnight. Bijumon, his friend Raju Narayan and I got into my car and went in search of food.

Raju used to be a very active member of the communist party of Kerala. Five years ago, when he was working at the district level of the party, he had taken leave of absence for five years to come to the City. 'I had some debts and I needed to repay them. And afterwards I just did not return. That's how it goes in this city,' he said. 'It doesn't let go of you. The way I look at it is when human life achieves a certain standard, that's socialism right there. At the minimum, socialism has been achieved in my own life; I paid my debts and now I have some savings in the bank. So why should I return to my old life?' I couldn't really understand what Raju was saying.

On the way to the restaurant, we got caught in traffic. Several police vehicles were buzzing around in front of us, their lights flashing. Other vehicles with blaring alarms were trying to get around the traffic by driving up the sidewalk. At first I thought there must have been an accident. Though Biju and Raju asked me not to, I got out of the car, unable to tamp down my newshound curiosity. A few vehicles up,

I saw a fire on the street. Maybe a car had caught fire? But when I got up close, I saw that tyres had been set on fire and were blocking the road. Police were trying to put out the fire. At the same time, lit torches were being hurled at them from behind a nearby wall. The police were fighting back with tear-gas bombs. I felt my eyes tearing up. I ran back to the car.

Biju and Raju laughed at me. 'Told you,' they mocked. 'Then we thought, why not let the Canadian learn the hard way.'

Within ten–fifteen minutes, the fires had been put out and the traffic started moving again.

'This is a regular Arab custom,' the communist leaned in from the back seat to inform me. 'This is how they celebrate weekends. Some fire on the streets, some tear-gas bombs. Maybe a few bullets to go around. Most weekends a couple of them will get slaughtered. The next day they will get a grand burial. That's how they live. Don't give it another thought.'

'Have you ever tried to understand what the real issues are?' I asked Raju, swallowing my anger.

'What's there to understand?' Raju asked, genuinely surprised. 'They are just a bunch of rowdies and religious fanatics. They destroyed this country. You have no idea, Mr Pratap, how peacefully and happily us foreigners lived here under His Majesty's rule. There was no country more beautiful. It was like the Garden of Eden. And His Majesty saw us as his own subjects. We had every freedom we could possibly want. We had churches and temples and gurdwaras and schools and bars and our own Malayali Samajam where we elected our own administration. In fact, Mr Pratap, the communist party of Kerala has a branch committee here. Every year we donated lakhs of rupees to the party fund in Kerala. No one stopped us or questioned us. I don't think we would have had this much freedom in a communist country. And still these locals wouldn't stop moaning about how they had no freedom. They kept crying for democracy. I don't understand what more they could possibly want.'

Raju was getting more and more excited as he spoke.

'Do you know why we are telling you all this? Short-term visitors like you see all this noise in the streets and get scared and report that terrible things are happening here.' Bijumon took up the conversation now. 'And that's exactly what they want – to ruin the country's reputation. And then destroy the economy. There is an international agenda behind all this. If this were happening back in India, they would all be dead. His Majesty is too good for this world, that's why they are still alive.'

That night we ate chicken tikka and lamb chops and beef kebabs and hummus in a Lebanese restaurant. But I could not stomach it. When I returned to the apartment, I threw it all up. Alongside all that roasted meat, there were some undigested words as well in my puddle of vomit.

Flash Mob

The remaining two members of our team arrived over the next couple of days. Vinod Chopra from Mumbai reached first.

When I heard that he had resigned from his job at Reuters to come here, I wondered if like me and my long-lost love or Edwin and his romantic notions, he too had some other motive. Compared to a job at Reuters, what we offered was peanuts.

'No, nothing like that. I just wanted a change of scene. I don't work anywhere for more than three years. By then I get tired of the organization and the organization gets tired of me. After that I have to leave, never mind how tempting the offer is. That's what happened in Reuters too. I caught the whiff of a rumour that they were planning to transfer me to some rural office. Before that axe fell, I fled from there. In all honesty, I hate Indian villages. All the problems in the country – terrorism, religious fundamentalism, caste, superstition – start in the villages and in those huge joint families. If it were up to me, I would burn down every village. I love cities, where you can breathe the fresh air of democracy and secularism. Now that I am here, I can breathe safe again. What a great city. I am looking forward to living here and breathing its fresh air!' That was Vinod Chopra.

Next came Riyaz Malik. The oldest among us, he was from Sindh in Pakistan. Till he got here, he was the bureau chief of the *Pakistan Chronicle* in Karachi for fifteen years. He also had some experience as a lexicographer at the Urdu Institute. 'There is a huge Pakistani population in this country, which is one of the reasons I got this job, along with the fact that I can handle Arabic. And, of course, it's a nice dollar salary and the opportunity to work in a foreign company, with a chance to meet some friends who live in the City. Nothing more. Not even the desire to live and report from a war zone. I don't have to leave Pakistan for that. Just walking up and down a street in Waziristan or Peshawar would give me enough material for four novels.'

I don't know if it was Abdullah Janahi's decision or an instruction from *Toronto Sunday*, but there was a certain discrimination in our living arrangements. This caused a rift between us right at the beginning. They gave Edwin a flat, while the rest of us had to share another flat. Riyaz Malik and I did not make a big deal of this. We had a spacious three-bedroom flat with plenty of personal space for each of us. But Vinod kicked up a fuss. His contract did not specify that he had to share his accommodation; he yelled at Abdullah Janahi, saying he wanted his own flat. Riyaz and I felt it was justified. He had come here from the world-famous Reuters. Edwin was a mere copywriter. Abdullah Janahi said that Edwin got his own flat because he was the news coordinator. Vinod retorted that it was racism. As *Toronto Sunday*'s ambassador in the City, I had to get involved. I calmed Vinod down by telling him we would discuss this with the head office.

The next day Vinod asked me for a ride. Since his Indian driving licence was not valid in the City, he was not able to rent a car. I went with him to visit a friend of his, Priyanka Agarwal, who worked as a radio jockey at a radio station. She lived alone in a flat in the city centre. They knew each other from Mumbai, and they talked a lot about those days. I enjoyed the time I spent with them. Though they were talking to each other, they included me in the conversation. What Vinod had to say to Priyanka, he would say to me as well, and when Priyanka had something to say to Vinod, she would involve me. I never felt like I was the third wheel.

On the way back, Vinod told me how he had met Priyanka. It seemed everyone had an interesting story about how they met their friend in the City. 'I first met Priyanka at the Chhatrapati Shivaji Terminus. I was living in Delhi and had come to Mumbai to report on an international business conference. I was waiting for the train when suddenly a young woman came running into the station and started dancing. Was it some film shoot? A crowd gathered around the woman to watch and I joined them. Suddenly another woman joined her from the crowd. Then two young men, then four more, then ten. Soon all of us on that platform were dancing. There were some people like me, a bit hesitant. But our neighbours got us dancing too. You know those Mexican waves you see in football stadiums? I had never seen people move in such synchrony, without any practice. It was an example of how easy it is to manipulate a crowd. You could start a riot that easily. Or you could start a dance party. Imagine the magnetic pull of a crowd if it could get a serious journalist like me dancing.

'My partner in that flash mob was a young woman, maybe twenty years old. We were holding hands, but we did not even notice each other. We were simply two souls without bodies, swaying to the music. Only when people started leaving after the dance did we come to our senses and pull back, and finally looked at each other.

'I have a very special skill. I know how to tell someone's character from the shape and appearance of their toenails. When I was a student, I got obsessed with Ayurveda and the Puranas, so I joined a Siddha Ashram and started studying Samudrika Lakshanam. Bodies have their own language and you can understand a lot from looking at the head, face, forehead, eyes, lips, feet and nails. I focused on the nails. It's very easy to study someone's nails. The nail of your big toe can reveal a lot about your luck, health, good and bad qualities. But you have to study it scientifically.

'Since then I have studied every woman who has crossed me, as long as she was not wearing socks and shoes. They have no idea I am reading their souls. And Priyanka's nails had something I had not seen in the thousands of nails I had read till then. Though she appeared tranquil on the outside, she carried a storm of lust inside her. I was amazed at how strong her desire was. For years I had longed to see a nail like that.

'I could not let her simply disappear in Mumbai. I introduced myself. Within ten minutes of conversation, I had broken the ice and we were drinking coffee together. I used that half an hour to win her over with my words, and we went to a hotel. Three or four times after that, we shared a bed when I visited Mumbai. When Priyanka became an obsession, I moved to Mumbai. But by then she had moved to the City. I could not abandon her. No, I am not in love with her. Love is bullshit. I have fucked several other women, before and after Priyanka. But no one has ravaged my body the way she has. She is a beast in bed. So when I couldn't get her in Mumbai, I had to follow her where she went. If I hadn't got this opportunity to come here, I would probably have come here on a labour visa! So you see, I am not here to fulfil some white writer's fantasy book dream. I am here for sex. I want women. And I know that the City is like a safety valve for this conservative Muslim region. You can find export quality women from at least 120 countries in the hotels here. I want to taste at least fifty of them. Food and sex are my twin passions. Of course, one could spend one's life obsessing over art and literature. But there's a limit to those experiences. They are all external. You can't help tiring of them. There are only two experiences you can sense deep inside your body: food and sex. We will never tire of those two.

'I didn't tell you all this earlier because I immediately disliked those two bewakoofs,' Vinod continued. 'That Edwin is a racist white pig. His ancestors were thieving dogs who stole from our country. Have you looked closely at his face? He still has that entitlement. If you give him an inch, he will colonize us again. That's why I made a fuss about a new flat for myself. Not because I find it inconvenient to live with you. And that other guy, Riyaz Malik – you made a bad choice there. He is a thief and a fanatic. He will drag us into danger. Pratap, have you noticed his fingernails? As per the Samudrika Lakshanam, bud-shaped fingernails show a manipulative, deceptive personality. We have to be very careful, Pratap. We are two Indians. We must stand by each other. Don't tell anyone what I have told you . . .'

Vinod had created waves of suspicion in my mind. The tides started pulling them in.

Part Two

Rub'al-Khali

Cafe Radwa

The next day we assembled in the office for the first time. None of us knew exactly what we were supposed to do. Edwin was the only one who had participated in a project like this before. We were traditional journalists with traditional methods of reporting on a subject and sculpting it into a news story. It's a kind of pretend integrity that interprets each subject according to the vested interests of our news establishment. But would a creative writer be interested in news takes? What would he or she possibly do with a bunch of news items gathered ad hoc?

Edwin, however, had some clear ideas. He explained to us that we were free to report whatever we found in the City. It could be an incident, a conversation, legend or historic fact. And we didn't have to record them in words. We were free to gather images, sounds, even objects. When we left, it should be with a comprehensive idea of the City. But comprehensive did not mean organized. The writer was not looking for a neat summary. We were there to collect the raw material.

This was not the place to show off our composition skills and vocabulary. We were to leave that job for the writer who had hired us. What was expected of us was pure research.

'Mr Pratap, I don't understand why you chose the City. Is this the kind of material our writer wants?' Riyaz Malik said. 'As far as I can see, this is a very stable city. In fact, it feels safer than many other cities that are supposedly safe.'

'Says who?' Vinod leaped into the argument. 'Each and every person on the streets of this city is a dark continent. We can find a thousand stories here if we understand that.'

'We are looking for stories from conflict regions. Think of this city as a dry run. Let's finish this project soon so we can move on to the next place quickly,' Edwin said.

'Where shall we start?' I asked. 'I was thinking of interviewing some famous personalities in the City. By that I mean poets and artists and film-makers. They are the only ones left on earth who speak the truth without fear. I have a list here: Rashid Madani, Faizal Jazim, Ali Al Jalavi, Ahmed Al Qaid, Karim Radi. Of these, Ahmed Al Qaid has agreed to speak to us. Perhaps some of the others will follow suit. We should use our network in the City to meet these people and persuade them to talk to us. They will open the doors of the City for us.'

That evening Edwin and I went to meet Ahmed Al Qaid. All we had by way of directions was a name: Cafe Radwa. We used the GPS in Edwin's car to get there. We waited in the parking lot of the cafe. A few minutes later, a Nissan Cressida 90 arrived. A shrunken man, fully bald, emerged from the car. He did not look like a poet to me. This can't be Ahmed

Al Qaid, I thought to myself. But he recognized us. Nobody else was waiting for him anyway.

'Are you the people John Maschinas from the radio station told me about?' he asked us.

'Yes, John told us to seek you out when we got here.' Edwin shook his hand.

'John was one of the few foreigner friends I had in the City. There was nothing we didn't talk about. He too has left the City now. What a shame.'

'He didn't leave willingly. Circumstances forced him,' Edwin replied.

'How could anyone with any self-respect stay? Locals like us don't have an alternative. To be a migrant elsewhere . . . what a curse.'

We walked into the cafe. It was a quiet place and I guessed that it was probably expensive. Our new friend told us that this cafe was where the intellectuals and activists and unemployed of the City gathered, 'just like La Rotonde in Paris, or the Literary Cafe in St Petersburg'. I looked around. An old man who looked just like Einstein was sitting at a table in front of us, smoking and reading a book. A bearded young man was playing on his cell phone at the table to the left. Two young women in Western clothes were having a very intense conversation at a corner table.

'Do you mind if a tape recorder joins us as we talk?' Edwin asked, taking his phone out of his pocket.

'It has an unpleasant presence,' Al Qaid replied. 'It will make us cautious in our conversation. Talk has a way of not flowing spontaneously when there's a recording device nearby.

If I say anything interesting during our conversation, surely it will stick in your mind. You are welcome to take notes, if necessary. But I do not want this machine.'

Edwin switched off the recorder. I could sense his disappointment. I tried to signal with my eyes that it was okay, but he didn't get it.

We began with literature. Al Qaid was saddened that though literature was making a glorious comeback across the world, there was nothing of the sort in this country. There was a proverb about Arab literature, he told us. 'Egypt writes, Lebanon publishes, Iraq reads.' Nothing has changed. Our country has not managed to find a place on that literary map. Still, we have managed to make some literary history. Especially in poetry. That was the voice of our people's protest and resistance.' Turning to his own literary works he told us that he had published three collections of poetry, but in Arabic. 'I did edit an anthology called *Dreams of Deserts*. It has English translations of the most important poets of our country,' he added.

'I borrowed it from John Maschinas and read it. That preface you wrote for that anthology – it was really great,' Edwin exclaimed. 'Such a great perspective on the poetic history of the City and the craft of writing. That's why I was so eager to meet you.' I saw the poet's face light up in delight. It was the writer's pleasure at meeting two genuine readers. I was also impressed by how well Edwin had prepared for his travel to the City. Of course, he was experienced at this and knew how to prepare. I felt a little jealous.

I turned the conversation to recent events in the Arab

world. From there, I thought, we could slowly push him towards our own subject.

'The sixteenth and seventeenth centuries were dominated by Europe and the eighteenth and nineteenth centuries by India and China. But the twentieth and twenty-first centuries belong to the Arab world,' he said. 'Think about it. All the major historic events of this era took place in our region. The fall of the Ottoman empire, the rise of Israel, the discovery of oil, the Islamic revolution in Iran, the Iran–Iraq war, the fall of Saddam, the Facebook revolutions that brought down dictators in Tunisia, Libya and Egypt. While other countries of the world were having a long siesta, we were making history.'

'Yes, yes, exactly,' I said. 'And the protests in this country continue that tradition.'

'I don't agree,' he said. 'I do not support those protests.'

I was stunned. Surely a poet of the people should be leading the protests from the front line. At least in spirit. I couldn't help asking him why he was against them. He was silent for a long time.

'This was a protest by religious leaders,' he replied finally. 'There was no place in it for an unbiased citizen. And no good will come out of it for ordinary people. It will take years for the protesters themselves to understand what happened. But the main concern of the protest was whether this should be a Sunni country or a Shia country.'

'Is that really true?' Edwin interrupted him. 'In Egypt and Tunisia and Libya, the protests brought together ordinary people who wanted democracy and social reformers and communists. Isn't it a bit of an exaggeration to say that the clerics hijacked the protests?'

'Not at all. Perhaps you two were too young to remember this, but when the revolution in Iran took place, communists all over the world celebrated it as a victory for freedom and democracy. But very soon the clerics turned that revolution into a court jester's antic. The first president of that country did not rule for even two years. The parliament caved in to pressure from the imams and impeached him. There was an order for his arrest. The president had to disguise himself in women's clothes and flee his own country. What could be a more humiliating end to a revolution? Till a protest succeeds, they talk about revolution. The moment it succeeds, they start talking religion. A religion that teaches hate. That's what we learned from the Iranian revolution. And all these new administrations that have come to power in the name of democracy . . . the same fate awaits them too.'

I had to ask him then what his political persuasion was. 'I used to be a communist,' he said.

'Wow!' Edwin said as if he had heard something that should not be admitted so openly. I, too, was surprised. A communist in this Arab land? Especially in these days? He had just demolished some stereotypes we held.

'The world outside seems to think of Arabs as savage religious fanatics who are still stuck in the seventh or fourteenth century. The reality is very different. Until recently, we were conscientious about adopting laws and political ideologies that were responsive to the times we lived in. Take, for instance, the rise of the Ba'ath Party, which is an important political actor in Syria and Iraq today. You may not believe this but that party was formed out of legislative ideals and principles that had nothing to do with religion. They took as inspiration the constitutions of France and Turkey. Even the name Ba'ath, which means renaissance, was taken from the book *On the Way of Resurrection*, written by one of the founders of the party, Michel Aflaq. The party believed in socialism and Arab nationalism. When the party came to power in Iraq and Syria simultaneously, there was even discussion of uniting these two countries. All over the Arab world, there was support for Ba'ath. The party branched out into Jordan, Libya, Yemen, even into this country. Egypt and Syria did experiment with becoming one, and for a short time the dream of a United Arab Republic was a reality. That spirit was alive in this country too, and we had a strong communist movement and trade unions. In the 1970s, we, that is communist poets and activists and social reformers, led this country in the struggle against our British rulers. It was us, not clerics. The public heard our call. Students walked out of classrooms, workers abandoned factories, housewives shut down their kitchens. Teachers, advocates, doctors – they were all part of the protests. Our national petroleum company has stopped production only once in its life. That was during our protests. And we won.'

'So if communists were responsible for the country's freedom, then how come this country is still in the hands of one ruling family?' Edwin asked.

'Whenever you British left a colony, you did not hand over power to the people. You chose clans to take over, didn't you?

You made sure each country inherited your own monarchic tradition. What did you do, for instance, in this man's country,' he said, pointing to me, 'in India? You put one family in power. And that's what you did here as well. The British invested all their power in one family that had worked for them for generations. That was His Majesty's family. In the beginning, we were democratic to a certain extent. We held elections and voted in parliament. In his fifth year though, His Majesty's family declared an emergency and disbanded parliament. Communists were hunted down. Many of us were arrested. And just as the Ba'ath Party lost the trust of the people, we too lost trust in ourselves.

It was the greed for power that destroyed people's faith in the Ba'ath Party. Everyone knows how a party of socialism became a party of dictators when Saddam and Bashar al-Assad took charge. I think they modelled themselves on Stalin. It was around then that the Soviet Union started collapsing. For a generation that had implicitly trusted in communism, this was a slap in the face. The Iranian revolution had just taken place across our borders. When our young people got inspired by Ayatollah Khomeini's victory, there was nothing to offer them, not even a dream. If history had moved in a different direction, there would have been many socialist democracies in the Arab world today. Instead, we are mere slaves in the tents of our sheikhs . . .'

His voice was exhausted by now, and I could sense it was an exhaustion that went deep.

'Do you think communism is the solution to all this?' Edwin asked.

'I don't know what the solution is. I do know that returning to the seventh century, as the al-Qaeda and Taliban want us to do, is definitely not the solution.'

'Is the movement still alive here?' I asked.

'Yes, there are some committees working secretly here and there. They front themselves as human rights organizations and volunteer groups, of course. I am not really part of it any more. My own disagreement with communism began many years ago. The party refused to consider or even acknowledge our regional problems and focused on useless international debates instead. They were bigger Soviets than the Soviet Union itself. If it rained in Moscow, they rushed to hold umbrellas there. In the meantime, they forgot the hot, blazing sun here.'

As we bid goodbye to the poet, we asked him about other writers in the City. Could he connect us to them?

'It's no use. I can certainly connect you. But all you are going to hear is some hagiography. About themselves and about these rulers of ours. There are one or two who are different. But believe me, it's best to avoid them if you want to continue to live and work here. They are already on the government's radar. Right now, for instance, at least three of the people sitting at the tables near us are spies. I think we may be the only city where spies outnumber ordinary people.'

Argument

On the way back, Edwin was quiet. He focused on driving and did not talk much. I could sense that he was not ready to reveal his thoughts. I let him process them for a while. Then I opened the conversation. 'A good beginning, don't you think?' He looked at me quizzically.

'I am glad we began our interviews with Al Qaid. He has good judgement. We are moving in the right direction,' I explained.

'Honestly, I am disappointed,' said Edwin. 'How will these academic discussions help us? I was expecting a fierce poet who had actually participated in the protests. I wanted to hear his experiences, not his theories. That's what our writer needs. Also, I don't really agree with his assessment of the Jasmine revolution. It was not a revolution of clerics and fundamentalists. They were young people, thirsting for democracy. How can an old communist like Al Qaid understand them?'

'But what about Iraq and Egypt? Saddam Hussein must be laughing in his tomb. And Hosni Mubarak in his prison cell. Is this why the people overthrew those dictators – so that they could fight with each other for power? Saddam and Mubarak could well say this is why our people need to be ruled with an iron fist.'

'Yes, it's true that some revolutions did not succeed immediately. Some of them even went from one extreme to the other. That doesn't mean you just let dictators rule forever. Each country needs to find its own equilibrium through trial and error. Maybe it will take a few revolutions before a country gets the government of its choice. I think of this period in Arab history as a transition period.'

'What if the clerics simply take over?'

'But if that's what the people want, why not give it to them? Surely the people can revolt against the clerics and snatch the power back if the clerics take away their freedom? They are a people who have fought for their freedom once already. They know how to overthrow dictators. That is what is happening in Egypt now,' Edwin said.

'But there could well be international powers meddling behind the scenes there. We have seen it happen in so many countries.'

'That might well be. But then, again, it might not. It's easy enough to claim that international powers are responsible for every revolution except, of course, the one that brought your own faction to power. That's what the governments of Iran and China have been doing all these years.'

I had assumed that Edwin was annoyed by Al Qaid's harsh words about British colonizers. I realized now that he had been thinking of much more.

'It's too bad Al Qaid didn't let us record that interview though,' he said. 'I am beginning to forget all that he said.'

'I recorded it,' I told him, taking a pen out of my pocket. He looked at me in surprise. 'Every investigative journalist needs one of these.'

I had searched all over Toronto and Calgary for a compact pen camera recorder. I had been lusting after one of those for a while when I finally found it at a duty-free shop on my way here. What amazed me was that though it was tiny, it could record up to five hours of sound and three hours of video. And it looked like a garden variety Parker pen. 'And Edwin, you won't believe the price – ninety-nine dollars! You will never find anything this good for so cheap in Canada. I immediately bought one. I had a feeling it would come in handy on this trip . . .'

Edwin looked it over approvingly. I mentioned how I had been stuck at the airport because of flight delays.

'Why have you not claimed your travel insurance then?' he asked me.

'Oh, it's such a pain, all that paperwork and form-filling. And even if I do get something out of it, it will probably be pennies. Not worth the trouble.'

'Then why do we get travel insurance at all? Do you think we should claim it only if the plane explodes mid-flight? Doesn't matter if it is pennies or not, it is your right. In fact, you are doing a service by claiming it because it ensures accountability. A journalist like you should already know that.'

I felt a little ashamed of myself.

As soon as we reached the office, he asked me for my boarding pass and ticket and a copy of my passport. He downloaded the forms, filled them out and printed them and got my signature. Abdullah Janahi was dispatched to the insurance office with all the paperwork. 'Whatever. This is pointless,' the little Indian voice inside me murmured.

Unexplained Lives

It wasn't just Bijumon who insisted that I go see them. James Hogan too had instructed me that if the opportunity came up, I should definitely meet them.

Two people from my home town. Somehow they had heard I was in the City. Perhaps Bijumon had mentioned it. Or maybe someone back in Kerala had told them during a weekly call. They were determined to meet me. They got Bijumon on their side. Apparently they were students of my father's at our local school. We all had attended the same school but they had been senior to me by four or five years. 'If they want, they can come and meet me here,' I said. But Bijumon didn't agree. 'You should go visit them. It'll make them happy. And you'll get to see another side of the City.'

They lived in a crowded building in one of the narrower galis of the City. It was a dirty building with a broken elevator, a spit-stained staircase, and walls that needed painting. Their room was comparatively clean. A tiny room, which they shared with three others.

They welcomed their old teacher's son with tea and sweets and savouries. One of them even pulled out a bottle from under the bed, saying 'What about a sixty?' 'No, let's not,' I told them. They reminisced about our village and told me stories about my life that even I did not know.

Their lives seemed very strange to me. It had been seventeen years since they had arrived in the City. Their families lived in Kerala. They had shared a room from the time they came here. Even when they moved, they always moved with each other. 'Even our wives have not spent this much time with us in the same room,' one of them said. Adding up the two months of vacation every two years, the total was perhaps eighteen to twenty-four months. Far fewer than seventeen years. 'Nobody else knows us the way we know each other.'

I met the other three roommates, who had spent more than twenty years in the City. The last time I had gone to Kerala, I had taken in all the new tall buildings and wealthy houses filled with every creature comfort, and I had wondered how bizarre it was. God blesses some small Arab country with petrol dollars. And then a tiny sliver of land far away gets to enjoy some of those blessings. I had thought then how it was all a matter of random luck. But now I realized that it was not just luck. There was a long and lonely road between the two lands, and it could tell many stories of sacrifice.

I also remembered then what James Hogan had said before I came here. 'Man needs sex just as much as he needs food. Maybe there are one or two saints who can live without sex. But there are two million of your compatriots living in foreign countries, separated from their womenfolk for decades. You must find out how that is even possible.'

But how could I ask them? I could only wonder what made them lead the barren lives they lived. Was money everything?

Crabs

I woke up the next morning to Bijumon's phone call. Bombs had exploded in five different places in the City. Two deaths and several wounded. This was a first in the history of the City. 'Maybe you should go take a look?' Bijumon said. 'You might even find some research material.' I felt uncomfortable going alone, so I took Vinod along. We asked around and found our way to one of the places. People were gathered in small groups, and they told us the police were not letting anyone go further since one of the bodies was still lying where the bomb had gone off. 'Let's try,' Vinod said, walking ahead. A police car stopped us.

'We are from the press,' Vinod said, showing his old Reuters ID.

The policeman did not notice that the date had expired. 'Go quickly and take your photo and come back. The investigation is still going on.'

We walked ahead. The dead man's body was lying there, not even a cloth covering it. We took photographs.

'Make sure this news gets out,' another policeman told us. 'Everyone thinks these terrorists are fighting for human rights. At least now won't you media guys start writing the truth? Let the world see how ruthless they can be.'

He and the other policemen were angry. When we asked them about their lives, they told us how it had turned into one long battle on the street, with arson and stone-throwing and petrol bombs. Once they started talking, they could not stop. It was almost as if they had turned into ordinary cowards, like us. The streets were hardly under their control. Then a senior officer arrived in a police car and they fell silent, saluting him, standing at attention.

We swallowed our remaining questions and returned to the crowds that had gathered on the other side of the police barricades. They were staring at us, wondering how we had managed to walk all the way to the explosion site. We must be from the CID or high-ranking police officials in plain clothes, they surmised. They gathered around us respectfully, eager to talk. Among them were representatives from various embassies and human rights workers. We spent the morning talking to them and only after the body had been removed did we leave.

But as we drove back I realized that the news had not made any ripples in the City. The road was full of vehicles. Women bustled across the streets and labourers waited for the buses that would take them to work and school vans, stuffed with children, zipped across town. There were zero signs of panic. It was almost as if the bomb explosion had been folded into the ordinariness of everyday life. Perhaps the months before had brought them to this. I couldn't help but wonder about what they had already suffered that a bomb explosion had left their tranquil city unshaken.

'Pratap, have you been paying attention to that Taliban since we talked about him?' Vinod asked without any provocation.

'There's nothing to it. He is a religious man, that's all,' I said.

'I don't think so. He is a man of secrets. Have you seen how he often sits in his room with his door shut while we are talking? Or he goes about the City by himself. If he has come across anything useful for our research during those trips, he is certainly not reporting it. Don't you think that is a bit suspicious?'

'I don't think so at all, Vinod. Even yesterday, he was hanging out with us. And what if he wants to be by himself occasionally or go out alone? He is entitled to some privacy.'

'You NRIs are becoming more and more naive with each passing year. In the last few years you have reached the peak of such stupidity. Spend a few more years in Canada, Mr Pratap, and you won't be able to figure out India. You have no idea how to spot danger and handle it accordingly.' Vinod was either mocking me or warning me, and I had no response.

By the time we got back to the apartment, Riyaz and Edwin had already left for work. I felt a headache coming and didn't want to go to the office. But Vinod had to go off to the Indian Club, which was hosting the Indian foreign minister. Why did we rent an office space for such a short project, I grumbled to myself. Surely we could have used our living room or balcony as our office. Then we could have avoided our commuting troubles. But from the moment we arrived, Abdullah Janahi had pestered us to get an office. I called Edwin, and he had good news for me. Abdullah Janahi had hired a driver. We arranged for him to come and get Vinod.

Relieved, I went to my room to lie down. Sleep wouldn't come. Vinod's suspicions started raising their heads, like tiny crabs, out of the hole of my own mind. Was Riyaz a man of secrets? Was he hiding another life? And had I lost my sense of judgement by living abroad? The next minute, I chided myself. Vinod was suffering from Islamophobia. What did Riyaz do or say to deserve such suspicions? By giving ear to Vinod's nonsense, I was wasting my time on this kind of useless melodrama. When some people talk, you have to deliberately turn your ear away, I told myself.

Yachting

After a coffee, I felt a bit more alive and awake. I checked my email. And there, after many days, was a mail from Jasmine. The moment I saw her name in my inbox, I felt my heart, like a trapped bird, beat its wings to escape.

Pratap, as I write these words to you, I feel naked on the page. I was trying all this time not to tell you about my life. Or rather, my false pride would not let me tell you about it. Or maybe I was trying to convince myself that everything is fine. But I cannot hide any more.

I know there is no fairy-tale, dream marriage. I also realize that conflict is a reality in every relationship. I don't want to dramatize my own life. But you must see it for what it is worth. From the outside, it's a good life. My husband is handsome and rich. I have my own job and my own income. Two servants. But you know what, a slave girl would have a better life than me. The way he counts every penny I spend, the curses he rains on me, the way he farts in my direction. If he can find a way to humiliate me, he will do it. Even barbarians would treat their women better. In bed, he calls me by the name of my women friends or co-workers. I could live with that, but then, after he comes, he spits in my face. I have often thought how much better it would be if I was sleeping with a pig in the mud on the street.

Does this sound like the life of some sixteenth-century peasant girl? No, Pratap, this is the life of an educated career woman of your era in this city. What miracle do you think you could work in such a life? My time for miracles is over. In fact, I doubt that there is any me left. As you wrote once, my destiny is entombed in this marriage. I don't expect or aspire to any miracles. But thank you for your wishes.

Jasmine.

I sat there paralysed. It was as if a colourful curtain had suddenly unravelled, falling to the ground, unveiling the sordid truth instead of the Jasmine of my dreams. All these days of emailing and Facebooking, and she had never once hinted at all this. The affection she had showed me, the memories she had recounted, the regrets she had expressed – I had imagined that Jasmine, bored by the sweetness of her marriage, was reaching out to me simply for a thrill, just as the tongue longs for the heat of a pickle after drinking payasam. But now I saw she was trying to swim to the shore of love, fighting the waves that threatened to drown her in the turbulence of her marriage.

If she were near me then, I would have embraced her and kissed her. 'Here,' I would have whispered in her ear, 'take my heart and give me all your sorrows.' Twelve years ago, when I walked out of her life, I had hoped, Jasmine, may you have a big life, bigger than I could ever give you. Instead what she got was a life of humiliation. I wanted to see a Jasmine whose life was filled with many joys. I longed to know the City because it was the place that brought you happiness and fulfilment. How can I face you now, a hollow woman surrounded by the disappointments I had left you to face?

Yet I wanted to see her. I went out immediately, aimlessly driving around, hoping to run into her. But again, luck did not smile on me. Or her.

I found myself driving along the beach-facing street on the eastern side of the City. Several yachts were getting ready to sail, as if their owners had not heard or were indifferent to all the recent horrors in the City. Surfers enjoying the waves. Volleyball games on the beach. Crab hunters poking around in the sand. I watched them all.

In the bloom days of our love, Jasmine and I would go to the beach every New Year's Eve. We would gaze at the waves as we welcomed the next year. We saw in the ocean the infinity of our world, and the distances we would journey together and the new dawns that would rise again and again. How quickly the sun had set on those dreams that we thought were within our reach. I had one life now and Jasmine had another. There was nothing joining us.

What peculiar things our lives are. What strange directions they take. Would I ever find myself going yachting? Or fishing in the cold air or hunting for crabs? Or playing volleyball in a T-shirt and shorts? I looked at all the different men on the beach. Had any of them gone to the seaside with their beloved some New Year's Eve? Did he wander around a city that was not his, hoping to find her? Would he stand by the beach watching yachts, weighed down by the knowledge that her life was all grief? So many lives, so many dreams. Wasn't it this variety that made life sweet?

Contracts

On my way back, I saw a young man on the road put his thumb out to hitch a ride. I hesitated for a moment, but then my heart said yes. He came running and asked if I was going to a particular neighbourhood. 'No, I said, but if you show me the way, I can take you there.' He looked at me wide-eyed, before clambering into the car. Perhaps it was the first time someone had turned their car into a taxi for him. After all, he didn't know that I had no particular destination in mind.

'So what brings you here?' I asked him.

'I am returning from an interview.'

'How did it go? Do you feel optimistic?'

'It is not enough to have a good interview. If you want a job in this city, certain criteria have to be met – usually I never make it past those,' he said indifferently.

'What criteria?'

'Oh, you know, everything from your surname to what village you were born in to what colour clothes you are wearing,' he said cautiously.

'I don't know this place so well . . . Can you be more specific?'

'Well, if you are a local, they begin by asking you your surname. That's enough to tell them what tribe, clan and creed you belong to. The rest of the questions are all just for show.'

Traffic was not too bad that day. Certainly there were no signs of a city on alert after a bomb explosion. Other cities would have gone overboard with the police stopping cars, examining them, taking into custody anyone vaguely suspicious.

I said this to my new friend, and he laughed. 'The police know there is no need to search locals and their cars. They know better than anyone else where to find the bombs.'

I couldn't make any sense of that. He turned his head away and stared outside as if to stop me from asking any more questions. But I was determined to get more from him.

'I am new to the City. I don't know its history. As far as I know, this is a free place. You can worship whichever god you want to worship. You can ply whatever trade you want to. Or if you want to sing, dance, drink, smoke – the City doesn't stop you. So I don't understand why people are protesting against the rulers. In fact I think their kindness, their patience, their patriotism is quite exemplary. You think countries that call themselves democracies have something better to offer?' I asked, hoping to provoke him.

'I am not denying any of this,' he said passionately. 'You will get all that and more from the City. But let me ask you, do you feel brave enough to express an honest opinion in public about what happens here? In your own country, people can criticize the government, draw cartoons about them, mock them. Here have you heard anyone say a word of criticism about these supposedly patient, kind rulers? Try it for yourself and you will see their true colours. Everyone likes servants who won't utter a word. As long as you keep your mouth shut, they will keep feeding you.'

I realized that this young man had more judgement than I had given him credit for.

He had also been directing me all this time, pointing to streets and gesturing towards narrow alleys. By now we had arrived at a small village.

'The rulers cannot do what they do without coolie workers like you,' he told me. 'They have their reasons for keeping you around, including incidents like the one this morning. But the moment you have lived out your usefulness, they will throw you out. Don't expect to see any of this kindness and patience then. You won't be able to move even a finger against them. Do you know that the salary scale is still what it was in the 1970s and 1980s? If you question that, they will simply fire you and bring in new workers from other countries. India or Pakistan, or if not that then the Philippines or Korea. There's always Bangladesh. The entire continent of Africa. They even have their eyes on Vietnam. You think they are being patient and kind? They are thinking, hmm, where can we find the next generation of slaves? The fact that you are allowed to live here means they still need you. Get rid of any other hopes.'

He thanked me and got off at a bus stop. I said goodbye and drove on. Then I saw him hailing me again. I stopped and lowered the window. He put his head inside and said, 'Every child in this city knows that the bomb that exploded today was our own government's bomb. They have started killing foreigners to make the locals look bad. Beware!'

Edwin was wrong, I thought to myself, Arab young men were not just characters in an old folk tale.

Not for Sale

No one was home when I returned. They must be hunting big game, I thought. Or maybe they were sitting in the office gossiping. Anyway, I was done for the day. I ordered some food and was waiting for its delivery when I noticed what a mess the flat was. It was, in fact, the cliché of a bachelor pad. I thought of how back home in Canada I would scold Shanti if even a single thing was out of place. She would respond, 'A home is not a still-life portrait, Pratap. Let things move around, otherwise our life will feel as false as an ad on television.' Even she would be wonderstruck at the mess in which I was living now. If she were to see this, I would never dare to lecture her about tidiness again.

I started cleaning the flat as I waited for the food. Once the living and dining areas were a bit tidy, I turned to my bedroom. After getting it back into shape, I peeked into Vinod's room. The moment I opened his door, I was taken aback. God, was it possible for a human being to live like this? Papers in disarray, food crumbs everywhere, empty bottles and pan masala packets. Here and there were piles of dirty underwear – perhaps instead of wearing underwear, he simply shed them like a butterfly emerging from a pupa. This room was beyond me. I shut the door quietly and abandoned it to its fate.

Then I stopped by Riyaz Malik's room. That was the best of the three. Everything was in its place. The only mess was on his desk, where several books were scattered. I hadn't realized but Riyaz was a big reader. I browsed through his books. Most of them were in Urdu, with a few English detective novels. None of them piqued my interest. As I was leaving the room, I caught sight of another book – its corner was sticking out from under his pillow. I hesitated. Here I was walking around his room without his permission, invading his privacy. But then curiosity got the better of me.

The book was in English. *A Spring Without Fragrance*, by Sameera Parvin.

The cover was intriguing. A Patton tank in the middle of a road and a boy facing it, holding aloft an olive flag. His face was not visible to the reader, but we could see his strong shoulders and arms. Blood was dripping on his back from a bullet wound. It was not clear if he was shot from the back or from the front. It was clear though that the bullet had pierced his heart and had tunnelled through his body. This was his final act of resistance before death, the cover was telling us.

But the real creativity of the illustration was in a small detail. Where his blood was dripping on the ground, a small plant with a single flower had bloomed. The cover was a collage of both photo and painting. The cover was by Parvez Ahmed, I learnt when I opened the book.

'Based on the true experience of an expatriate Pakistani woman', said the byline on the cover. The blurb on the back called the book 'the story of a people whose lives were ground to dust by the wheels of authoritarianism'. A few lines of praise from public figures, as is typical with books in English. I looked for a photo of the author but there was none. Her biographical information was just three lines: 'Sameera is a twenty-four-year-old woman from Pakistan. An MBA graduate, she worked in a private company abroad for four years. She now lives in her home town, Faisalabad.'

Despite the extraordinary beauty of the cover, the pages were of bad quality and the printing reminded me of those photocopied books you find in second-hand shops on the sidewalk. But then I noticed something strange. Though the book was written in English, the writing was printed from right to left, the way Arabic, Hebrew and Urdu texts are written. So you had to turn the pages towards the right as you read.

An even bigger surprise awaited me when I got to the very first page. It said, 'Free proof, not for sale.' Beneath that were the words, 'This is an uncorrected book proof made available in confidence to selected persons for specific review purpose and is not for sale or other distribution. Original copy will be available soon.' In all my years of reading, I had never come across a semi-published book such as this one. I was turning the page when the doorbell rang. I almost had a heart attack. I quickly ran out of the room, leaving the book behind. The delivery boy was at the door. I burst out laughing at myself. He stared at me suspiciously as he took the money and left.

As I was eating, my thoughts kept straying back to that book. But I didn't dare to invade his privacy again. Any minute now my roommates would return. How would they react if they saw me pottering around in Riyaz's room or if Riyaz saw me reading that book? They might conclude this was what I did when they were not around. I didn't want to look bad in their eyes. I decided to do the dignified thing and borrow the book with his permission.

But the book had taken hold of my imagination. What did those mysterious pages contain?

Book

Two things bothered me as I sat on the balcony enjoying the lights gleaming in the harbour. The first was Jasmine's letter. The things she told me about her marriage. Pain stirred inside me whenever I thought of her. What was the point of the playful little surprise I had been preparing for her? She was in no position to enjoy games. I emailed her.

Jasmine, the life you described is the life of so many women in this city. But I never guessed that you, of all people, would have to endure it. Is this why I surrendered you to someone else? Until the moment I read your mail, I believed that you lived a full, rich life, blessed with every good fortune. Once again, life has reminded me that our beliefs can lead us astray.

I don't know how miracles work. But let me ask you this: what if someone very dear to you were to come to your city in search of you? Would that bring you joy? Excitement? If so, start believing that the amazing is about to happen. Someone has arrived in this city to catch a glimpse of you. His breath is part of the air of this city. Jasmine, he wants to see you.

I felt relieved as soon as I sent that mail. It was as if I had finally put down a burden I had been carrying all day. Almost immediately after that, I became aware of another burden: a book called *A Spring Without Fragrance*.

I had to read it. I went to Riyaz's room. In all these days of apartment sharing, it was the first time I had gone to visit him in his room. Riyaz stopped writing and greeted me.

'Are you busy?' I asked him.

'I write a couple of newspaper columns,' he said. 'It's the most annoying job in the world. But I have a small loan that needs to be paid, so I just have to do it.'

'I just wanted to see if you have any magazines I could borrow. I'm so bored,' I said.

Riyaz looked through his books and said, 'Sorry, everything is in Urdu. If any crap will do, here are a couple of detective novels in English.' He showed me the novels I had seen earlier that day. I pretended to look over them and shook my head to indicate I was not interested.

'But, Pratap, you should read detective novels and popular fiction. It's the best way to understand the underground culture of a society. I am a huge fan of genre writing,' Riyaz said.

But I was not persuaded. 'Do you have anything else? Maybe an interesting human story?' I asked, letting my glance go towards the pillow.

'Yes, but in Urdu.' Riyaz shrugged helplessly.

I almost said, 'What about *A Spring Without Fragrance*? But if he asked me how I knew, what would I say? I chose not to humiliate myself. I searched in his pile of books once more just in case, and left, disappointed.

All through dinner and in bed, I longed to read that book. Why had Riyaz avoided handing it over? What secrets did it contain? Or had he forgotten all about it? I had to know more about the book. I leaped out of bed and went to my laptop, wrote *A Spring Without Fragrance* in the Google search bar and hit enter. In the next 0.46 seconds, I got 60,000,000 results with the words 'spring' and 'fragrance'. Not one of them was about the book. I changed the order of the words and googled again – nothing. I tried the name Sameera Parvin. Google found 214,000 Sameera Parvins in 0.45 seconds. Which one of these Sameeras was the author of *A Spring Without Fragrance*? I kept playing around with the search terms, then crossed over to Bing, Yahoo Ask and other search engines. I had no luck even after carefully scanning Wikipedia, Answer.com, InfoPlease. From there I went to Facebook, Twitter, LinkedIn, MySpace, Google Plus, Google Hangouts, Orkut. Still no Sameera. And none of the online bookstores, from Amazon to BookFinder, had any trace of her book.

After an hour of futile searching, I finally had to accept that the Internet had no information about Sameera Parvin or the book she had written. And I was not just surprised, I was terrified.

In the morning, I was showered and ready before anyone else. I left just as they were waking up. I didn't want any company. Edwin and Vinod had both told me they wanted to take me somewhere. I wanted to avoid them. As I was leaving, I told Riyaz that I had to go see a friend urgently and would be late coming home.

For a long time, I drove aimlessly. Clusters of blue-uniformed workers were standing on the sides of the streets. As each company bus arrived, they ran into it, like a hive of bees, and clambered on. I marvelled at their ability to throw themselves into their lives. It is the poor and working class who are truly dedicated to living. The middle class and the rich squander life away. I parked by the side of the road to watch them. In a few minutes I was surrounded by a group of Pathans in kurtas. They told me that they were willing to work long hours for as little pay as I wanted to give them. I had to disappoint them. They must have thought I was a contractor trying to find cheap daily labour.

I drove on till I found a twenty-four-hour Starbucks. I whiled away some time there reading the newspaper. Finally it was ten o'clock, and I could be sure that everyone had left the apartment to go to work. I drove back. On the way, I confirmed that the flat was empty by calling Vinod and asking him if they needed the car. He said they were all going somewhere else with the new driver. Feeling more confident, I let myself into the apartment. Even so, my footsteps, the way I turned the key, the way I shut the door – a thief could not have been more careful.

First, I went to my room and lay down. Maybe I needed some mental preparation before committing my crime. Or maybe I was trying to talk myself out of it. But the book had become a dream by now. Finally I got up, summoned all my courage, made sure the apartment door was locked, and went into Riyaz's room. I checked under the pillow. But the book was not there. I went through the books on his desk. It wasn't there either. Riyaz had hidden it. My heart started beating faster. Inch by inch, I went over the room. I could not leave without that book. I searched inside the wardrobe and under the mattress and even in the toilet. Finally I found the book between some clothes in a suitcase under his bed. I was holding *A Spring Without Fragrance* in my hands.

I ran to my room as if escaping from a monster. Only when I got back to my room did I start breathing again. Surely nothing in life takes more courage than stealing. After checking the doors one more time, I opened the book.

Part Three

The Believers in the Pupa

Black Hole

The novel was narrated by Sameera, a young woman who worked at a radio station in the City. Though her storytelling was simple, the novel was well paced and had a gripping quality. I quickly got used to flipping pages from right to left. When I looked at the page numbers, I was surprised to find that I had read almost one hundred pages in one go. I had not paused even for a bathroom break. When was the last time I had read a book that had held my attention like this? Not in ten years. My passion for reading had remained frozen for years. This book had thawed it within seconds, and I delighted in this.

I had never been a voracious reader. I would read one beautiful chapter and then pause for a reverie. My imagination would transport me into the universe of that book and I would live there alongside the characters in the book. I would read a little more and return to enjoy my imaginary universe. Then back to reading. That was my reading style. As the end of the book neared, I would get very anxious. Soon I would have to leave my beautiful story universe and return to real life. Each book was a new life for me and every time a book ended, a small part of me died too. So I would do my best to extend the life of the book I was reading.

But with this book, I couldn't pause. Left alone, I might have finished it in one sitting. But the thought of being caught reading this book if someone came home suddenly made me stop. I went back to Riyaz's room and replaced Sameera's novel. The tightness I felt when I thought of my theft loosened a bit. No, I had not stolen a book. I had merely succumbed to the desire to read it. And now it was back in its place.

Before I went out to find some food, I did one more Internet search for the book. Again, I was disappointed. And astonished. It was as if the book had been born inside a black hole and it seemed to have died inside it too. It is readers who radiate the light of a book far and wide. But no one had done that. At a time when even a fourth-rate book was given hundreds of reviews and showered with opinions, why was no one telling the world about this book? Why was the whole universe ignoring Sameera and her book? Did every reader who read this book dislike it? Or had no one in the entire world read it?

Even more astonishing was that Riyaz had not even hinted about such a book to any of us. Considering we were researching stories for a write, this book seemed like a worthwhile find. It's not as if he had read it long ago. This was one of the books he had carried on this journey to the City. There was no way it could have slipped his mind. In fact, since it was under his pillow when I first saw it, chances were that he had been reading it in the apartment. Then why? Was he shrouded in secrecy, as Vinod had suggested? Who was Riyaz? What was his relationship to this book? A fog of suspicion enveloped me, and I couldn't breathe.

A Pile of Dogshit Called Democracy

Our destination was a Turkish restaurant called Pied Piper. Bijumon had recommended it. 'It's in the third gali to the left of the City's main gate.' Arab men were sitting on benches and tables on the street, smoking hookahs and eating kebabs. Some were immersed in chess games while others were playing cards or carrom. A young man with a long wispy beard was playing the oud, while another man sang. Their music was so soft that it seemed they were making it for each other.

We found a table and joined the hustle and bustle of the street. The people at the next table were playing a strange game.

'What is this game?' Edwin asked me, throwing a glance at them.

'I was about to ask the same,' I told him. Vinod also shrugged his shoulders.

'It's domino,' said Riyaz. 'It's a kind of dice game. Very popular in the City. You will see people playing it all day.'

Then the hookahs arrived. Edwin and I had chosen an apple flavour while Riyaz and Vinod had picked strawberry.

As soon as we inhaled the smoke, Edwin and I started coughing. 'Smoke slowly, you'll be fine,' Riyaz said.

The Arabs at the next table were laughing at our struggles with the hookah.

Within a few minutes though, we started enjoying the delicious smoke, and went back to discussing religion and politics.

'Let me ask you this,' said Edwin. 'Why is it that so many countries in the Middle East are still dictatorships?'

'You know those who have studied this topic extensively say that those countries are not ready for democracy,' Riyaz said. 'The people in those countries do not yet have the skills required to face the initial chaos of democracy or to use their voting power sensibly. Often, the economic systems in those countries will not be able to handle democracy either. If an immature public goes to vote, chances are they will elect another dictator or a religious demagogue. The price they pay then will be much higher than if the country had stayed a dictatorship. You can see this with Hitler, Saddam Hussein, Colonel Gaddafi, Hosni Mubarak, the Iranian revolution ...'

Perhaps he had misunderstood what we were talking about, but suddenly one of the Arabs who had been playing domino at the next table turned to us angrily.

'What is this fucking democracy? Some people here say they are the majority. How are they a majority? Because they all belong to the same sect? So adopting sectarianism is what the world calls democracy? If you think it is bad when a minority rules over a majority, think how much worse it will be when the majority oppresses the minority. Am I right or not?' He looked as fierce as a fire-breathing dragon.

Then someone else entered the fray.

'And anyway, can you name a single country that doesn't oppress anyone? Or discriminate against any of its citizens? Someone is always getting screwed, whether it is the Shias, or the Sunnis, or the Christians, or the Protestants, or the communists or the Kurds or the Serbs, or the indigenous. The faces may change but aren't all dictatorships the same?'

We fell silent. But he was not about to stop.

'I have a question for these Jasmine revolutionaries. Everyone knows that oil prices have been going up around the world, making all other prices go up too. So if people are starving because they cannot afford food, we can blame it on oil prices. Right, you Englishman?' He pointed at Edwin. 'Twenty years ago, a barrel of oil cost ten dollars. And today it costs two hundred dollars. How do you think that happened? The manufacturing cost has definitely not gone up. So what is it? It's the speculation games played by these OPEC sheikhs. So how come these Jasmine revolutionaries never protested about that?' He spoke accusingly, without letting Edwin or Vinod get a word in edgeways though they tried.

'If you find any protesters willing to protest against profiteering and market-rigging, I will happily join them. But these dogs only want a share of the profits for themselves. What they are saying is, "Give us our half of what you are looting." What justice do they care about? Will one of these holier-than-thou Islamic states agree to stop inflating oil

prices? Can Iran do that? No. Then stop talking about a pile
of dogshit called democracy. Democracy is justice for all the
people in the world. Democracy is not a choice between
ayatollahs and sheikhs and imams and sayyids.'

Another kebab-eater joined the conversation, directing
his speech to Edwin.

'Listen, you English have gotten into the habit of blaming
Islam for everything. What do you know of us? When
Khomeini issued a fatwa against Rushdie, fifteen Islamic
countries stood together to declare that it was illegal. Has
that been written about anywhere? So many Muslim scholars
have spoken out against Ibn Taymiyyah's Mardin fatwa, which
Osama and other terrorists use to justify jihad, but none of you
acknowledge that. You need Khomeini and Osama so that you
can keep scaring your people and making Islam the enemy.'

Yet another was pointing his finger at us now.

'You have no right to teach us what democracy is. We have
seen what your democracy looks like and we are not interested.
Who are you anyway to say that democracy should look like
this or that? We have our own models of democracy.'

We were all in shock. What had happened here? The
conversation had lost all logic. I realized that these men were
spoiling for a fight. I picked up the car keys and got up. The
others followed suit.

'Oh, you are leaving now? We have so much more to tell
you.' One of the men tried to block us, but somehow we
escaped. As soon as we got to the car, we burst into laughter.

'This is even more ridiculous than the time we went to see
Musa Alavi,' Riyaz said.

'This reminds me of the Hindi proverb "Bandar kya jaane adrak ka swaad". God knows what else this country has in store for us,' Vinod said.

Jasmine

The next day Edwin proposed a little game on the balcony. 'Get a piece of paper and a pen. I am going to read your mind,' he said. 'A Chinese sage came up with this technique. Asmo taught me the other day. She says it works 98 per cent of the time. Let's try it out.'

Vinod and I grabbed a pencil and paper. Riyaz hesitated. 'I don't believe in these things too much,' he said. 'Oh, come on Riyaz, what do you have to lose,' said Edwin. Finally Riyaz gave in.

'So I am going to ask some questions and you should write your honest answers. You don't have to show them to me, but you must write them down. Ready?' He went through the questions.

1. What is your favourite colour among red, black, blue, green and yellow?
2. What is your favourite number?
3. Write down the name of someone of your own gender.
4. Do you prefer the sea or the lake?
5. Write down the name of someone from the opposite gender.

'Done? Good. I am not going to look at your answers. I will leave it to you to decide how far this technique worked on you. So is everyone ready for my answers?' We all said yes, and he went through the answers.

1. If you wrote that your favourite color is red, you are careful and alert. Your life will be full of romance. If you like black, you are a traditionalist and a hothead. Blue: you are needy and require constant displays of affection. Green: you will always be tranquil. And yellow: you are always cheerful and provide good advice.
2. Whatever number you wrote down, that's how many close friends you have.
3. This person is your best friend.
4. If you like the sea, you know how to make others happy. If you prefer the lake, you are trustworthy.
5. You are in love with this person.

'So what do you think? Did the Chinese sage get it right?'

I sat there paralysed, unable to answer Edwin. Whether or not the first four answers had any truth to them, I could not deny the precision of the fifth answer.

I wanted to see Jasmine. How stupid was I to have wasted all these days not seeing her. Who exactly was I trying to defeat? Do we all walk on a perfectly straight path, without any deviations? Then why such stubbornness?

I looked at her photos on Facebook. Her face. Her eyes. The gleam of love in her eyes. Her cheeks. My kisses sleeping on her cheeks. Her smile. The sorrows hiding behind that smile. Though it had been three years since she returned to my life, we had not talked even once in that time. All these days I had been satisfied with emails and messages. But now suddenly I wanted to talk to her.

I sent her a message. 'Jasmine, send me your number, please. I want to hear your voice.'

Then I waited and dreamed.

I thought of the many women who had offered me their love. They promised me everything they had. Yet they did not move me in any way. Dancers, singers, artists, actors, writers, great beauties . . . but my mind and body were left cold by their sweet words or their creative talents or the curves of their body. But now I realized that true love always waits. I thought I was no longer capable of love. But now love had resurrected within me, it was sending its roots into my heart and blooming into the world, sending its flowers towards the sky. I see butterflies flying from my heart to dance around you. I never realized that daydreaming about a beloved could bring me so much joy. My darling, my life, you have returned love to this body. I feel blessed. Jasmine, I must see you.

A Disease Called Poetry

Ahmed Al Qaid had not forgotten us. He sent us some news items about a young woman called Ayat Al Omran. Edwin was eager to interview her and we asked Al Qaid several times to put us in touch with her. At first he refused. But finally he agreed and set out two conditions. The interview must take place in the presence of her parents, and we must go to her home to see her. We agreed to both.

Armed with the address he gave us and our GPS, we set out. After some time on the highway, we had to turn on to a narrow village road. Gloom lay heavy on that road, as if it were a bombed-out city street. The houses we passed on either side were like tombs, with doors shut, no signs of life. The few faces we saw on that road were scarred with fear and distrust. Eventually the tar road ended in a mud path and the GPS announced that we had arrived. To the right was a house with tall walls. This had to be it. We parked and pressed the bell next to the gate. A middle-aged woman opened the gate. 'What?' she asked irately. Though she was wearing a grey purdah, her face was uncovered. Her eyes were sunk deep, as if they had dug themselves into the depths of pain.

When we explained who we were, she took us inside. It was Ayat's father who opened the front door of the house. He wore pants and a T-shirt. His face was marked by indifference and a grey stubble. We waited for a few minutes. A little later, Ayat came out to meet us.

She was wearing jeans and a top and a headscarf. She was very thin. But her eyes were shining and there was a broad smile on her face. She sat in front of us, flanked by her parents.

Edwin and I didn't know where to start.

'What do you need to know?' her father asked.

'Did you start writing poetry at a young age?' Edwin asked.

'Yes, I started when I was six, right, Baba?' she said, looking at her father for confirmation. 'I wrote about rain and desert and wind and flowers. When I was in seventh grade – wasn't it, Mama? – we had hail in this country for the first time. Our poor car was damaged. Wait, what was I talking about? Yes, I wrote a poem about hail. That's when my poetry was published. An Egyptian publisher put together a collection of about a hundred poems of mine. There were two editions, right, Baba?'

'She has trouble remembering things, often forgets what she was talking about. The doctors have said she needs some coaching. That's why we are not helping her – so that she can use her own memory,' Ayat's mother explained.

'So have you published only one collection?'

'No, there were two more collections. One was *The Wind Mumbles*, the other was *Walking to the Horizon*. Right, Mama? There must be around three hundred poems altogether. Those two books were published in Lebanon. We went there for a vacation. It's such a beautiful place, right, Baba? I always wish Baba had a house there. Then I would write love poems like Khalil Gibran. Or I would sing like Fairuz. Have you heard her songs? What songs they are! I am crazy about her. One day I hope I will meet her. I would just kiss her.'

'What else have you written? Did you write any political poetry?' I asked.

'No, no. I always wrote about the beauty of life. About the green earth and rainbows and stars in the night sky. About giving this earth to the flowers and cats and worms. Right, Baba?'

She looked at her father. Her father looked at us.

Ayat continued, 'My first political poem was the one I read in Pearl Square. Were you there? What a big crowd that

was, right? It was such a wonderful opportunity to read to
them. How many poems are blessed like that, right, Mama? I
realized that day that only political poets get that lucky. Like
Pablo Neruda or Mahmoud Darwish or Ken Saro-Wiwa or
Ben Okri or Federico García Lorca. You too should write
political poetry. Only political poetry can go beyond titillating
a few intellectuals and inspire ordinary people.'

'But was it really a blessing? Didn't it completely change
the course of your life?' I asked, remembering the news items.

'No, it was not a blessing. I had forgotten. What miserable
days followed that, right, Mama? What was that poem I read?
Hmm ... oh right, "His Majesty". I wrote two more poems
after that. The first was "Traitor". The other one ...'

She tried hard to remember the name of the second poem.
But she could not. Her parents gave her hints but she still
didn't remember.

'Ayat, don't you remember ... it was called "Backbone",'
her mother said finally.

'Yes, "Backbone",' she said. 'That was the most famous
poem. I don't remember how many streets I read that poem
in. In fact, the protest would begin in each village after I read
that poem. Baba and I were so busy in those days, going from
village to village.'

'So when did the police come in search of your daughter?'
I asked her father.

'We were expecting that from the first time she read her
poem in the street.' Ayat's mother was the one who answered.
'One day two CID officers came and asked her to report to
the police station the next day. What else could we do. I took

her there. They questioned her for a long time, without me.'

'They wanted to know who was making me write these poems,' Ayat said. They kept telling me if I gave them a name, I could go. But I don't need anyone to make me write poems, right, Mama? I wrote three hundred poems! Poetry comes to me naturally. How could they question my talent like that? I told them no one has to teach the bird to fly.'

'After they had been gone for hours, I called her' – Ayat's father pointed to her mother – 'I was so worried. I had wanted to go with them, but everyone said it was too dangerous. I might never come back. Women are treated a little better. They are not thrown into prisons.'

'But his calculations were wrong,' Ayat's mother said with tears in her eyes. 'They told me they had more questions for Ayat and sent me home. I waited for a long time. I begged and pleaded with the senior police officers that she was a small child and should not be imprisoned like this. But they ignored me.'

Ayat's father added, 'That night, we ran around the City, knocking at the door of every politician we knew. All of them shook their heads. Someone mentioned a member of the royal family who was very influential with the police. We spent the night searching for him, and finally found him after midnight, drunk in some bar. I fell at his feet and asked him for help. "Your daughter will be back home in an hour. But I will need some compensation from you," he told me. "Anything," I told him. "Any amount of money, and I'll get it to you somehow." He laughed. "Money! Who needs money! Send your wife with me to London for a month's vacation. Agreed?"

'We wept when we left that bar. Those days are seared into our memory forever.'

Ayat took up the narrative. 'That night many different officers questioned me again and again. I have forgotten so much of it, to be honest. I do remember them shining bright lights into my eyes and beating me with an electric baton. What a horrible night. That was the first night I ever spent outside my home. And on the bare floor, right, Mama?'

She looked at her parents, and seemed reluctant to continue. Her mother suddenly got up and walked out of the room, saying, 'Tell them, daughter. Let the world know what happened. What's the point of hiding it?'

'In the night, two policemen entered my cell,' Ayat said.

"You look like a little girl, but your boobs look like they are bursting out. So who plays with them?" one of them asked.

"No one," I said, trying to cover my chest from his shameless gaze.

"Oh, right, you are a poet, aren't you? So you prefer doing it to yourself, I suppose."

'I didn't even understand what he was saying.

"So how do you like to masturbate?" the other policeman said and smiled lewdly.

"I don't know what you are talking about. Please . . . I am just a child," I said, crying.

"As if. I bet you enjoy this all the time. That night when you read your poem in Pearl Square . . . didn't you spend the night in a tent?"

"Yes, and my Baba and Mama were there too."

"You must have been in a good mood after reading your poem. So how many people did you pleasure that night?"

'It didn't even make sense to me. I stared at him uncomprehendingly.

"Who did you sleep with?" he roared.

"With my Mama," I answered.

"Why, is your Mama a dyke? Tell us the truth. Which one of those guys fucked you that day?"

"No one did anything to me," I said.

"Stop lying. We'll call the doctor right now and examine you. He knows how to spot the difference between what you do to yourself and what others do with you. Do you know what the sharia says your punishment will be if your hymen is broken? Write down the name of some guy if you don't want to get into trouble."

"No one did anything to me. Call the doctor if you like," I said, summoning all my courage.

'They kept talking dirty to me and asking me all kinds of obscene questions, but I had no more answers for them. They took me to a cell with some other female prisoners. We were asked to take off all our clothes. When I hesitated, they hit me with the electric baton and tore my clothes off my body. Then someone with a camera took photos of all of us while the other police officers beat us if we tried to cover ourselves. They said they were going to publish the photos online if I didn't sign a charge sheet.

'Then they brought a piece of paper and asked me to sign. I did not. Right, Mama? I did not sign.'

'But, Ayat, we read in the newspaper that you signed a confession,' I said.

'Yes, I had to do that in the end,' she said slowly and looked at her father.

'She finds it difficult to talk about it,' he said. Ayat got up and left the room. Her father sat there with his head bowed.

'The next morning, we ran to the police station. They were expecting us. They asked Ayat's mother to wait outside and took me inside. "What a brave daughter. She didn't confess anything after a night of questioning," a policeman told me in a mocking tone. "But let's see if the father is just as brave." They showed me photos of Ayat naked. "If you don't want these published all over the Internet, do what we say," they threatened.

"I will do anything you say," I begged. "Please, please let go of me and my daughter."

'They made me take off all my clothes. Then they pushed me towards a cell with four or five girls in it, all of them naked. Ayat was among them. They asked me to face the girls and masturbate. I cried like a child. Ayat could not bear that. She said, "I'll sign whatever you say." She signed a confession that said some rebel leaders had encouraged her to write poems insulting His Majesty and then used her sexually. Those poor men – they are still under trial. We all know how that is going to end. Here, judgement comes first, the trial after.'

Ayat's mother and Ayat came out with some juice for us. 'Can I also have some juice, Mama?' Ayat asked.

'My trial was seven months long,' Ayat said, 'and then they sent me to a mental asylum. The judges found I had some

kind of mental illness that made me write poems. Poetry . . .
it is a disease, isn't it, sir?'

Ayat's mother said, 'They made her spend more than three
months in the asylum. Every day she had to take pills and she
was given electric shock treatment. In the meantime, we were
petitioning all the international human rights organizations.
She became a public cause. Everyone was talking about it.
And that is the only reason they released my daughter. But
by then the trauma had left its mark on her memory and her
intelligence. There's no going back to who she used to be.'

'Yes, Mama is right. I can't read or write like before. It's
like there's always some fog inside my head. I keep seeing
yellow everywhere and I want to spit all the time. I'll begin a
sentence and before it's over, I'll forget what I meant to say.
I guess they have fixed the poetry disease forever,' Ayat said
with a weak smile.

What could we say to that child? It is God's will?
Everything will work out? No, all we could offer was silence.
The best we journalists can do at times like these is listen.
We have no words of comfort or solutions. This helplessness
is one of the occupational hazards of journalism.

'We agreed to this interview only because you are from an
international newspaper,' Ayat's father said. 'Newspapers such
as yours had such a big role to play in her release. We felt so
supported by human rights activists around the world. In our
time of pain, that was a big deal. We were completely ignored
by our local media. Who needs the support of those dogs
anyway? They are far too busy eating from the royal trash bin.'

As we said goodbye to Ayat and her father and drove

back, that question kept ringing in my head. 'Poetry . . . it's a disease, isn't it, sir?'

Daisy

When I was a teenager, we friends would tease each other when we got acne. 'Someone somewhere is longing for you,' we would say, 'look at that "love boil".' We knew all the scientific explanations – hormone changes, oily skin, fried foods, etc. But it was more fun to tease each other with this silly superstition. But was it just a superstition, I wondered when I woke up the next morning and saw a pimple on my face, as tender as a baby leaf that had sprouted after the first rain. In twelve years this was my first pimple, and I had thought of you, Jasmine – who else could I blame for this?

Then I remembered Daisy. Daisy John who was my classmate in Delhi University. Pimples might make most people look bad, but on Daisy's face, they had a seductive beauty of their own. On her face the pimples looked like black spots on a full moon. We would tease her, 'Who could be in love with you so much that your face is always covered with pimples?' Had Jasmine not been the fire in my veins those days, Daisy would surely have become a part of my life.

I knew that she too lived in the City. I found her number on Viber and sent her a message, 'An old classmate has crossed oceans to come to your city. Please arrange a red carpet and a marching band to welcome him.'

She called me back immediately. She was convinced this was one of my usual tricks. So I had to prove that I was indeed in the City. But once I persuaded her, she got very excited. 'Please cancel whatever evening plans you have made. I am coming over to pick you up,' she said. But when I gave her my address, I could almost hear her mouth fall open. After all these years, she had no idea how to go anywhere other than her workplace and her regular shops. Like an ant, she had her routes and she never deviated. In the few days that I had been here, I had got to know the City much more than she had. Finally we agreed to meet at five in the evening, in front of the central post office that was next to the city gates.

I got there a bit early. Our new chauffeur, Faisal, dropped me off. That was the first time I encountered him. His driving was kind of crazy, full of sudden turns to the left and right, constant change of lanes and ignoring of red lights. 'Aren't you scared of getting into trouble with the police?' I asked, fed up.

'Pratap sahib, do you know what these colours actually mean?' he replied. 'The green light is for Europeans and Americans, like our Edwin sahib. The yellow light is for you and Riyaz sahib, and other Indians and Pakistanis. The red light means we locals can go.'

Then he laughed.

'Anyway, the police here are too busy to look at who is breaking traffic rules. In countries where the police have nothing else to do, they might come after you for this kind of stuff. But the police here have plenty to keep them hard at work . . .'

Perhaps he was right. The police probably thought good riddance to those who were killing themselves in road accidents.

In front of the post office was a portrait artist. He was lost in thought and cigarette smoke. I admired his pictures. Two Filipinos passed in front of us, holding hands and giggling. He asked if he could do their portraits. After a little persuasion, one of them agreed. As I sat there watching him sketch her, a young man came by selling coins. 'Only five dinars.' He handed me one.

'What is so special about this coin?' I asked.

'See here, this coin shows the Square of Pearls, where the revolution began. It was one of our important monuments. But the government tore it down after they suppressed the protests. They also withdrew all coins and stamps showing the Square. So this is a pretty rare coin. You won't get it anywhere else for five dinars. But I am fed up of carrying them around, so I am practically giving it to you.'

'What would I do with this coin?' I asked.

'Don't you want a souvenir of this city? It's going to be remembered in history because of these protests. It would be stupid to pass up this opportunity to own a piece of history ...'

We went back and forth, with me refusing and him persuading. Then a Lancer stopped in front of us and someone waved from the window. It took me a minute to recognize Daisy. Her hair was shorter and her skin was clear. But somehow, with all the acne gone, it looked like something was missing from her face.

'What is this? Have all your lovers dried up since you got married? Not a single pimple on your face,' I teased her as I abandoned the coin seller to his fate and climbed into her car.

'I think your hair must be greying so rapidly at a young age because you still have romance in your heart,' she served right back at me.

I asked her the usual questions. 'Husband Alex Perumal, thirty-seven years old; one daughter, Shweta, eight years old. Three days of the week, our marriage is on a high, and the sex is amazing; the other four days, we are ready to murder each other. I teach English in an Arab university. There, that's ten years of my life in a nutshell,' Daisy said.

I told her about Shanti and her job plucking innocent people's teeth and Aditya and Shankar and *Toronto Sunday*.

Every five years a human being changes fully, inside out. So when we see someone after a long time, they seem completely strange to us. But there are very few people who never change. Their character and personality and even gestures remain the same. Daisy was one such person.

We spent the rest of the ride reminiscing about our Delhi lives. I was amazed at how vivid Daisy's memories were and how eloquently she remembered them. It was as if she had stored each moment in a treasure box. Some of us look back at the past with pride and joy. Others only have relief at having escaped its clutches. But either way, the past is what gives meaning to our life.

Non-believer

Daisy's car came to a stop outside a huge villa with its own garden and compound, in a suburb of the City.

'Don't be taken in. We didn't get this villa because we are rolling in money. It's just extremely convenient for both our workplaces. The only problem is there is no school bus. So Perumal drops off Shweta at her school every day,' Daisy said as she opened the door.

'Mama!' Shweta came running. 'Don't run!' The maidservant came running too.

Even the Vatican probably didn't have as many photos of Christ and the saints as there were in Daisy's living room. There were at least five different idols of the Virgin Mary, in different poses. A special prayer room, an altar with a lamp . . . altogether it felt like a church.

'How does a sinner like you lie amid all these holy men?' I asked her.

'This is exactly what Perumal and I fight about!' Daisy said. 'And now you too had to point it out the minute you stepped in. There are two things in the world that are beyond explanation: the first is love and the second is faith. If you are not feeling it, it looks weird. But to the ones who are feeling it . . . nothing is holier. So just let it go. Otherwise we'll also start fighting!'

Shweta was a fun little kid. Within a couple of minutes, we had become pals. She sang a song for me and showed me a few Bharatanatyam steps she had learned. Before long, she was sitting in my lap and introducing me to Sweetie and Lucky, her favourite dolls. 'Uncle, don't tell anybody. At night Mama and Dada talk in Malayalam,' she told me in strict confidence.

Daisy left me in Alex Perumal's office and went to get tea. It was a spacious and inviting office-cum-library. A wooden plaque inscribed with Sartre's famous question *Qu'est-ce que la literature?* hung on the door. Through a floor-to-ceiling glass window, I could see the lawn and the garden. Another wall was all books, arranged neatly by subject. Lounge chairs were scattered everywhere for comfortable reading. And in a corner there was a treadmill in case you wanted to walk while reading, I suppose. The third wall was mostly framed portraits of writers. There were also pictures with the signatures of many great writers. A print of 'Guernica'. And, of course, a computer and a printer and other conveniences on the desk.

While I was drinking tea and browsing through the books, Alex Perumal arrived. His face showed all the tension you would expect in a chartered accountant. But he greeted me warmly. 'Oh, I was expecting an old man when I heard you were a classmate of Daisy's,' he joked. 'Now I am thinking she must have failed a few classes.'

'Oh Pratap, isn't it ironic to see someone who took two five-year-plans to finish his chartered accountancy studies make fun of a Delhi University rank holder?' Daisy retorted.

'Sorry I was late. The traffic was worse than usual. The protesters have started a couple of fires.'

'Oh, are they still at it? I thought things were back to normal,' Daisy said.

'Oh no, it's not going to end that fast. Now they are

addicted to rioting. They are not thinking how fast they can end it; they are thinking how much more they can prolong this.'

'Violence, arson, bombs . . . what next? When will these jerks be satisfied?' Daisy said. 'And what are the damn police and the military doing? Why don't they just shoot all these rioters?'

But Perumal's voice suddenly changed. 'Now, Daisy, you must not say that. I may be a non-believer, while you are a believer. But that means you should hold yourself to a high standard.'

Both Daisy and I looked at him, not understanding.

'Patience, love, mercy . . . these are not just words to be read in some holy book. We have to put them into practice, especially in times like these. Surely your Christianity is not simply about putting up pictures of saints on walls and making the cross sign before eating? Should it not extend to every person on the street? How easily you condemned the rioters to police execution. What do we want? Do we want them to protest in their own country only according to our convenience? Or should they stay silent all their lives? And what about those who get killed by the police? What about their families? Are they not human? Do you wish my fate on others? Even if they are our enemies, you must not. Otherwise this Christian faith that you carry around will be an empty shell.'

Daisy went over to Perumal and hugged him. 'Sorry, Perumal. That's not what I meant.'

'No need for sorry or thank you between us,' Perumal said tenderly.

'Then thank God that you reminded me of this.'

'Daisy, if mere mortals like us feel bored of formalities such as thank you, imagine how bored God must be with our gratitude. Only acquaintances say thank you to each other, which means if anyone should thank God, it is me, since we are not very close.'

'See, Pratap, this is classic Perumal. He has defeated me by my own logic. Never mind all that. In case you are wondering, he is an orphan. He lost his parents in the Delhi riots. He gets very passionate about these issues. Please forgive him,' Daisy said to me, but it was almost as if she were consoling herself.

Then Perumal asked me what I was doing in the City. I told him all about Canada and James Hogan and the novel whose research I was leading.

'I wonder why writers feel the need for research. We readers have enjoyed so many books that have come entirely out of the imagination of their authors. We never complained that those works should have been fact-checked. In fact, we loved the wildness of their imagination all the more,' said Perumal.

'Maybe fact is stranger than fiction,' I said. 'Maybe writers think readers are bored of imagined worlds.'

'Or maybe some writers no longer feel confident about their imaginations,' Perumal said.

'Let writers write whatever they want to write,' Daisy interjected. 'Perumal, you are too critical.'

'Pratap, did I say anything you found annoying?' Perumal asked. 'I only made a general comment about writers. I am a good reader, so I have the authority to comment on them occasionally.'

'We don't need to overthink this,' Daisy said. 'Let's talk of something else.'

'This is just work as far as I am concerned,' I said. 'James Hogan challenged me to do this and I took it up. I haven't given this a lot of thought otherwise.'

Perumal went away to freshen up and Daisy and I fell back into our conversation about Delhi, or rather, she talked and I listened.

'Daisy, if you keep sitting here going over all your Delhi epics, we'll have to take refuge in some restaurant,' Perumal said when he returned shortly. 'Don't you think Pratap would prefer a couple of chapattis and some korma made by your own hands?'

'This is a husband's jealousy speaking,' Daisy said. 'He cannot bear to see me simply sitting around and relaxing. Especially with a man friend. All right, I hereby give you the baton of conversation. But please don't kill him with your literary criticism.'

Perumal and I stepped out into the backyard. The lawn was fringed by flowerpots, and beyond it was a small vegetable garden.

'I did this for fun,' Perumal said as we walked through that garden. 'But back in Nashik in Maharashtra, I have sixty acres of farmland. All vegetables. I didn't do it for an income, Pratap.

Part Four

The City Without Doves

Ismael

'Pratap,' said Perumal, 'my dearest friend in the City is a man called Ismael. We are not classmates or co-workers. We don't eat together or drink together or visit bars. Neither do we talk on the phone or chat online. And yet, our friendship runs deep. What binds us to each other is something that goes beyond all these usual clichés: books. I am a reader and Ismael is a bookseller. He sells out of a shop that he shares with a paan vendor in a narrow gali near the gold souk. In fact, only his usual customers know about the existence of his shop. You can barely stand upright in his shop. But it is all you need. Ismael has every one of the great classics of world literature. And it is he who tells me about newly published books I must read.

'I know I boasted that I am a reader. But I am merely a worm before Ismael's reading. That man knows books like nobody else does. He could defeat anyone at the book criticism game. Whenever he gets hold of a good book, Ismael sets aside a copy for me. He probably understands my taste better than I do. When I am browsing, he'll give me advice. "Don't bother with that one, you won't like it" or "That book is a waste of paper, sir. Don't be taken in by the big name on the front cover," or "That one's good for passing time, but it has no depth to it." On the other hand, if he sees me bypassing something worthwhile, he cannot bear it. I have never taken a loss on one of his tips. It was he who made me read Saramago's *Blindness* and Malika Oufkir's *La Prisonnière* and J.M. Coetzee's *Summertime* and Ayan Hirsi Ali's *Infidel* and Ismail Kadare's *Broken April* and Mo Yan's *Republic of Wine* and Axel Munthe's *The Story of San Michele* . . . He introduced me to Bolaño and Toscana and Jonathan Franzen and Nadifa Mohamed and Maaza Mengiste and Nadeem Aslam and Mohammed Hanif and Taiye Selasie. Now do you see how wide and deep his reading is?

'If he didn't see me for a while, Ismael would call. "Drop by soon, I have a couple of books you might be interested in." Sometimes I would ask him to find me a book, and no matter how rare it was, no matter where in the world it had been published, within two weeks, he would have it ready for me. A bookseller who can read your mind is a blessing. No wonder he was my best friend.

'About six months ago, I got a call from Ismael. "Sir, I found a very special item. I have set it aside just for you." Now, you must understand that Ismael is not the kind of guy who calls a book an "item". I knew that the book must be something remarkable. I wanted to go right away, but then I got busy with work. Besides, it was a book. It wasn't going to run away, was it. A week later, Ismael called again. "Sir, I can't keep this around for much longer. Come soon."

'The next evening, I went to Ismael's shop. He asked me to wait while he dealt with the customers. When the shop had emptied, he took the book out from under a pile of books. He had been hiding it there. "Sir, I have only one copy. Read it quickly and then return it to me. And don't show it to anyone else." But I got lazy and I didn't get around to reading it for a few days. I would keep picking up the book, gaze at the cover, inhale its new book smell, run my eyes over the introduction, flip through a few pages and then put it back. I am always reluctant to begin reading a book. Even with a book that I have bought eagerly, I keep it around, touch it every now and then, develop a relationship with it, and only then can I start reading it. I am like a dog that smells its way around a new kennel, hesitant to enter it right away. So the book stayed on my desk unread.

'Two weeks later, I was at home alone. Daisy and Shweta and the servant had gone out for some shopping. I had just gotten back from work and was about to change out of my work clothes. The doorbell rang. I opened the door to a couple of strangers, both local young men. They walked into the house smiling, without asking for permission.'

"What a beautiful room. Looks like you are a big reader, sir," the first one said looking over my books.

"Not really . . . I try to whenever I have free time," I said.

"What do you prefer? Fiction or non-fiction?" the second one asked.

"I am sorry, but who are you?"

"Oh, really sorry. Forgot to introduce ourselves. We are both just a couple of readers. I am Rashid, he is Jafar. We heard so much about your love for books and wanted to meet you."

"How do you know me? Who told you I was a reader?"

"What do we not know, sir? Who can keep secrets in this city? Aren't we all under surveillance by machines, including some living machines? All you need to know right now is that we know a lot about you. Don't bother with these silly questions. After all, we have something wonderful in common. Our love of reading . . ." Jafar answered me.

'I fell silent. Words simply failed me.

"So what are you reading right this minute?" Rashid aimlessly flipped through a magazine on the coffee table.

"I am reading *You Are Here*, by a new Indian writer. Maybe you have heard of her, Meenakshi Reddy Madhavan? It's probably a good fit for new-generation readers. But not for old-fashioned readers like me. But that's not the writer's fault. It is the reader's fault. The old ways of writing are inadequate to describe the new world that is forming under our feet. It is a kind of obstinacy to expect the writer to bring that world to us. Instead we must go there, where she is . . ."

'Never mind how strange the circumstances are. Ask me about reading and I'll talk.

"Yes, yes, these new-generation writers are not good for people like us. They are very shallow, aren't they? Too lightweight. We want writers who can show us the unseen depths of life. If you can't write like Dostoevsky, what's the point?" Jafar said.

"So, sir, where do you get your books from? Do you buy them online or do you have a bookshop you like?" Rashid asked.

"Usually I go to a shop in the souk. But I also order online. And, of course, friends often give me books."

"Oh, that reminds me. Did you read that new book, *Jasmine Wind from a Foreign Land*? I hear it's good," Jafar said.

"How could he have read it? I have been searching high and low for that book. It's not available anywhere in the country," Rashid said.

"Yes, this damn city never gets any good books. We only get the crap that says 'No. 1 bestseller in the world' and '10 million copies sold' on the jacket," Jafar agreed.

They kept talking of reading and books. I remained silent.

"You don't mind, do you, sir, if we take a look at your book collection? Don't worry, I won't borrow anything. I just want to see it. Surely no one in the City has such a great collection." Jafar stood up and walked to my bookshelves without my permission. So did Rashid. I followed them, like a cat whose space had been invaded. The book that Ismael had said nobody must know about was splayed open on the desk. I was praying that they would not see it.

Then Rashid noticed *The Moor's Last Sigh*. "Hmm, how did you get hold of this one?" he asked. "This book is banned here."

"But Rushdie is not banned," Jafar said. "Only one book of his is banned."

"No, no. It's very hard to find any Rushdie in this country," Rashid said. "Let's ask sir. He would know for sure." They turned to me.

'Honestly, I had no idea whether Rushdie was banned entirely or if it was just one book of his. Whatever be my answer, they would want to know where I got the book and I would have to mention Ismael. I knew that would be a betrayal.

"I don't know for sure whether Rushdie is banned here," I said. "A friend in Canada sent me this book."

'They seemed satisfied with that and went back to browsing. But it was not a reader's leisurely curiosity that I saw. Instead they looked at each book with a quick investigative glance. I felt deeply suspicious. Who were these two "readers"? How did they find me, a peaceful citizen whose only pleasure was some reading? Were they some kind of con men? But I felt helpless to stop them.

'And then finally, my luck failed. Contrary to every hope I had, they spied the book on my desk.

"Oh my god, look, Rashid, there's that book you were looking for," Jafar yelled. "Do you know how long we have been searching for this book? Couldn't find it anywhere. Sir, you are a lucky reader to have such good friends. I am jealous."

'Rashid snatched the book from his hands. "I had a feeling. Remember I told you on the way here, Jafar, if anyone in the City has the book, it would be him. So, sir, where did you say you got this book?"

"A friend . . . in Canada . . ." I trotted out my old lie.

"Lucky you. Extremely lucky, in fact. Your friend must love you a lot to make sure you get these kind of books. Could you share his details with me? I only ask because, you know, I love reading so much . . ."

"Well, he can't really be expected to send books to anyone who contacts him. He is not a publisher or bookseller, just a friend of mine. Besides, this book is not as special as you seem to think. I read a few pages and found it quite boring." I was hoping to underplay the book.

"Oh, is that what you thought? We heard quite otherwise. People have been talking of how you can't put it down once you start it. Anyhow, we better read it ourselves to find out. We have a saying in this country, when it comes to books and brides, listen to your own heart." Rashid put the book under his arm.

"Well, you are in for a big disappointment. This book is a big bore," I said desperately. "Also, I don't like to lend out books that I have not read. Leave it here for a couple of days so I can read it. Then you can come and get it." By now I was almost pleading with them.

"You know how it is with books, sir. They don't belong to any one person. Books belong to those who want to read them. In fact, I think it is high time they criminalized private libraries."

"No, I cannot give it to you." I tried to snatch the book from Rashid.

"Sir, please don't embarrass yourself. We are taking this book with us." Jafar held me back.

"Look, mister, if I know how to get hold of a book, I also know how to keep it. Please give me the book and leave my house."

'I growled like an angry cat and lunged at Rashid again.

'Then Jafar took out a small gun, smaller than anything I'd ever seen a villain wield in a film, and aimed it at me.

"Stop talking. And don't make any noise. We are taking this book away. Go sit quietly on that sofa or I'll have to use this bullet."

'At first I thought they were joking. I may even have laughed out aloud. But Rashid gave Jafar a single look and a bullet whizzed by me into the wall. My laughter evaporated. Like an obedient little lapdog, I went and sat on the sofa.

"We are taking this book away. We will return it to you when we are done. Do not try to find us."

'When they left the room, it was as if a hurricane had passed through.'

Station

'What could I do, Pratap? Nothing like this had ever happened to me, not even in my dreams. Imagine — two readers walk into your house, they take a liking to a book, and steal it at gunpoint. To think I had lost that book before I had even read a word of it made me want to cry. But to think that such an absurd drama had taken place over a book? I couldn't help see how ridiculous the whole incident was. And here I was, a character in this absurd drama. Who would believe me if I told them what had happened? Well, whatever, let them read it and bring it back. Please, let them bring it back, I hoped. A part of me selfishly worried that if they liked it, they might never return it and then I would never get to read it. Worse, they might lend it to somebody else. This is the fate of every good book, isn't it? But, of course, my real worry was Ismael. What would I tell him?

'Two days later, when I was busy at work, I got a call. It was Jafar, the one who had aimed his gun at me.

"Sir, thank you so much. We read that book in one sitting. What a gift. How nice of you to offer it to us. We'll get it back to you as soon as possible. In the meantime, I have a request. We are organizing a discussion about this book. You must come too. It will be in English and there will be lots of international readers. Rashid and I are not so eloquent as you. So you are going to introduce the book at this discussion."

"But I haven't read the book. You ran away with it before I could," I said innocently. To be honest, Pratap, my anger had completely melted by then. They may have pointed a gun at me, but they did it for a book after all.

"But that day you said you had read most of it. Are you trying to avoid us, sir?"

"No, Jafar. You took the book away before I had read even one line of it."

"I don't believe you, sir. A book lover such as you would never leave such an amazing book unread. Now if you don't want to come to our discussion, just say so. I can find someone else. But if you read the book, why lie about it? Also, there were some parts that were not so clear to me. For instance, let's see, yes, in chapter forty-four, the narrator talks of cars honking in a particular rhythm – pi, pi, pipipi. What does she mean by that?"

"Jafar, I swear I have not read the book."

"Okay, never mind that bit. What about the beginning where Ali does not go to the Justin Bieber concert? Why do you think that is?"

"Jafar, you are very suspicious. All I did was skim through the introduction. Get it back to me as quickly as possible and I'll read it and answer these questions."

"Okay, I'll get it to you right away," he said and hung up.

'Nothing for a week. No calls, no book. In the meantime, Ismael called. "Sir, if you have finished reading the book, can you bring it back?"

"I have a few more chapters left, Ismael. As soon as I finish . . ." I lied.

"Be careful, sir. That book is a bit dangerous. Don't let it leave your hands," he reminded me again.

'My insides caved in. What would I tell him if I never got the book back? He had given it to me so trustingly. I should have at least taken a number for Jafar and Rashid before letting them walk away with that book.

'Two days later, I got another call. This one was from a petty officer at the police station. He asked me to report to the nearest station the next day and answer some questions. I asked what the matter was, but he refused to say anything more. "Make sure you come," he said brusquely a few times. I smelled a threat in those words. I was annoyed. Why should I run to the police station because some guy called up and said so? I am not a petitioner or a defendant in any case. I am a well-regarded senior employee in a well-known firm in the City. If they wanted to ask questions, they could come here. The next day, I did not go to the police station.

'The day after, I got yet another call, reprimanding me for not turning up. "Who do you think you are? When we ask someone to come to the police station, we expect them to turn up. Or else we know how to make them come here. This is the last and final call from our office. You must report at the earliest." He slammed down the phone with a force that made it clear how angry he was. That's when I got scared. Till then I was under the impression that there was some minor issue and I must stop by sometime to clear it up. But now it was a matter of my record as a law-abiding resident in the City. I had no desire to stray towards the wrong side of the law. I ran to the police station.

'At the reception, they asked me who had summoned me and why. "All I know is that I have to report here," I said. He went inside and made inquiries. Then he came back for my identity card and some primary information. "You can wait here," he said, pointing to a bench.

'I waited. From around eleven in the morning when I got there all the way till afternoon, I waited. Many officers arrived and left during that time. They all ignored me. I got up several times, annoyed, ready to leave. But each time, the policeman at the reception told me, "Just a few more minutes. The officer was just asking about you."

'At some point, I was called in and asked to sit in a big room all by myself. I waited a long time there.

'By then I was also starving. I waited awhile thinking it would be good to be done with the police station, but finally I could hold out no longer. "Okay, go eat and come back soon," said the policeman at the reception. "By then the officer will also be free.'

'After having some snacks and juice, I came back to the police station to continue waiting. Time crept slowly. I had left the office saying I would be back in half an hour or so. And here I was twiddling my thumbs while everyone ignored me. I even wondered if someone had been playing a practical joke on me. Four, four-thirty, five, five-thirty. The policeman at the reception called me. "You can go home now. The officer was very busy today. Report back at eight-thirty tomorrow morning. He will see you first."

'I was so frustrated to hear that. But what could I do? Who could I express it to? If I were in my own country, I would have thrown a fit and yelled at the policeman. But this was a foreign country. Here I was a guest. Here I did not have the right to express my emotions freely. All I could do was obey. So I left the police station with a long face.

'My dog wouldn't come back, I muttered to myself as I left. They can do whatever they want. Let them come to my office and arrest me. But I am not returning here. The next day I woke up determined to show them what's what. But when I left home to go to office, I somehow ended up in front of the police station.

'I shouldn't let a small thing like this ruin my record, that's what I was telling myself now. The mind knows how to rationalize every decision.

"Nice to see you so bright and early," the policeman at the reception greeted me.

"I hope I can leave early too," I said, unleashing some of my resentment.

"Definitely. He is going to attend to your case first thing this morning. He said so yesterday. Please sit down."

"Do you have any idea why he called me here?"

"Only he knows that, sorry."

'I went back to my bench of the day before. Police officers arrived. Police officers left. I watched people come to report incidents, press charges. I saw the police bring in a couple of arrestees. I wondered what my situation was, which category I fell into. Two hours passed. Tired of being a spectator, I asked at the reception a few times. "What can I do? He is not here yet" was the answer I got.

"Then call me when he is here and I'll come right away," I said. "I need to go to the office now."

"No, no, no," the receptionist said. "He was very annoyed that you did not come on that first day when you were summoned. If he hears that you couldn't be bothered to wait for him today, it will be enough to get you into serious trouble. It's best you wait." A threatening note had crept into his voice. I couldn't pretend not to hear it. I went back to my bench.

'Finally around noon, the police officer who wanted to see me arrived. He recognized me the moment he walked in and gave me a stern glance. "So you came in the morning? Good. Wait here. I'll call you right away." Then he disappeared into the station while I continued my wait.

'That was a tough wait, because I was on pins and needles expecting to be called in any moment. I wanted to lash out at someone and scream, "It would be better if you put me in prison." But, of course, I did not want to be misunderstood.

As the moments dragged on, I became uneasy. Was I being mocked or scammed? Once or twice, I walked out of the station. But then I remembered the stern glance the officer had given me on his way in. Evening came and he still hadn't called me in. I couldn't help lose my temper. I went to the reception and made a scene. "What kind of game are you playing with me? Why have I been sitting around here for two days? At least you could do me the kindness of telling me why you called me. Do you think the police can do anything?"

'Hearing all the commotion, a couple of officers came out and asked me what the matter was. I explained everything. I was so angry that I was in tears by this point. They laughed as if they had heard a good joke. Then they went inside. I went back to my bench. The man waiting next to me on the bench smiled sympathetically at me.

"I have been waiting for seven days," he said. "If you think two days is too much, then imagine my situation. But in this country, if they ask us to wait, we wait. There is no other option. They make the law."

'I looked at him with surprise, and then terror.'

The Scream

'Do you know when I finally met with the police officer? In the afternoon on my fourth day of waiting. I followed a policeman down a labyrinthine corridor, marvelling at how big the police station was. Finally I ended up in a big hall, with a single table and a single chair in the middle. The policeman asked me to sit down and left. I felt as if I were trapped in a mine by myself.

'I sat on the chair and pondered what crime could have brought me here. Why had they shut me up in this room? Uneasy, I began to walk around, before I got scared that I might be breaking some rule and went back to my chair.

'Then, from the next room, I heard crying. I held my breath and listened carefully. The sound was a kind of frightened whimpering. The volume increased. It became a kind of grunt, as if someone were choking down something difficult. But very soon, it turned into a scream. A scream of unbearable pain. Then it stopped. I listened very closely but I could not hear anything any more. I ran to the wall and held my ear to it, while my heart raced with panic. Nothing. I ran back to my chair and sat there as if I had heard nothing.

'A few minutes later, a police officer entered the hall. He was wearing all his police insignia. He locked the door behind him. I stood up. He placed several files and papers on the table, sat down on the chair and asked me to sit on the floor. The humiliation of it shrunk me. Here I was, an important man with an important job in an important firm. How could he ask me to sit on the floor? I hesitated, but he insisted. I sat down. To sit on the floor comfortably requires an agile body. I could barely do it. Within a couple of minutes, my feet were trembling. All I wanted was to get up. But he gestured with his hand that I was to continue sitting there.

'"I apologize for delaying our appointment," he finally said.

'I gave him a wan smile. "That's okay."

'"We will take care of this matter right away," he said. "I have a busy day. You too?"

'I nodded my head, as if I had not been sitting in this station like a statue for four days.

'He took a book out of his folder and threw it in front of me. "Then tell me, where did you get this book from?"

'It was the same book. The one those two young readers had taken from me at gunpoint.

'I finally began to understand the truth of what was happening to me. So those two were . . .

'A thousand lies rose on my tongue. But I knew they were futile, that he knew exactly the path this book had travelled to reach me. Each lie I uttered would only incriminate me more. Yet, how could I tell him about Ismael and his little shop and how he had given me this book? It would be better to accept defeat than to betray a friend. So I told the police officer about my Canadian friend sending me books.

'Just then the scream from the next room sounded again.

"Don't worry, that is the scream of someone who lied to us. We know you are a very respectable person. You know that it would be impossible to get away with lying to a police officer who has been trained in the science of interrogation. So yes, you were saying?"

'A few moments later, the screaming subsided.

'I tried to establish my innocence by saying that I had not read even a line of the book and that it had been taken away by the two men.

"Okay, but we hear that you get most of your books from a shop in the City?" the officer asked.

"I do visit that bookshop in the City occasionally. But this book came from a friend in Canada."

"What is your friend's name?" came the question.

'For a second, I was taken aback. Of course, there was no such friend and I had no name to give him. He knew that as well and repeated the question.

"His name is Pratap," I said.

'Don't ask me why, Pratap, but your name was the one that popped into my brain in that moment. We had never met, but Daisy has told me so many stories of her college days. There was a character called Pratap in those stories, and eventually he moved to Canada and started working for a newspaper. And so I said, "He is a friend of my wife's. He is the one who sends me books." There was no way they could hurt you, I thought to myself.

"What is his address?"

"I don't know. We only use email."

"Don't try to spare your friend," the police officer said. "Tell us the truth. After all, we cannot do anything to him in Canada."

"No, I am not lying," I said, feeling the ground under my feet become a bit firmer. "Who uses postal addresses these days."

"You are an educated man of the world. Why do you have this banned book in your possession?"

"I had no idea it was banned. Give me a list of books that are banned in this country and I'll make sure to avoid them," I said, eager to prove how much I loved following the law.

"In other words, we might find other banned books in your library?"

"Possibly. But I don't have any books in my library that

I know for sure are banned." My confidence was returning minute by minute.

"In your library, meaning you might have those books elsewhere," he mocked me.

"Well, I do have homes in other cities in other countries. If a book is banned in the City, that doesn't mean I can't read it anywhere else in the world."

"So you have other copies of this book, but safely stowed away elsewhere?" He raised his voice.

'But I stayed calm. "No, I don't. What I mean is that if I came by another copy of this book, I would probably keep it somewhere else."

"So Ismael was right . . ." he said as if to himself.

"What? Which Ismael?"

"So you know Ismael?"

"Of course. I used to buy books from him."

"So he and you are partners in this book smuggling?"

"Book smuggling? Me? Definitely not. Some day I dream of owning a small bookshop myself, but the only relationship I have with Ismael is the one between a vendor and his customer. And I can prove that anywhere," I said loudly.

"Don't think that we didn't know about Ismael till you told us about his shop. Just know that he is in custody and has made some important revelations. Keep that in mind when you talk to me."

'Now he had me scared. What a time we live in. No one can be trusted. Maybe Ismael had betrayed me?

'For the third time, I heard screaming from the next room. It sounded even more pathetic now.

"No one who cooperates with us in the first phase of questioning will have to scream like this. But those who lie … we have the power to make them suffer," he said, looking deep into my eyes.

'I knew he was trying to scare me. But I had to stand firm.

"I don't need to open my fist every now and then to check if I have stolen something. And I am not scared of what someone else might have said about me. I know what I have done and what I haven't. You can definitely trap me in a false case. But everyone will know there is no truth in that."

"So should we not believe Ismael?"

"It's up to you who you want to believe. It is easy to arrest someone on some trumped-up charges. But your duty is to investigate real crimes, get to the bottom of the truth. That is much harder work."

"We believe that you are an important link in an international book smuggling network."

"You are free to believe that. But till you can prove it, these beliefs are not real."

"Why did you go to see a prominent lawyer recently? Why did you spend time with him?"

"A lawyer? Your spies are not doing a very good job. I have not needed a lawyer in all my years in the City."

"Who trained you then to answer so precisely to police questions?"

"No one needs training in simply telling the truth. Only liars need training."

"Cool down, man. We have to ask you all kinds of questions as part of our interrogation. That doesn't mean we are charging you with those crimes. But that doesn't mean you are not guilty of possessing banned books."

"If reading is a crime, yes, I am guilty. And I am ready to accept my punishment for that."

'He was silent for a minute. Then he gestured at me to stand up. My legs had gone numb from sitting on the floor. I rose up with difficulty. He took a paper from his folder and placed it in front of me.

"Our conversation has been recorded. This is an affidavit saying that everything you said was voluntary and you were not under any duress. You can sign here."

'I signed.

"You may leave now. That doesn't mean you are free forever. We can call you back any time and you are expected to show up immediately." He left.

'I sat there for a few more minutes waiting for the blood to return to my feet. Then I, too, walked out, my bones aching as if I had laboured all day.'

Parallel Lines

'I stayed home from work for two days. I couldn't tell anyone what had happened to me, not even Daisy. The previous couple of days when I had gone to the police station, she had assumed I was going to the office. So my fatigue and silence and sitting at home was all a bit of a surprise to her. "What happened? Some problem at work? Or did you quarrel with a friend? Any financial troubles? Or maybe some cute woman confessed she has a crush on you and you are scared of running into her?" Her questions were so innocent that even with how I was feeling, I burst out laughing.

'The next day, I was back at work. Slowly, those bitter memories of the police station faded. But that book had tightened its grip on my imagination. What was so unique about it? Why was it banned? The police were like bulls that had been shown a red cloth. The only way to answer those questions was to read the book. What had happened had happened. What else could they possibly do if I read the book? Maybe they would torture me again? Maybe a few days in jail? But I had to read it. I had to know what was in it. But where could I find that book?

'Only one person could help me, and that was Ismael. So that evening I made my way to his shop in the souk. But just as I had feared, the shop was locked off and sealed. A notice in Arabic was pasted on the shutters. I returned home disappointed. Whenever I travelled abroad after that, I looked out for the book. But I have never found it since. And then, not even six months later, I heard you were in town. You can imagine what I felt. I was sure you must be coming to seek revenge from me for having given up your name to the police. What a strange series of incidents.

'You know, I may not believe in the God that Daisy is constantly praying to, but I do believe in destiny. There is some meaning to our silly little lives. Otherwise, how did you get here, in front of me? Our lives were like parallel lines, fated never to meet, but here they are intersecting. Pratap, you are an investigative journalist and a world traveller. Won't you find that book for me? I'll pay any price. Just tell me where I can find the book. Here you are, on assignment for a writer. Consider this an assignment from a reader. Aren't we both equally important?' Perumal took hold of my hand, begging.

'But Perumal, you haven't even told me the name of this book.'

'Oh sorry, I forgot in the excitement of telling you the whole saga. The book is called *A Spring Without Fragrance* and the writer is Sameera Parvin.'

It was as if the sky had fallen on my head.

'What happened, Pratap? Do you know of this book? Where can I find it?'

I wanted to say an eager yes, that I knew about this book, and had even read some of it. About a hundred pages, perhaps. But luckily my tongue held back. A banned book? Why? Was it the story of this country? But none of the pages I had read indicated anything political. And how did Riyaz get hold of it? Would it be stupid to let Perumal in on all this?

In half a second, I had asked myself a thousand questions.

'Pratap, what happened? Have you heard of this book?'

'No, I was trying to remember if someone had sent us a review copy of that book. But the name doesn't ring a bell.'

'Oh . . . when I saw your face, I thought I was in luck. I was sure you knew this book. Well, surely you will be able to find it.'

The rest of the evening felt like a shadow play. Daisy announced that dinner was ready; we ate and reminisced some more about Delhi. Perumal dropped me off at home.

None of it seemed important. All I could think about was that book. I had to read the rest of it.

Terrorists

As soon as I returned to the flat, I went to Riyaz's room. Had I a gun in my hand, I would have done what those two readers did to Perumal. I would have pointed a gun at Riyaz and said, 'Give me the book you were hiding under your pillow.' I was that ready. With or without a gun, my plan was to ask Riyaz for the book. But he was not alone. There were three or four strangers in his room and they were drinking soft drinks and eating snacks. For a minute, I was stumped.

'Come join us, Pratap. Where have you been?' Riyaz said more warmly than usual.

'I was visiting a friend.'

'Good. We are all beginning to find our friends in the City. These are my school friends. I finally tracked them down today.'

Riyaz introduced me and I gave the obligatory handshakes and smiles.

'Did you need me for anything urgent?' Riyaz asked.

'Oh, nothing like that. I thought I'd borrow one of those crime thrillers you showed me.'

'No problem, here you go.' Riyaz gave me the books. 'We are going to hang out for a bit.'

'Goodnight.'

'Goodnight.'

I returned to my room, annoyed with myself and with life. I turned to the Internet for one more desperate Google search. Nothing new came up. I kept hoping Riyaz's guests would leave. But their laughter and talk could be heard all the way in my room.

A bit later Vinod came to my room, looking sulky.

'Who are these terrorists who have come to visit Taliban?' he asked. 'I am trying to sleep.'

'They are old classmates of his. You know how it is meeting old friends after a long time. Let it go.'

Vinod, however, was in no mood to let it go. 'I, too, can find some old friends to come and sit in my room at night. But when it's a shared apartment, you have to have some manners. Is this some cheap hotel? Either you should put an end to this or arrange another flat for me,' he revived his forgotten demand.

'Vinod, just let it go for tonight. I'll talk to Riyaz.' I calmed him down and sent him off.

On many nights, Vinod and Edwin and I had got drunk together in the apartment and behaved like boors. Riyaz had joined us in those moments, always perfectly calm. Not even once had he expressed any resentment about those gatherings that he was on the sidelines of. But today he had two guests, and suddenly it was a crime. What selfish creatures human beings are, thinking constantly about their own comforts and conveniences.

I started on the thriller that Riyaz had given me. The opening scene reeled me in. Two men are cleaning the streets and watering plants by night when a speeding car passes by and throws a corpse at them. It is the body of a young woman. One of the street cleaners recognizes her as a woman he had once loved. She had mysteriously left the City one day.

Somewhere in between those lines, I fell into a memory of my own. Isn't that one of the pleasures of reading? There are always pathways and alleys inside every paragraph that lead you back to your own life. I imagined that I was the young man, and it was Jasmine whose body had suddenly appeared in front of me. How horrible that would be. Why hadn't Jasmine written back? What danger was she in? Every day I would check my inbox eagerly, only to be disappointed that she hadn't mailed me back. Back when I was in Toronto, things were different. She would reply within a day or two. I had put so much faith in this friendship when I came to the City. But she had abandoned me to this emptiness. I sat down and wrote another email.

Jasmine,
Sometimes silence is a good response. But it has the fatal flaw of being open to interpretation. So whatever your opinion, it would be best if you told me what it was. I am surprised by your coldness. I thought you would explode with happiness when I told you that I was in your city. Instead, you withdrew deeper into the recesses of silence. I don't understand. We are not strangers. We loved each other deeply for twelve years. Can you imagine the joy I felt when you appeared in my life again, like the gleam of a pole star far away. But that joy was not the joy of a greedy

lover. It was the joy of finding a part of myself again. It was the joy of knowing that not all losses are permanent.

I was reading your old emails just now. The dreams you shared with me. How many times you pleaded with me to stop over in the City when I went to India. All you wanted was a glimpse of me, you said repeatedly. You even joked, 'Can I borrow some of your seeds and grow them in my stomach?' And now, when life has brought us together, you want to stay away from me? Has my arrival frightened you? Do you prefer the safety of distance? What are you afraid of – me or your marriage? Or is it society?

Jasmine, however much you turn away from me, I want to find you. Like those tiny crystal fish that chase whales into the deep sea, some day I'll swim all the way to the darkness that surrounds you. When I find you, I'll remember this journey with joy.

But if you'd rather not be found, please write to me frankly. I thought I understood you. Maybe I don't. But I am at least capable of accepting your decision. If you cannot count on me to follow your wishes, then I am not a good friend.

Whatever is frightening you, please tell me. Jasmine, I live in hope.

Pratap

Fear

The next morning Riyaz sought me out. 'There's a place we need to go to today. One of my friends from yesterday is going to introduce us to a very important person in the City.'

'Who is it?' I asked without much interest, because I had been hoping to sneak into his room like a thief and read his book after he left.

'He is a doctor, very influential in the government here.'

'Riyaz, why don't you take Edwin with you? I am fed up of this research. Wandering around the City, asking people stupid questions. There is zero creativity in this. This is fine for people without much experience. But I am wishing I hadn't taken this assignment.' I made my indifference clear.

'But, Pratap, even gold mines are filled with dust. Yes, these factoids we are collecting might be boring. But tomorrow when the writer turns it into a narrative, we'll see the beauty of the dust.'

'I like this philosophy, but right now I am in no mood to apply it. I just want to be left alone.'

'I am not criticizing you, Pratap – I am just being candid with you. If you accept an assignment, you have a duty to it, whatever it is. The middle of every task is boring and difficult. It is best to foresee that and say no to assignments you are not interested in.'

'But, Riyaz, I am not shirking my duty. I am trying to find a new way to explore this city. We are rushing around interviewing people and collecting their stories, but are we truly experiencing this place? We are merely floating on the surface and we will leave the City with some hearsay. If we must truly take the pulse of this city, we must experience it.'

The words were just popping into my head as I spoke, but now that they were said, I couldn't help thinking they made sense. Sometimes our mind reveals what we don't know that we know.

'I agree one hundred per cent,' Riyaz said. 'You have all my support for this new idea. We should discuss it more this evening. For now, let's go meet that doctor.'

'Why? Why do you need me? Edwin or Vinod would love to do this.'

'I have nothing against either of them. But sometimes you feel an affinity for one person that you don't feel for others. I feel like we are on the same wavelength . . .'

What could I say to that? I gave up and we drove off. On the way, Riyaz picked up one of his friends. Politely, I asked him his name.

'Oh, did you already forget? We met just yesterday.'

'Please forgive me. I might have to ask you another twenty times. I have a terrible memory for names.'

I was not exaggerating. For years I had tried many tricks to remember names, but none of them had worked. Sometimes I would forget the name of a co-worker who would have sat across from me for five years. Why, once I forgot Shanti's name. I had even gone to the doctor to find out what was wrong with me.

'Whether or not you forget it again, this is the last time I am going to tell you. My name is Jahangir.'

'How do you and Riyaz know each other? Were you classmates in school?'

'Yes, we were in the same class for two years after matriculation. Then we were in different schools for our intermediate years, but we would still meet up. However, yesterday was the first time we met since then.'

'What do you do here?'

'I run a cable television service. To be honest, it is not legal here. But I know a few people in the police service. Even so, once a year, they come and confiscate my receiver and cut the cables. And I begin all over again. What else can I do? There's law and then there's life.'

'Ah, okay. And who are we going to see now?' I had resolved after meeting Al Qaid with Edwin that I would do a little prior research before interviewing people. But Jahangir refused to tell me who we were meeting. 'Just come with us. Don't worry about who and what,' he kept saying. I was annoyed but did not express it.

While the car was waiting at a signal, some Arab boys walked among the vehicles selling this and that. One boy was selling water bottles while the other had strings of jasmine flowers. Still others were selling strawberries and little toys and dates. As the lights turned red at the different corners, they ran up and down streets and between cars, risking their lives.

Whenever I see these sellers at a signal, I feel a whirl of panic rise within me. I don't know why. Each time I resolve to buy something from them, but then I worry that before I can give them the money, the lights will change and the car will have to leave. When I see them handing over whatever they are selling to someone inside a car, my panic increases. I pray that the lights stay red, the customer inside the car finds his or her wallet quickly, and they have the right change for the transaction. I was constantly afraid that someone might choose to trick them and drive away. This is not a new anxiety. When I was in school and college, if a teacher called on someone to answer a question, I would panic on their behalf till they finished answering. If someone was asked to recite a poem, I would recite the poem under my breath with them. If someone got on stage to make a speech, I prayed that they wouldn't get tongue-tied, that their words would flow easily and naturally. In college, if a friend was acting in a play, they would not be as stressed as I was, sitting in the audience praying that they got all the dialogues right. And now that fear had reincarnated at signals such as these.

Most drivers ignored the boys. Perhaps they were also panicked like me. Or perhaps they were indifferent to them. But Riyaz lowered his window and got two bottles of water.

'Are you mad?' Jahangir asked. 'If you wanted water, we could have gone to a shop. This is probably bad quality.'

'I don't need water. I just want to encourage them.'

'Encouragement for what? Do you think they support their families with your money? They are going straight to the drug dealers.' Jahangir's voice was cynical.

'And do we not misspend our own hard-earned money?' Riyaz replied. 'We have to look at their hearts, Jahu. Every time a fancy car passes by ignoring them, they feel their lowliness keenly. Poverty and resentment are what makes terrorists. After all, we are all products of our systems. And if we don't want to breed tomorrow's terrorists, we should spare a thought for these kids.'

Yellow Lines

Eventually we arrived at the City's medical college. On either side of the gate, an enormous armoured tank stood guard. With upright guns on either side like horns, the tanks looked like giant wild bulls. We entered and saw a tarpaulin tent, where masked soldiers, their fingers on the triggers of their guns, examined each vehicle. Police dogs sniffed some vehicles, while a soldier studied identity cards and registered each visitor. Since Riyaz and I did not have national identity cards, we had to show our passports and were subjected to cross-questioning.

'Is this a hospital or an army camp?' I muttered to Jahangir.

'Well, it was much worse a few days ago. Every visitor had to undergo a physical examination. What else could they do after the rioters attacked the hospital.'

'Attacked?'

'Don't get me started. We can talk more about it on the way back,' Jahangir said as he led us down long corridors with yellow and blue lines on the floor to show the way.

Jahangir was a master of secrets, I thought. He found a peculiar pleasure in hiding and hinting.

We reached a consultation room in the emergency section. By then we had walked through a confusing series of corridors. If I had to find my way back alone, I would have to follow the yellow line. If only life too came with yellow lines, I thought, I would have traced my way back to Jasmine walking on the yellow line of desire.

A number of people were waiting to see the doctor, but

in all the time we waited, only one person was called in. I wondered how the doctor would get through all the patients if each appointment took so long. In any case, we didn't have to wait too long. An ancient doctor sat inside. He seemed to have gone completely grey with age. His hands were wrinkled and trembling. One did not expect to see such an old man in government service. He invited us to sit, but there were only two chairs. Riyaz and I sat down while Jahangir went up to him.

'Mamuji, this is the Canadian I was telling you about. Here he is trussed and bound. Ask him whatever you like.' Jahangir kissed his hand.

Why did you choose Canada? Why aren't you bored of living there? What does it have that other countries do not have? How did someone raised in the tropics survive those cold winters? What kind of precautions do you take in the winter? How much does a house cost in Canada? What would be a month's expense? How were Asians treated in Canada? Was racism a problem in Canada? How were Muslims perceived there? Were there any disadvantages to migrating in old age?

The questions came quickly without any preface. In all those years of journalism, I had interviewed many people, but no one had interviewed me. Though I felt a bit uneasy, I did my best to answer his questions. But what were his intentions?

'I am planning to migrate to Canada,' he declared at the end of the questioning, as if to answer my unasked question.

'At this age?' The words just slipped out of my mouth.

'Yes, unfortunately at this age,' he said in a melancholic voice.

'What brought you to this decision, doctor?' I asked.

He was silent for a while before answering, 'I migrated to this country in the early 1960s, having barely received my MBBS degree. I was twenty-four years old then. In those days, there were only English and Indian doctors here. I have worked in this hospital for fifty-two years. I am the oldest person here. I should have retired nineteen years ago. But the government insists that I stay. And I was happy to agree. This hospital is my entire life. I find joy in spending time with my patients.

'Around two years after I started working here, I had the privilege of treating His Great Majesty, the father of the current ruler. I was only a junior doctor. You know, there's no point saying I have an international degree, I am a specialist, I know how to diagnose and prescribe. There's more to healing. Just like some cooks have a special magic in their hands, some doctors also have magic hands. There's someone I know. A very smart surgeon who studied abroad. He knows how to perform neurosurgery even on newborns. But what's the point? He has no luck. Whatever he has operated on turns septic, despite all precautions. Every single surgery he has performed requires a follow-up, whereas me – I have this magic. I can prescribe water and it will work as well as an antibiotic. As luck would have it, I treated His Great Majesty and took care of a breathing problem he had had for a while. Since then I have been the palace physician. In this time, I have taken care of five of the most senior members of the royal family. If I don't have any pressing jobs at the palace, I come to the emergency room here. Because in all honesty, I get much more joy from treating poor patients.'

He paused.

'Forgive me, Pratap. Mamuji has been long asking to meet a Canadian. So as soon as we met yesterday, I decided to drag you here. Please excuse the suspense,' Jahangir said. I smiled at him to show that I didn't mind.

'A migration at my age . . . you can imagine that I am a bit nervous. So I thought why not find out from someone who has real experience, instead of looking at photos,' Doctor Mamuji continued. 'But I am worried about two things: the cold and air travel. I am terrified of planes. If only there was a ship to Canada.'

I laughed. Looks like I had found another friend in this foreign country. True, he was old and afraid of planes, but still.

The doctor took a call. 'I'll come tomorrow . . . ask him to calm down . . . tell him if he doesn't take his medicine, I am going to beat him up.' He was laughing as he hung up. 'That was His Majesty's private secretary. That scaredy-cat insists on seeing me at least once a week. You know, I am one of the three people in this country who can call him by name and scold him. The others are his mother and his uncle. And do you know why I have that privilege? Firstly, I have known him since he was a boy in shorts. But secondly, and even more importantly, I have never accepted an undue favour from him. Several times he has offered me citizenship, rewards, prestigious positions. But I refused them all. I have lived my life within the parameters that are applicable to any foreign resident in this country. The only benefit I have accepted is my house, and only because it made it easier for me to get to the palace. Living with integrity is the best medicine for a long and happy life,' he said.

'So what is wrong with His Majesty?'

'Oh, he's a hypochondriac. But on top of that, he now has something new called "tunnel disease".' He laughed.

'What's that?' I asked.

'It's a brand-new infection that has been spreading from one head of state to another. He can't sleep. If he does sleep, he dreams of being chased through a dirty tunnel. Eventually he is caught, dragged through the tunnel like a rat is dragged out of its hole, punched and violated, and in the end, shot. At this point, he wakes up suddenly and examines his body for bruises. Where did I get shot? Is this blood? Am I in the palace or in the tunnel? He is not able to sleep again. He complains of a heaviness in his chest. Counselling and medication don't work. What can I say, he is a coward. This is the first time he has seen a protest. I keep telling him, you need to practise facing your people. But he has always lived in the palace, surrounded by flattery and luxury. Do you remember that one time he addressed the country? His hands were trembling. His father and his grandfather were all lions. Nothing could shake them. But this one didn't get those genes. He will die of a panic attack. Once a week, he needs to see me.'

'Mamuji, if you have such a close relationship with him, why would you abandon that and emigrate to a strange country?'

'I, too, hoped to live out my days here and be buried in a qabar here. But the recent incidents in this country and in this hospital have shaken me. I know I don't have much longer. But I would like to be far away from these memories. A dying man deserves a little peace of mind.'

I remembered what Jahangir had said about the attacks by the rioters. And now here was Doctor Mamuji, a man of principles, shaken by recent incidents in the hospital. What had happened here?

Butchers

'This very hospital was the epicentre of the riots that took place all over the City,' Jahangir told me on the way back. 'I doubt what they did here has any precedent in all of world history. And it wasn't just happenstance. A lot of planning and preparation went into it. They also got a lot of support from some other countries. People keep talking of how the Arab Spring began with a random incident. Well, at least in the City, it did not. The truth is they were waiting for an incident like that. And by "they" I mean the same doctors who had taken the Hippocratic oath to put healing above all and to uphold medical ethics. You would be shocked if you knew how they conspired. First, they emptied an entire hospital ward in the name of renovations and made it their headquarters. Then they started collecting weapons and hiding them in the lab, the mortuary, the operating theatre and the wards. They used ambulances to smuggle weapons. They even stole blood from the blood banks and poured it in the protest zones to create an atmosphere of panic. This should be called the first hospital revolution in the world.

'But what made Mamu really sad was how the doctors behaved with patients. They tore into wounds and dressed them with chemicals that would turn them infectious. They pushed some patients towards death when they could have saved them, because the protests needed martyrs. They didn't do this to people in the opposite faction; they did it to their own. It was a drama they performed to show the world: look how cruel His Majesty's soldiers and policemen are.

'That one month, Mamu told me, the hospital was a place where every medical ethic was trampled on. It wasn't a hospital any more. It was a slaughterhouse. His faith in his profession was shattered. These are not healers, these are butchers, he said about his fellow doctors. He could not continue amid them any more.

'There were about three thousand foreigners working in this hospital. The protesters were planning to take them all hostage and bargain with the administration. They hoped that there would be international pressure on His Majesty to step down. But their calculations were incorrect. When the military retaliated, the first place they attacked was the hospital. Can you imagine, the army of a country attacking its own hospital? But it became necessary.

'You know, Mamuji saw the trouble coming long before anyone else did. When the government started appeasing these religious fundamentalists, he gave His Majesty a few pointed hints. But rulers will do anything to keep ruling. I still remember the day the protesters poured petrol on women who participated in a marathon in the City. Then they turned to bars and hotels and liquor shops. Still, the government did nothing. Maybe you think, good riddance to alcohol, women should wear purdah – what's wrong with what the protesters are asking for. But the protesters were using these issues to consolidate their power. Luckily our police stamped them down. Otherwise we would be in the middle of chaos now. At least for the next ten years we can expect some peace and quiet.'

The minute Jahangir stopped talking, a boy jumped on to the road in front of us from a high wall. If the car hadn't braked suddenly, he would have been crushed underneath it. Unflustered, he got up, raced towards a police jeep that was heading in our direction, and threw a flaming bottle of petrol at its bonnet. The bottle exploded, but the jeep was unharmed and the policemen simply ignored the incident and kept driving. The boy slowly walked back to the wall. Suddenly I wanted to talk to him. I leaped out of the car and ran after him, calling to him to stop and talk to me, in every language I knew. He gave me a mocking glance and disappeared behind the wall.

I thought then that if Mamuji had a reason to leave the City, the boy had his reasons to throw that bottle.

Cat

I longed for a day alone in the flat when I could read the book that was Sameera's, Riyaz's and now Perumal's. Just as a man who has decided to commit suicide dreams about death, I dreamed constantly of reading that book. Everything else vacated my mind. Researching the City, meeting Jasmine: none of this mattered any more. Like a cat with its eye on a fish, I circled Riyaz's room, but the flat was never empty. If Riyaz and Vinod left the flat, there was Edwin sitting around. It was almost as if they were taking turns guarding a treasure.

A few days later, I finally got the flat to myself. The relief I felt! It was as if I were no longer handcuffed and bound. I locked the apartment door and ran to Riyaz's room. First, I looked in the box under the bed. The book was not there. Under the pillow. Not there either. I was flummoxed. I remembered putting it back in the box. Did Riyaz know that I was reading the book? Had he hidden it elsewhere? Did he realize it was a banned book? How did he get hold of it in the first place? Why did he bring it here knowing that it was banned? Was it a coincidence that he had the book, or was there some intrigue behind it? Who was Riyaz?

I started searching the room carefully. I looked on the desk and inside its drawers. The bookshelves, the bed, between Riyaz's clothes. I even looked under the cushion of the chair and inside the pillowcases. As each new place turned up nothing, the anxiety in my heart increased.

By now I had messed up the room in obvious ways. But I was too far gone to care. As a last resort I searched in the bathroom. At first I found nothing. Then I noticed a few bath towels neatly folded on a shelf. I shook each one. And then from the towel at the bottom, the book fell out.

Eureka! I ran to my room as if I were tearing down the walls of reading heaven.

Part Five

Pirated Copy

Riddle

In one sitting, I finished half of Sameera's novel. I realized that the city she was writing about was the City. Her words described the heated days of unrest in the City beautifully. One thing was certain: she had lived here. She knew the City in the detailed, particular way that long-time inhabitants come to know a place. I felt as if I had met some of her characters in the few days that I had spent here. I decided to ask Bijumon and Priyanka and Abdullah Janahi and Faisal about the stories in the book. But I also knew that I had to keep the book's existence a secret, otherwise I, too, would become a criminal.

One day Vinod put forward an idea, 'It's been many days since we got here but we haven't done any sightseeing. Let's abandon work for a day and be tourists in the City.'

'Four men sightseeing. What a bore. Shouldn't we have some female company? Can I invite my girlfriend Asmo?' Edwin said.

'Why not. And I'll invite Priyanka as well. The more female company, the better.'

'Too bad these two don't have any female friends who can come along,' Edwin said about me and Riyaz. Perhaps it was true of Riyaz. But I wanted to tell them that I had a secret friend in the City and it was in search of her that I had come here at all. I didn't, but the thought of Jasmine immediately darkened my heart, like a raincloud gathering in the west. I had not progressed even one step in my search for her. I had never faced such a failure in my life. I felt stupid for promising Shanti that I would not seek anyone's help in finding her. What was the point of sticking to a promise like that? I decided to seek help from Vinod who seemed to know his way around such things.

'A name and email address. If that's all you have for someone, how would you track down them?' I posed the riddle to him that night on the balcony.

'Well, you could write to the person and ask them for their location,' Vinod said.

'But what if that person does not tell you their location? I am not joking. How would you find someone who does not want to be found?'

He stared at me. 'What's going on?'

'Never mind that. Do you have a solution?'

'It's a bit tricky but if you can get them to send you an email, you can use it to track down their IP address. Then you'll have to get the local IT cell to assist you. But it's a lot of hard work.'

'I have to track someone down in this city using this trick. Can you help?'

'I can try. It won't be easy, but it's worth trying. However, first, just like a lawyer needs to know the whole story before taking on a case, I need the whole story too. Who is this person? What do you want from them?'

I told him about Jasmine and how she had come back into my life after twelve years and how I longed to see her and how she had suddenly gone silent.

'Hmm. I see what you are saying, but no one is going to give an IP address because you want to check in on an ex. We need a better story. We should say that the person has cheated us financially or that she's harassing us via social media. Tell them we need the IP address so we can complain to the police.'

'Oh, that's a bit extreme, isn't it?'

'Sometimes we have to take some extreme steps to get to where we want to go. Remember, the end justifies the means.'

'No, Vinod. I don't want to find Jasmine by complaining about her. I cannot hurt her in any way.'

'Then she will just have to remain a mystery.'

'That's okay. I prefer that to besmirching her reputation.'

'This is the problem with true love. God, save me from ever loving a woman too much.'

Vinod paced up and down the balcony thinking aloud, 'Hmm, how can I bring these lovers together?'

'Don't call us lovers,' I said. 'Our relationship has gone well beyond that. It has no comparison with what we call "love".'

Vinod stopped and stared at me. 'Don't mind my asking this, but do you have any problems in your marriage?'

'Shanti is my best friend, my guide, my adviser, my manager, my partner.'

'Then why are you chasing this other woman?'

'That has nothing to do with whether my marriage is good or bad, Vinod. I don't know if you will understand. Adam is always looking for his lost rib. Jasmine is my lost rib.'

'I don't know . . .' Vinod shrugged. 'Maybe my rib was scattered among many women. In fact, from my broad experience as a first-class skirt-chaser, I can tell you that most of the women I have bedded were not single women, but seemingly happily married domestic goddesses. They found a special delight in taking revenge on their husbands in my bed. There is no system more broken than marriage.'

I had no answer to that. I believe in marriage, in its stability and its love and its togetherness. But then we all have pet theories about systems. It is best to believe in them. Otherwise how would we bear life?

'Oh yes,' Vinod said happily, 'what if we say that the woman with that IP address is your sister and that you have been out of touch with her for years? That kind of sentimental crap always works on people.'

I, too, liked the idea. Vinod helped me write an email about my sister who had been missing for years. It was full of brotherly love. He put his language and persuasion skills to good use. We sent it off to the service provider right away.

I sat there on the balcony long after Vinod got up and left. I felt a closeness to Jasmine again, although all I had done was send off an email in search of her. She did not know this, but every time I visited our old city, I would go, like a pilgrim, to the restaurant where we first met. I would sit in the same chair that I had sat in across from her many years ago and, like a prayer, talk to her in silence. The place where I met her for the first time, before worshipping her for twelve years, was a place of pilgrimage for me. Remembering her was my prayer.

I don't know how long I sat there, feeling her presence. The night advanced but the City continued its hard work. From where I sat I could see a new billboard, on which an ad called City of Joy glittered every now and then, announcing forthcoming cultural events. Russian ballet. Syrian music concert. Egyptian theatre. Peruvian folk drama. Chinese magic show. Pictures flashed on the screen. Further away in the harbour, huge cranes picked up containers. Bullhorns sounded from the ships. A flyover was being constructed under floodlights and giant diggers were excavating the ground. Metal vessels ran along an assembly line towards the aluminium company in the distance. Machines and only machines were running the City, I thought. Not a human being anywhere. I longed to see one. Both Vinod and Riyaz were sleeping. I left the flat and went for a long drive. When I returned, I emailed Jasmine.

Dear Jasmine,
It's three in the morning. You are probably floating on the wings of a sweet dream right now, your head resting on a soft pillow. I just returned from another drive in your city. Yes, in the middle of the night. To know a city, one must know it at different times. Cities wear different faces at different times of the day and night. While you

are sleeping, Bengali workers are cleaning your streets. Others are watering the trees and plants that fringe those streets. Some are pouring tar on the highways so that your car can speed over them. Your bridges are being repaired while underneath those bridges, fishermen are waiting with nets and tackle. There is music in the dance bars and no one is sleeping in the fast-food shops. The old men who can't get enough of dice games are smoking hookahs while Lebanese young men are roasting kebabs on a spit for them. The money exchanges are open, waiting for the last dollars, and the security guards are sitting in between the coolness of the sea breeze and the heat of their cigarettes, dreaming with their eyes open. The bakery vans are making their rounds and newspaper boys are counting the stacks of newspapers and the police have their fingers on the trigger, ready for any unexpected enemy.

Beloved, are you sleeping? Wake up. Let's roam around this nocturnal city.

Dilmun

Finally there came the day we became tourists. Faisal was our driver and he had rented a minibus for the day. For a moment we considered inviting Abdullah Janahi, but everyone agreed he was a bore and must be avoided. We picked up Asmo and Priyanka from their flats. It was the first time I was seeing Asmo after the airport. 'I gave you my number, but you never called,' she reproached me. Riyaz was meeting them for the first time, and Vinod was meeting Asmo and Edwin was meeting Priyanka for the first time. After the introductions, we all fell into an easy companionship.

Faisal first took us to a place called Barbar, which was famed for an ancient temple. We were expecting a magnificent temple, the kind that are littered all over India and Indonesia and Malaysia, but when we got there, all we found were some limestone structures.

'You brought us all the way here for this?' we teased Faisal.

A young man happened to hear us and came over to introduce himself. 'My name is Yanik Appalaswami.'

'Are you Indian?'

'No, I am a French citizen.'

'Sorry, you looked Indian to me,' I said.

'My ancestors were Tamils taken from India to Mauritius to work in the plantations. From there we migrated to France. That's why there's an Appalaswami in my name. That was my grandfather.'

'Are you a tourist or do you work in the City?'

'You could say both. I study ancient cultures and their gods. I did my doctorate in how the qualities of Sumerian and Phoenician gods such as Tammuz, Osiris, Athes and Adonis were integrated into Christ. Currently, I am studying the relationship between the Mesopotamian and Hindu cultures. That's what brought me to this site.'

'Oh really? What's special about this site?' Edwin asked.

'Oh, don't you know? This is an ancient city from the Mesopotamian era. This place used to be known as Dilmun. Even *The Epic of Gilgamesh*, considered the oldest surviving work of literature, refers to this place. Dilmun is a motherland in the Sumerian origin story, a place without death or disease. Later, the Semitic religions developed that into the Garden of Eden. If that is true, then we are standing in what most people living today would consider Paradise.'

'My God! I had no idea this country was such a holy place,' Asmo exclaimed.

'These ruins are what remain of three temples consecrated to Enki, the Sumerian god of water. They were discovered by Danish archaeologists in 1954.'

'Is there a connection between the Hindu civilization and these Barbar temples?' Vinod could not hide his excitement.

'Scholars who have studied sun worship in the Mesopotamian era have proved that Barbar and the Tamil Parpar are both the same deity. And Parpar is another name for Shiva. There is an inscription in Chidambaram that refers to Thilai Manar which could well be the same as Dilmun. According to that inscription, Thilai Manar or Dilmun is where the soul entered the body. So if we connect the dots, we can see that Shiva emerged from Enki.'

'What is the crux of your arguments?' Riyaz asked.

'None of the gods we know of in human history are independent. They all have some connection to other ancestor gods. In other words, all the gods and prophets we worship today are updated versions or pirated copies of older gods.'

'Can you give me an example?' Asmo asked.

'Let's take Jesus Christ. The Sumerian god Tammuz was born to a virgin. Another god, Mitras, was born in a cave, and shepherds brought him presents. When those gods faded from memory, humans amalgamated their best qualities and combined them with the life of Jesus Christ to create a new myth. Allah, the God of Muslims, is a pirated version of Yahweh, and Yahweh is an update of Yah and Bal. You can see the concept of the return of the Messiah in the Shia belief in the return of the Mehdi, the Twelfth Imam. And of course, as I said earlier, the Sumerian motherland transmogrified into the Garden of Eden.'

'In other words, don't take too much pride in your gods,' said Edwin.

'Why do gods go out of fashion? Why do we keep updating them?' Asmo asked.

'As time goes by, science grows, but gods stay still. They are very limited in what they can do. When humans realize that, the gods go out of fashion. We have been doing this since we worshipped the sun and the moon and the trees and the mountains. We find new gods to match the times we live in.'

'Will the religions that are dominant today also die out?' Priyanka asked.

'We might find it hard to believe but that's exactly what human history suggests. So many religions that were popular in the ancient world have completely disappeared now. So many gods have died out. Sometimes when a civilization decays, its gods also fade away. Or they get washed out by a natural disaster that annihilates entire populations. Or maybe they simply go out of fashion, like I said earlier. In fact, the three Semitic religions understand this all too well. They have remained strong by constantly updating themselves. If you just look at the last five hundred years in their history, you will see huge changes. That is how they have stayed relevant.'

'Yanik, do you think humans will ever be free of religions?'

'I don't think so. Humans will keep inventing new religions and gods to suit the new circumstances they find themselves in. Humans cannot survive without faith. At least till they find all the secrets of the universe!'

As we were walking back after taking photos with Yanik and saying goodbye to him, Edwin told Asmo, 'Here we are in Eden. Maybe it is time to commit the Original Sin.'

'But don't we need a forbidden fruit and a serpent?'

'Here's the forbidden fruit,' Riyaz took out an apple from his bag.

'And here's the snake,' Priyanka pointed to Vinod, who had thrown back a couple of shots in the morning. We burst into laughter.

'Though I did not understand Appalaswami's theories fully, I feel ashamed to think of how we humans fight over religions and made-up myths,' Priyanka said.

'We have to preserve these ruins to dead gods. Otherwise how will we understand the futility of our own religions and gods, and the fact that they too will die some day?'

That was what I was thinking too. As we got into the car, Riyaz said, 'I wonder how long these ruins will last. This is a Wahabbi stronghold and they have no tolerance for idol worship. They even razed down the home of Prophet Muhammad and made it into a library. It's a miracle that these ancient temple ruins have survived. But as the country grows more fundamentalist, they probably won't last forever.'

Pilgrim Centre

Priyanka sang a Hindi song for us, and then Asmo and Edwin performed an English duet. As laughter and music and conversation filled our bus, my thoughts turned to that book. It was Priyanka's song that reminded me of it, for Sameera, the protagonist of the book, was a radio jockey. In fact, given the clues I had deciphered, she had been a radio jockey in this very city. Perhaps Priyanka knew her. I almost asked her, but then remembered that Riyaz was sitting right there. If only I could get a moment alone with her.

Faisal wanted to stop by his village to pick up something, so we headed that way. I was struck by how much poverty existed in the streets and houses of such a developed nation. It was as if we had entered a tunnel in the twenty-first century and emerged at the other end in the tenth century. But in front of those crumbling houses with peeling paint were colourful pictures of His Majesty. Every house was flying the national flag. It was as if a servant in cheap clothes was waiting for the arrival of the master.

I had noticed before how workplaces and supermarkets and petrol pumps and government offices and even barbershops made sure to show their loyalty by prominently displaying his picture. That was not surprising in the least. But I wondered what these poor folks in this rich country felt about loyalty. When we finally got to Faisal's house, I was especially surprised. His Majesty's pictures were all over the house on banner decorations. The house looked ready for a celebration.

When he returned, I asked him about it. 'Oh yes, loyalty. There was a contest recently in connection with our national day. Five thousand dinars for the best decorated house. Why not try out, I thought. And anyway, there's nothing to lose. Even if you don't win, the government will compensate you for the expense of decorating. What can I say? His Majesty has some very sly advisers. The whole point is to make outsiders like you believe that we are all in love with him. Besides, who would want to stand out as belonging to a house that was not decorated? That is all you need to be called in for questioning by the police. You know, they have banned pictures of any other leader, from anywhere in the world. Only one flag and one picture is allowed.'

Next we went to see a bridge, supposedly one of the marvels of the City. Perhaps someone who had never been anywhere else, never seen any of the engineering marvels of the world, could enjoy looking at it for a few minutes. In the middle of the bridge, there was a man-made island and a revolving restaurant. What a trick the government had played on its poor people.

Luckily, I got a quiet moment with Priyanka when we got out to look at the bridge. Vinod and Riyaz had gone to the restroom. 'Do you happen to have a co-worker called Sameera?' I asked her without any preface.

She thought for a moment and then shook her head.

'She's from Pakistan. I heard that she was a famous radio jockey in this country.'

Priyanka shook her head again.

'Do you have any other Hindi stations?'

'No, we are the only one. The other radio station is a Malayalam one. Do you know if she's still there?'

'I don't know if she's still there. But she used to work at your station. Is there some way of finding out for sure?'

'Oh, now I get it. She must be from the old team. Till about six months ago, we had a different production team. Then the government asked for new bids and our management won the bidding. So the old team left. We are all from the new team,' Priyanka said.

'Have they all left the City?' I asked sadly.

'Probably. What other options do radio jockeys have? They are probably working in FM radio in their own countries. Anyhow, I don't know anything about their whereabouts.'

'So your management did not retain any of the old team? Sometimes they keep a few people around, just for continuity. Maybe on the Malayalam side?' I could not bear to give up hope.

'Nope. The management made it clear they wanted fresh voices,' Priyanka said indifferently.

Vinod and Riyaz had returned by then and our conversation ended. My hope of finding Sameera, if not her book, also ended with it.

'There's a place I'd like to go to, even if none of you might be interested. Shall we drop by there as well?' Edwin asked as we were leaving.

'If it is another yawn like this bridge, then I object,' said Asmo.

'It will make you yawn even more,' Edwin said. 'But hopefully you will understand its historic importance.'

'What is this? A fun sightseeing trip or some kind of field study in history?' Vinod asked.

'Bear with me on this. In return, we are going to give you all an amazing surprise this evening,' Edwin said.

'Who is "we"?' I asked.

'That will be another surprise,' Edwin said.

'Are you at least going to tell us where we are going?' Vinod's voice was impatient.

'All in due time,' Edwin said, giving Faisal some incomprehensible directions.

We drove across the bridge and started moving in a new direction. In a bit, we were travelling through barren lands. Soon we could see intersecting pipelines running all over the ground.

'We are now riding over some of the most valuable soil in the world. You have all heard a lot about oilfields, but have never seen them, right? Well, take a good look,' Edwin said. 'Over there in the distance, those things that look like donkeys shaking their heads? Those are borewells bringing up the oil.'

'Are you serious? This is an oilfield?' Priyanka exclaimed. 'All these years I thought an oilfield looks like our fields of wheat or paddy. And when people talked of oil wells, I imagined a hole in the ground and people with buckets.'

'This idiot has no idea what he is talking about. You are right, Priyanka. That's exactly how it works. Every day the Arabs come here and haul up oil in buckets and sell it in the evening. They even have a special market for that. It's called OPEC,' Vinod said.

We all laughed, but Priyanka was still confused.

'Please . . . which one is true? Is this really an oilfield?'

'You are something else. Just perfect for a radio jockey job,' Vinod said.

'This is one of the few oilfields that ordinary people like us can visit. In other countries, they wouldn't let anyone enter something like this,' Faisal said. 'The amazing thing is that despite all the problems we have had in the country, no one has laid a finger on these pipelines.'

'That is strange indeed. Why is that?' I asked.

'Everyone knows this is our common wealth. Whoever comes to power needs this.'

'The Arab people are hungry for democracy. Their rulers know their days are numbered. So their policy is to get as much oil as possible while they can,' Riyaz added.

The moment the car came to a stop somewhere in between those pipes, Edwin opened the door and ran out with the eagerness of a child visiting his grandparents. The rest of us got out slowly, unburdened by any excitement.

There was an abandoned pit in the middle of the desert. An old stone plaque stood next to it. We walked towards it.

Look!' Edwin yelled at us. 'I never thought I would get here. But here I am, in this place where my grandfather's hard work left its mark on history. No one in my family has ever seen this. I am lucky, I am so lucky!' He fell to the ground and kissed it.

We still had no idea what he was going on about.

'This was the first oil well in the Gulf peninsula.' Edwin

was so elated he could barely speak. 'That's what this plaque records. This place changed the course of world history. Yet it lies here ignored by everyone. Surely this is the most important place of pilgrimage in the Arab world. All Arabs should perform a hajj here too. Is there another place on earth that has completely changed their lives? All you see is a hole in the ground, but this was the door to their dreams!'

'In other words, this is where their peace and contentment descended into hell . . .' Riyaz added.

Pasta Art

'So I am treating all of you to dinner. Where should we go?' Edwin said on the way back.

'Is this the surprise you were planning for us?' I asked. 'Any special reason?'

'No, there is another surprise. But where should we eat?'

'Well, obviously if we don't go to the Sheraton or to Le Meridien, you are going to feel that we didn't take you seriously enough.'

'No, no, I am not wealthy enough to take you Asians to places like that,' Edwin retorted.

'We Asians might have to give you a piece of our mind,' Vinod muttered.

Where should we go? Copper Chimney, Johnny Rockets, Nino Italian, Cafe Radwa, Kudooz, Foodruckers, Polp, Loco Mexican, Pizza Hut, Ceasars, Senor Pacos . . . we debated the merits of different restaurants.

Then Asmo said, 'Let's stop arguing. One of my co-workers left his job to start a restaurant. Why don't we give him a chance?'

Everyone liked that idea and we drove off to Pasta Art. The restaurant was in an old building outside the City. It looked very quiet. Did we just leave behind all the good restaurants in the City to come out here, I wondered. But as soon as we entered, it was clear Asmo had made the right choice. From the reception itself, the restaurant was decorated masterfully with beautiful Arab art. As soon as he saw Asmo, the owner Abdul Nabi came running to greet her. She introduced us one by one. When he heard we were journalists, Abdul Nabi was thrilled. He took us to the special guest room. The walls here were covered with murals. As I was admiring them, Abdul Nabi told me, 'They are all my own drawings. The whole time that I was a bank officer, what I really wanted to do was cook and draw.'

My eyes widened. Those drawings were far above the level of an amateur painter. My respect for Abdul Nabi increased rapidly.

'Shall I order for you? I would like you to taste the restaurant's speciality,' Abdul Nabi said. We all agreed. His speciality was ravioli pasta.

When the food arrived, Edwin stood up. 'Before we eat – remember I had a surprise for you?'

'Yes?'

'This Lebanese beauty sitting next to me and I are going to get married.'

We cheered at the unexpected good news. Vinod hugged Edwin. 'Congratulations, you lucky man. With the Father and the Son and the food before us as witnesses, I give you permission to enjoy the valleys of Lebanon.'

He took Asmo's hand and placed it in Edwin's. The happy couple took out rings and put them on each other's fingers. They embraced each other.

'Friends, Romans, countrymen, let me ask you a very relevant question. What does a husband seek in his wife?' Riyaz Malik asked.

'Love?'

'No.'

'Trust?'

'No.'

'Sex?'

'No.'

'Then?'

'Peace of mind!'

'When a man comes home after fighting the entire world, the best welcome gift he can receive from his wife is peace of mind. In difficult times, one's home should be a refuge. It is those who do not have that refuge that end up drunk in a bar.'

'Okay, fine. Let me ask you the same question about women,' Asmo said.

We tried the same answers – love, trust, sex. 'No,' she responded. 'Then?'

'A good ear for listening. She might have a lot of things to talk about. But most men simply want to drag her into bed. That's when she goes in search of other ears that are willing to listen.'

We agreed.

'On the guarantee that you will give each other peace of mind and listen to each other, we approve the world's shortest engagement ceremony and declare you both engaged,' Riyaz Malik said.

With that we turned to the delicious food.

Abdul Nabi

On the way back, Asmo told us how Abdul Nabi had gone from bank officer to restaurant owner.

'Abdul Nabi used to work in the loan section at our bank. He started as a document controller, but eventually ended up becoming indispensable to the section. His loyalty to his work was something unusual in natives. Though he worked under supervisors, Abdul Nabi was fully responsible for that section. His word was the last word there. If anyone wanted more details about an old case, they needed Abdul Nabi. If they wanted to find a folder, they needed Abdul Nabi. Only he knew exactly where an application was. You could ask him any question and he would have an answer. The newcomers to the section simply had to slip into the system that he kept running smoothly. He was that systematic. That's how it was till the protests started. Then someone in the bank decided to put an end to Abdul Nabi's rise. For no other reason except that he was of the second class. Abdul Nabi never took time out of his working day to participate in any of the protests. But still, a case was made against him for not reporting a couple of younger men in his section who protested while they should have been working. Maybe someone speculated that by sacrificing a Shia who worked in the bank, they could ingratiate themselves to the government a bit more. Or maybe they were simply avenging some old slight. This was a good time for old slights. And the management did not simply demote him or fire him. They made up a new post called technical consultant and appointed him to it. Then they stopped giving him work. So Abdul Nabi, who used to spend all his day running from one floor to the other, became someone who sat in a chair twiddling his thumbs all day. He was reduced to drinking tea and reading the newspaper and playing Sudoku. Outside his cabin, the new employees were destroying the system he had perfected over fifteen years. Within two months, his system was gone. Even then, he could have sorted it out, but no one asked him for any advice or opinion. Slowly he realized that he was being ignored. That's when he resigned. As he was stepping out of the bank for the last time, I saw his tears fall on the threshold. He must have asked himself, "What was my fault?" But no one in the office cared enough to hear that silent question. What does a corporate management care? As far as they are concerned, employees are merely machines for making money and one of their machines was being disposed of.'

Silence filled the car. We, too, were machines, we knew, and any moment we, too, could be disposed of. Faisal dropped us off at our flats. As Vinod and Edwin got out of the car, Faisal stopped me. 'Pratap sahib, do you have any alcohol? Can I have some?'

'Alcohol?' I was shocked. 'Aren't you a Muslim? Isn't alcohol haram for you?'

'Yes, I am a Muslim and it is haram. But tonight, I need it. If you don't have any, can you give me some money so I can get some?'

I stared at him again, trying to make sense of what he was saying.

He took off his shirt and asked me to touch his shoulder and back. My fingers could feel lumps; something was trapped under the skin. 'The police shot me,' he said. 'They were rubber bullets, so they did not go in deep. Now my skin has grafted on top of them. If I go to the hospital to remove them, the police will catch me. So I just have to carry them around. That's not all.' He hiked up his trousers and showed me his ankle and heel. I was taken aback to see that they were covered with infected, pustular bruises.

'What is this? Do you have leprosy?'

'Yes, looks like that. But no, this is the result of getting beaten up by the police. They hit me with a cane and a lathi and an electric baton. Then they poured acid on the bruises. Now the bruises won't heal. They are always infected. And the pain . . . it is unbearable.'

'Why did they do all that? Did you participate in the protests?'

'We don't want to overthrow His Majesty or bring the Shias to power. But we must be recognized as citizens of this country. We must be given the same rights as others here. You know, when we have holidays, my friends go to Jordan or Lebanon or Syria to have fun. They go to Iraq to observe Ashura. Or they go to Iran to visit relatives. Or to Dubai to celebrate festivals. But I have never left this country. How can

I travel without a passport? And if we ask for passports, they beat us up. I have to report at the police station every week. I have to sit through their interrogations. I have to lie down and take it if they want some more action. Pratap sahib, I am a twenty-four-year-old man. A very ordinary young man. All I want is a life like yours. But I don't have a life worth living. I don't have any dreams or hopes. And my only crime is that I was born in the City.

'Only alcohol can put a half-human like me to sleep, Pratap sahib. But there is another reason why I need it desperately. Today when you were having fun with your girlfriends, I was remembering my girl.' Faisal opened his wallet for me to see. A beautiful face smiled at me from the photo in it. 'Fathima,' he said. 'We studied together, played together, grew up together. We wanted to live together for the rest of our lives. But I am a Shia and she was a Sunni. Do you know what her family did when she insisted on marrying me? Her own father and her brothers drowned her in their swimming pool. Today I kept remembering her. Her face. Her smile. Her sulks. Her squabbles. Her kisses. Her tears. Her death. I cannot survive this night without some alcohol. Am I not a human being, Pratap sahib?' he cried.

We do not understand some people until it is too late. And some others we never understand at all.

Novelist

For days Bijumon had been inviting me to hang out some evening. Every day I would plan to go. But by the time evening rolled in, I would feel lazy. It was not easy for a Canadian to adjust to the City's heat. All I wanted by then was to sit still somewhere. But I was not being courteous. I had visited him only once, immediately after my arrival in the City. And I had barely talked to his wife, Liji.

When he called again that morning to invite me home that evening, I tried as usual to get out of it. But this time he insisted. 'Don't worry, this is not just about getting drunk and wasting time. I have big plans. You have to come.' I had to agree. He picked me up in the evening.

As we drove to his place, the radio in the car was on and Priyanka was hosting a live show. That was the first time I heard her on the radio. She had a great voice and the right personality for radio. I remembered Sameera.

'Have you been listening to these programmes for a while?' I asked Bijumon.

'Yes, haven't you noticed? I am crazy about the radio. As soon as I get into the car, I switch it on. I feel transported home when I listen to the radio,' he said.

'Did you ever listen to a Sameera? Sameera Parvin?'

'Oh yes, she used to be on Orange Radio. Her programmes were a huge hit. But that team has left.'

'Would it be possible to dig up information on them?'

'Why, are you guys planning to start a radio station?'

'Yes . . . possibly. Find someone I can talk to.'

'Definitely. Their managing director, Rajeevan, is a good friend of mine. We can ask him for more information.'

Even as he was talking, Bijumon had dialled Rajeevan's number from the hands-free phone in the car.

After the initial greetings, he introduced me as a journalist from Canada.

'Hello, Mr Pratap,' Rajeevan's voice came through the speaker phone.

'Hello, Mr Rajeevan, I have a small question for you. You were the director of the Hindi radio station here, right?'

'Yes, that institution was my dream come true,' he said. 'I spent five years building it. But unfortunately, we lost it in last year's auction. It was a huge loss. I don't even like to remember it. Why do you ask?'

'There was a Sameera who used to work there. Do you remember her?'

'Sameera?'

'Yes, a Pakistani woman. I heard that her programme was a huge hit in the City.'

'Yes, she was a brilliant artist. Her programme was our biggest hit. Why are you looking for her?'

'We are thinking of starting a Hindi radio station in Canada. Maybe we can hire her.'

'Really sorry, Mr Pratap. It was painful but we had to send away all our artists. However, if my memory is correct, she left for personal reasons even before we lost the bid.'

'Do you remember hearing anything about her afterwards?' I asked, thinking about the book.

'Nothing at all.'

'Any chance you could connect me to someone who knows her?'

'Sorry, I don't know anyone like that.'

My investigation had reached a dead end. Sameera and her book continued to be a riddle.

Bijumon was taking me to an event hosted by a local organization with ties to the far left movement in India. He was a member. In fact, there wasn't an organization in the City that was spared of his membership. He belonged to everyone and everything. I guessed that he would soon become a famous writer.

There were fifty or sixty people gathered there to honour the memory of an international leader who had died fighting authoritarianism. The event was inaugurated by a prominent Malayali in the City, a young writer with multiple awards to his credit. Bijumon told me that his latest work was selling like hot cakes. It was getting translated into multiple languages and had been added to the syllabus in many universities. His name was new to me, because for years I had ignored literature. In fact, in the last few days, I had heard more about Malayalam and Malayalam literature than in the last ten years.

The novelist gave a rousing speech about the revolutionary leader and the path of resistance on which he walked. He concluded by reminding everyone that as long as humanity existed, there would be a special place in history for the leader and his struggle for freedom. We should all walk in his footsteps, he exhorted us. Martyrdom is meaningful only if we can use our death to bring about more social justice than we could achieve in our lifetime. Through his death, the revolutionary leader had effected a change in society, and that made his death meaningful. I loved the novelist's perspective.

After the event, Bijumon introduced me to the novelist. He had been living in the City for twenty-five years. This city made me a writer, he told me proudly.

Another Bijumon, I thought to myself.

'Can I talk to you for a moment?' I asked him, and he agreed happily. I wanted his perspective on the protests in the City. We went to a restaurant. Bijumon went to pick up his kids from dance class.

I began by asking him about his famous novel, which, I freely admitted, I hadn't read. He told me it was about the tragedies in the life of a Malayali who had arrived in the City, full of dreams of a good life. As someone who had lived in the City for several years, why not write a novel set against the background of the protests, I asked. Surely, I thought, he would do a much better job than our own novelist who was sitting in some faraway place waiting for notes from his research team.

'Yes, I suppose I could write a novel like that, and indeed, I have enough experience for something like that. I considered the idea very deeply. As someone who believes in humanity, I secretly support the protesters and their struggle for democracy. Any novel I write on this subject would be against the government of this country. And that would affect not just my life here, but the lives of hundreds of thousands of Malayalis in the City. Remember Idi Amin? It was over something extremely trivial that he asked all the Indians in Uganda to pack up and leave within three months. The dictators of the world have not changed. As a writer, don't I have a responsibility to my own people? Shouldn't I keep in mind their future? The businesses they have built over years, the jobs that feed so many families . . . what if they were to lose all that because of a novel of mine? They look at me as their spokesperson, their pride and joy. How can I throw away that affection and that respect? I owe it to them to unsee some things. I don't see the protesters. What I see are immigrant Malayalis and the lives they have built here.'

I had nothing left to ask him. Knowing his biases, I knew that it was pointless to ask him anything about the City. Bijumon arrived soon after. The novelist gave me a copy of his famous book. Tell me what you think, he said.

I pitied him. My storyteller friend, you may be a great writer and your book may have won impressive awards, but I have no inclination to read it. A writer should not discriminate between his people and other people. A writer should see only human beings, their hopes and their disappointments. If you can turn away from these bloodstained streets because you prefer to think of the survival of your people, then your writing is meaningless, your literary life is pointless.

When Bijumon dropped me off in front of my flat after dinner, I tossed his book into the trash can.

Part Six

Monocle God

Mail

That night Vinod came to my room with alcohol on his breath. 'I have been hanging out with your friend, the businessman–poet Bijumon. We went to a couple of dance bars. He knows the best girls in each bar. Now he is a good friend of mine.'

They had met each other a few times when Bijumon came to see me in the flat or to pick me up. How quickly they had become friends and were now close enough to visit dance bars together. Vinod and Biju were equally talented at this. I have seen it happen in so many cities – friends of friends will bond over common interests. People of the same wavelength will find each other.

For a few minutes, Vinod was busy praising various bar dancers. Then he asked if I had seen my email. I had not checked it for a couple of days. People with no hope of love or friendship have no need to check emails or social media.

'Why do you ask?' I asked him.

'What can you lose? Check your email,' he insisted.

I understood when I opened my inbox. There was a reply to the email I had sent to our Internet provider. For a moment I was surprised at Vinod's intuition. Then I remembered that we had given his email as an alternative address and they had copied him on the response.

'So looks like you are not that anxious to find your lover. When I heard you that day, I thought you wouldn't be able to sleep till you found her,' Vinod teased.

'No, it's just that I did not expect such a fast response. Also, I promised my wife I would not seek help to find her. So when I took your help, it felt as if I had betrayed her.'

'What kind of man are you? Even if you keep every other promise, you must never keep promises made to a wife,' Vinod said. 'In fact, you should betray that promise at the first opportunity. Otherwise, with each promise, you are simply turning into her slave. A man should not sink so low.'

'Well, that's your opinion. Mine might be different. Let's leave it at that,' I said.

But when I read the email, it was nothing more than an official acknowledgement that my complaint had been received. To take action, they needed me to forward a police report on the same complaint. I looked at Vinod helplessly.

'We'll go to the police station tomorrow and register a complaint. Then we'll ask them for a report and send it to these guys.'

'Is that really necessary?'

'Life moves forward, Pratap. This Vinod has never taken a step backwards. Especially when it comes to women. No question of accepting defeat. One way or another, we are going to smoke out this lover of yours. Now this is a matter of my pride.'

I was annoyed at the way he kept characterizing Jasmine as my lover. The affection and friendship between us was much more complex than that simple word allowed. I had made this clear to him already. But Vinod could only see things from his single-track perspective. When you share your life with people who do not have the same paradigms, you have to be prepared to be humiliated by their misinterpretations. That's the lesson I learned from this experience. But some lessons come too late.

'I'll come with you to the police station tomorrow,' Vinod said.

'But, Vinod, when they find that our complaint is not valid, won't we be in trouble?'

'My friend, is your IQ really that low? Are we lifers in this city? We are not going to stick around long enough to get into any trouble. By the time they figure it out, we'll have found your lover and we'll be home safe.'

Vinod's words gave colour to my dream again. Perhaps it was within reach after all . . .

'So maybe we should move on this . . .' I said half-heartedly.

'Let me tell you this from experience. If you are chasing women, you have to be obsessed in your heart and strong in your gut. Women and opportunities don't wait around while you dilly-dally.'

Chasing women. I wanted to kill him for his stupid insults to our relationship. Then I remembered the last time I had seen Jasmine, and my anger was forgotten.

I had just got a cell phone that could capture images and audio. It was a rainy day and we had one umbrella to share. Half in the rain, half under the umbrella, we went to the beach. We gazed at the rain falling around us and the sea flowing in front of us. Then we ended up in the same restaurant where we had first met. We sat on the same seat as that first meeting and shared their special biriyani and a sulaimani tea. We talked and laughed and floated through the city like rainbirds. I have never had another day of pure joy like that. Through the day, I took photos of Jasmine, smiling in the rain, by the sea, under the umbrella, savouring her biriyani, sipping her tea. Before we parted, she sang a song for me. Forever after that, those pictures and that song lived with me, as much a part of me as my heartbeat. They travelled from phone to phone as I switched phones. Whenever the banality of my life made my soul dry and dusty, I would look at those pictures, I would listen to that song.

I went to my room and played the song.

'Mera jeevan kora kaagaz kora hi reh gaya . . .

Jo likha tha aansuon ke sang beh gaya . . .'

Every time I heard that song, I felt the slow burning of my heart.

After that final day together, the next message I received from Jasmine was 'I am getting married'. There were no explanations or rationalization. And I did not ask for any. Twelve years of silence followed. And then she returned into my life, again with no explanations.

Jasmine, you returned to me at a time when I had begun wondering if marriage was a netherworld that makes us forget who we used to be. Your return was nothing short of a miracle for me. Of course, I can understand your commitment and your closeness to your family. I can even understand the limitations within which you live. If I didn't, what would be the meaning of the word 'friend'? I have always tried to see others' point of view. For my part, I have a request. Please don't misunderstand me. All I want is to be a true friend to you. I do not expect or desire anything more from you. You have walked a lot on your path and I have walked on mine. But what is left for us in these little lives of ours? Except this friendship where we can be absolutely honest and transparent with each other. Every human being should have a few empty spaces in his or her soul for friendships such as these. But if I am crossing borders I should not cross or stretching limits I should not stretch, and harassing you, then here's an apology from the bottom of my heart.

Jasmine, there are a few sorrows in my life. Sorrows I cannot share with anyone else. If we do badly in an exam, we talk to our classmates. If we fail in a work assignment, we can share that with our colleagues. But if we fail at life itself, if we lose in love, then who do we share that with? If the one person who will understand bolts her heart, what can we do? You know how words stew in our heart when they go unspoken. Is it helplessness or bad luck that makes us say to the whole world via our Facebook walls words that should only be shared with one person?

Jasmine, I still believe that one day you will return to me. I live in hope.

All night I listened to that song.

'Mera jeevan kora kaagaz kora hi reh gaya . . .
Jo likha tha aansuon ke sang beh gaya . . .'

Complaint

The next day I went to the nearest police station with Vinod.
But they had no idea what I was talking about. Their mouths
fell open when they heard the words 'cyber cell', 'complaint',
'email provider' and 'report'. We had changed our story by
then and made it about a woman emailing me, as Vinod had
suggested earlier. We went from table to table, policeman
to policeman, but no one could help us. If someone hit you
or stole your money, tell us and we can try to help you. But
can anyone make a case out of a woman emailing you? If
you don't want to email her, give us her address, we'll have
fun emailing her. This is how they scorned us. It was almost
sweet, such naivety. Eventually we ended up at the same table
where we had started, thereby proving once and for all that
the earth is round. But luckily a police officer who had just
arrived intervened and told us to take our complaint to the
cyber cell in the CID office.

As we left the station with the address of the CID office,
I wondered if government workers everywhere were exactly
the same. Nobody else has their talent for not knowing what
is going on within their own department if it does not apply
to their work. In fact, many of them take special pride in this
indifference. Knowing this, I was ready to return. Moreover,
Perumal's account of his police station days lay heavy in my

head, like undigested food. But Vinod was still on fire from the previous day's alcohol.

After some runarounds, we finally got to the CID office. At least people there had heard of the cyber cell. We followed their directions and eventually reached that section. The police officers there were willing to listen. Vinod explained the matter for me. The story was by now quite embellished. After he had finished, they asked us to write up a complaint. Don't do it, my heart murmured. There shouldn't be a complaint against Jasmine. That would be an injustice to her and to our friendship. But by then, I was trapped. They gave me a format but I chose to write up my own complaint. I stressed that the complaint was not about ending harassment but more about my curiosity to find out who was emailing me. I insisted that they should not register a case or take any action. All I wanted was simply to find out who was sending me these messages. If I didn't have that much integrity, I knew my conscience would not let me rest for the rest of my life. By then, I had decided that this was definitely the wrong way to go about finding Jasmine. The policemen advised me that my complaint was very weak. Their senior officers would dismiss this complaint. They asked me to write that I was receiving obscene messages from the address. But I wouldn't do it. So they were a little annoyed to register my complaint and sent us off with an indifferent 'we'll let you know when the report is ready'.

Naturally, Vinod was upset with me. But as I stepped out of the CID office, I felt a small twinge of satisfaction. I was finally on my own path to finding Jasmine. I did not realize then that I was tying up my life in knots.

Survival

I visited Bijumon again. Liji was full of reproaches, saying I had avoided them deliberately because they were poor and I didn't like their food and their tiny flat was not luxurious enough for me. I kept telling her that it was just my laziness, but she would not accept it. I felt bad for not visiting more often. Friendships need constant updation. The interesting thing is that even old friendships can be updated easily enough. A call, an occasional visit, a birthday greeting or a best wishes. That's all it takes to make a tarnished relationship gleam. Theoretically it's very easy. But in practice, I am too lazy to do this.

We talked for a long time. At some point, Liji heard me refer to the Jasmine revolution.

'I have been hearing about this a lot. What is it?' she asked.

'You nurses. You won't understand anything,' Bijumon mocked her. He turned to me. 'Look, Pratap, I always tease her. There are two kinds of human beings on earth. Regular human beings and Malayali nurses. I have never seen anyone with less general knowledge than this second category.'

'Yeah, right. We nurses certainly have more general knowledge than you airy-fairy writers. Anyway, what is the point of general knowledge? Does it put food on the table?'

'Then why are you asking about the Jasmine revolution?' Biju asked.

'I have work to do in the kitchen. Are you going to tell me or waste my time?'

'Liji, it refers to the protests that took place recently in this country and in the neighbouring countries,' I told her. 'Different revolutions have different names. For instance, the Orange revolution in Ukraine, the Rose revolution in Georgia, the Velvet revolution in Czechoslovakia, the Cedar revolution in Lebanon . . . this will now join that list.'

'Oh, I see. So it's like when there's a wind in America and they give it names like Katrina and Thresiamma.'

'Yes, exactly. That's all you need to know,' Biju said.

I remembered what Jahangir and Doctor Mamu had said about the protesters in the hospital, and asked Liji about it.

'That was something else,' Liji recalled. 'At first we thought, oh, there are some demonstrations in the country and hospital workers were participating occasionally. We had no idea they were storing weapons in the lab and the blood bank. And they used ambulances to bring them inside the hospital, so no one suspected. But never mind all that. The way they behaved with the patients! I can never forgive them for that. They deliberately caused the deaths of so many of their own wounded people so their movement would have enough martyrs.

'Then they took the blood from our blood banks and poured it on the streets and on people's clothes and bodies so that it would look like the police were being violent. We were taught that during wartime our loyalty is to the wounded. But what we saw there was the wounded being tortured further. I still remember a seven-year-old. He only had a small bruise on his shoulder. But they cut off his arm and injected germs into his body. Then they took photos of it and spread it all over social media. They killed him on the fourth day. All so that they could have a seven-year-old martyr.

'They admitted their own people to the wards, calling them patients. The plan was to carry out an armed attack on the hospital and imprison all of us. We could guess some of this. But what could we expatriate staff do? They had all the control. And we were afraid that if this government fell, they would form the new government. Then what would they do to those of us who betrayed them? So we pretended that we didn't see anything or hear anything. What else could we do? Later, everyone blamed us. Easy for them. Try working in a foreign country to understand our plight. We needed both the government and the protesters. Till the military came and took over the hospital, that was the situation. If they hadn't, who knows how many of us would have been killed. But luckily the military captured all the protesters. Many of them have never returned. Some of them were fired. We too were taken in for questioning. A few people used the opportunity to settle some old scores. A few innocents have fallen by the wayside because of all that. But we didn't have the luxury of figuring out what is just and what is unjust.

'You know, I remember a funny incident that happened in those days. Well, it seems funny now, but it was scary then. So the protesters would claim the streets after noon every day. People had to finish whatever they needed to do by then and get home. Otherwise we would end up sitting in traffic for the rest of the day. One day, I got a bit late when I left the hospital. The highway was jam-packed with vehicles.

Flags were fluttering in the breeze. Constant honking. Loud slogans. Noise everywhere. I couldn't even tell any more whether I was in the middle of pro-government protests or anti-government protests. Both groups used the national flag. Both groups held car rallies. Both groups had women and children participating enthusiastically. In fact, both protests seemed like celebrations. Even their slogans sounded similar to us who do not understand Arabic. I know just about enough Arabic to get through my day at the hospital. Bijuchayan can speak Arabic like he is drinking water. Anyway, I thought I was in the middle of a pro-government protest, and I got into the car rally so I could keep moving. But then when I saw the people in the next car and their angry gestures, I realized that I was in the wrong place. I was in the anti-government car rally! Those protesters were full of resentment towards foreigners like us. I was terrified. What if they attacked me? All I wanted was to get out of that rally. I kept looking for exits to leave the highway. But the protesters would not let me get to those exits. They had me trapped on all four sides. They found it fun, to have this hapless foreign woman struggling to get out of their rally. For them, it was like playing ball. At one point, it looked as if I would have to accompany them all the way to the end. Then I got desperate and started driving recklessly so that I could get out. What if I hit someone or got hit, I thought, but what was more important was to escape. Finally, I managed to find my way into a small by-lane. I parked my car there and waited for my heart to stop racing. Only then did I drive home. I was thankful that I had been in the car and that the doors had been locked. If anyone came to harass me, I could at least run over them. But what if an innocent pedestrian got trapped in a demonstration?

Margarita

Children love guests. This is true, be it in Canada or in the City. Firstly, they know that they have full rights over the sweets and snacks the guest does not eat. Secondly, guests allow you to take liberties with them that parents don't. The third happiness is going to a restaurant for dinner in the guise of hospitality towards the guest. Biju's children were no different. They insisted on going out for dinner, preferably to a Chinese place. Liji wanted Indian food. Biju wanted a place with a bar. I was okay with all of these.

'In that case, follow me,' Biju said. 'Children, there will be your favourite prawn fry. And Liji, you will get your onion rings and mayo sauce. And Pratap, there will be something new and special for you. What do you say?'

Everyone agreed.

On the way, Biju said to me secretly, 'To know a city, you have to taste three things: their best food, their best alcohol and their best women. As a friend of Vinod's, you must know by now that the City has high marks in the first and third categories. Now let me show you that it is no less in the second category.'

I smiled but didn't say anything. May his faith help him. I could see now how his friendship with Vinod had progressed so quickly.

Just then we saw the yellow cones arrayed across the street and blue lights flashing on top of police vehicles. The police were stopping cars and checking identification cards very thoroughly. When Bijumon's vehicle approached, the policeman looked once into the car and gestured that we could keep moving.

'Just look at the respect we Indians get here,' Bijumon said proudly. 'In your Canada and other Western countries, they would have made us take off our underwear. That's why I keep saying this is such a good place to live in.'

I wondered at the policy of letting the foreigner pass quickly while a local would be examined from head to toe.

We went to a Mexican restaurant in a small alley. 'I have passed through this alley so many times but I never noticed this restaurant. Is it new?' Liji asked.

'This restaurant is about twenty years old. If you didn't see it, it is not their fault. Women! They walk around like horses with blinders on. All they see is clothes shops and gold shops and handsome men.'

The restaurant was crowded when we got there and it looked like we would have to wait. But Biju knew one of their section managers from the Samajam and he managed to get us a table.

'This is the benefit of social service. Wherever you go, you find someone who can help you,' Biju said.

The kids ordered pizzas. Liji asked if they had masala dosa.

'Why stop with masala dosa? Let's ask them if they have Mexican puri bhaji as well,' Biju retorted. He ordered margaritas for the two of us.

It was late when we got out of there. As we were heading towards the car, a young woman was walking in our direction. She had almost passed us when Liji and she realized that they were co-workers from the hospital.

'Where are you coming from so late?' Liji asked her, holding her hand.

She stared at us in silence. Then she said, 'Why? Do people like us not have the right to walk on a street at night?'

We blanched. What a response to an innocent question.

'No, no, Zainab. I was just wondering seeing you alone . . . in this alley . . .' Liji tried to cover up her embarrassment.

'What do you know about an Arab woman's life anyway?' Zainab's voice hardened. 'We are women who have brought home the dead bodies of our fathers and sons and husbands before the blood dried on them. Every day we have to walk through rioting streets before we can get to our homes and go to sleep. Why would I need a chaperone to walk through a small alley like this?'

We had handed her a stick to beat us with. We had practically begged for the beating. 'Well, see you then,' Liji said, and we hurried off.

'Look at that bitch's arrogance,' Bijumon spat in her direction. 'Is it any wonder that the army wants to shoot them at sight?' For the rest of the ride home, he kept cursing her. But I felt the sting of her words deep inside me. Like the boy who had thrown the bottle of fire at the police car while I was travelling with Jahangir and Riyaz, I suspected that she too had her reasons. I wanted to know what they were. Before leaving, I got Zainab's number from Liji.

Zainab

The next day I called Zainab. At first she did not want to meet me. But finally she agreed and said she would meet me in front of the hospital during visiting hours. I took Riyaz with me. After all, we had already gone to the hospital together once. She was waiting for us when we got there.

'So how did you get hold of my number?' she asked without any preface.

'I was with Liji when you met her last night.'

She burst out laughing. 'I must have scared you . . . I realized later that my reaction might have been too much. But when I met you, I was not in a good frame of mind.'

'So are you on duty today?' I skirted the subject.

'I have been on leave for a few days.'

'Then why did you want to meet us here? Are you visiting someone at the hospital?'

She smiled sadly. 'So Sister Liji didn't tell you anything about me? I guess not. Or maybe she doesn't know as well. It never ceases to amaze me how hard you foreigners will work not to know what is going on in the City. Maybe the politics here does not mean much to you. But surely, human questions are the same everywhere. Or are you simply too busy making money?'

Riyaz and I had no response to that.

'I am not blaming you. We are standing on opposite sides of the same wall. We don't try to understand each other. You are essentially living inside a Third World country within this country,' she said. 'It is not just here. Immigrants are always living in the Third World. If they start interfering in domestic issues, they will not be able to survive.'

'No one in the world gets angry for no reason. I am here to find out why you were angry last night,' I said.

'For two months now, my father has been fasting in prison. All he wants is a fair trial,' Zainab said. 'He was arrested and imprisoned without any charges. His only mistake is that he is a human rights activist. Yesterday, finally, I got to see the thirteen-page charge sheet that the police had cooked up. I was in shock.

'As his daughter, I can assure you that he has never committed an act of violence or supported it. When we were young, he was constantly talking to us about the lives of Gandhi and Mandela. He told us to follow the example of Aung San Suu Kyi. Of all the career options in front of us, he encouraged my sister and me to choose nursing because we could be of service to large numbers of people. Please don't think that we Arabs don't know a life without violence and rioting. My father is the best example of someone who stood for peace. But despite all that, he was arrested on the charge of inciting violence,' Zainab said as we walked into the hospital.

'We have a recording of the speech he gave at Pearl Square, which, according to the government, was inciting protesters to be violent. We sent copies to Amnesty and the UN. They asked the government to let him go because it was clear that he had done nothing wrong. But the government completely ignored them. And what can the UN do when this government has the backing of the US and other Western powers? The UN! They are exactly what Khomeini called them – a paper factory for useless declarations.

'They moved my father to the hospital when he was finally close to death. Yesterday when you saw me, I had just visited him. Starvation has a reality of its own. He had shrunk so much that I started crying when I saw him. But he continued to be cheerful. That thin, shrivelled body could still smile. I know he is dying slowly. You know, the sudden death of a loved one can be a shock to our system. But to watch someone die slowly is painfully unbearable.'

For the first time since she had started talking, Zainab's eyes gleamed with unshed tears. We went to the ward with her to see her father, Khalil Mohammed.

Criminals

Three armed Pakistani policemen were standing guard outside the room. Their grave, alert expressions suggested that a major criminal was inside. They told us that Khalil was a political prisoner and no one had permission to see him. Riyaz told them he was Pakistani and spoke to them in Pashtun, but to no avail. Only Zainab was allowed inside, and that too just for ten minutes. We left on realizing how hopeless it was to wait. But when we got into the elevator, by a stroke of good fortune, we found Doctor Mamu there. He didn't recognize us at first but when we told him about Jahangir and Canada, the light bulb switched on. 'Oh, Canadawala, what are you doing here?'

We told him about wanting to meet Khalil and the police not letting us in. He came back with us to the ward. The policemen suddenly transformed from tigers to pussycats. That's when we realized the respect he commanded in the City.

Zainab was surprised to see us inside. Of course, she didn't understand when I told her that we ran into one of the gods of the City in the elevator. Khalil Mohammed tried to rise when he saw us, but his feet were chained to a leg of the bed. Laughing at himself, he said, 'Arab activists have trained themselves to protest while lying horizontal. There are locks on all our feet.'

Zainab had described things accurately. He was feeble from lack of food. Riyaz and I sat next to the bed, and Zainab sat on the bed. He spoke to us in his feeble voice about his work as a human rights defender and the way the government and the courts had obstructed it. 'Our organization has been recognized by Amnesty. And even so, this year, we had to shift offices four times. The police found us each time. Finally we started working from inside a civil consultancy office. People would come to talk to us pretending they were coming for building and architecture consultations.'

Twice while we were speaking to Khalil, the policemen came to inform us that we had run out of time. But knowing that Doctor Mamu had our backs, we ignored them. Zainab cursed them soundly.

'What was your inspiration to begin this human rights work?' I asked him.

'I am embarrassed to call myself a human rights activist

today. There are so many counterfeits among us. Everyone from government spies to terrorists introduce themselves as human rights activists. And many international agencies are funding them. That's what most people who get into this work have their eye on. But my history is different. I came to this field because of something horrible that happened to a young law student many years ago. The police took him and his five friends into custody because they had gathered in one place. They were tortured and charged with treachery, conspiracy and a coup attempt. In truth, what brought them together was nothing but football and cinema and cigarettes. But after they had been tortured enough, they admitted to all the crimes. Everyone, even the judge who was a government stooge, knew they were innocent. The judge told the police to bring them back to court another day. When they returned, the students declared in court that they had been tortured and denied the crimes.

'But the government prosecutor argued strongly, calling for life terms or executions. He had no proof except for the police accounts. Everyone in court knew the truth and expected the students to be discharged. When the judgement came, those gathered in the courtroom gasped. Ten years of exile.

'Looking back, I see the judge was being merciful,' Khalil said. 'Even today, the judgements are written long before the case is argued. You might ask why we still take our cases to the court. Only so that the world might know of the existence of this case. That judge could have sentenced the five students to death, and no one would have raised a voice against it. But for a moment his integrity rose above the pressure he was facing from the government and he limited the punishment to expulsion from the country.

'That judgement woke the students up. They realized that in a country with such weak laws, the government could do anything. Without impartial judges, there could be no democracy, no human rights,' Khalil said.

'What happened to that law student?' I asked.

'From the moment that judgement was issued, he decided to dedicate his life to human rights. During his exile, he started an organization called We Are Watching You. When he returned, he continued that work in the City. The organization's motto is "Monitoring is our tool; the media is our weapon". We have identified many corruption issues. We were the ones who broke the story of how some people in the government were able to buy prime real estate for one dinar.' Khalil's eyes gleamed as he told us this.

'You were that law student, weren't you?' I asked after a moment of silence.

Khalil gave me no answer except a wide smile.

'Baba, I understand all this. I know you must work for your ideals and we will always support that. But what is the point of this fasting? These kind of protests only work when the government has a conscience.'

'If this is how I die, so be it, Zainab,' he said holding her hand. 'Let the world see that Arabs know how to die non-violently and not only in riots.'

Tom and Jerry

After many days, I had another opportunity to be alone in the flat. Riyaz left early to meet someone. Vinod got up after a while and flexed his muscles. 'Priyanka is not working today. She is alone in her flat. See you later.' Edwin had not been around much anyway. He was spending all his time with Asmo these days. I was overcome with desire for Sameera's book. I had forgotten about it for a few days but now that opportunity had come knocking, I was eager. Waiting impatiently for Vinod to leave, I switched on the television. As I hopped like a hare between channels, I suddenly saw Tom and Jerry on the screen. Two characters that I never tire of. When my kids would watch that cartoon, I would often sit with them, enjoying a rare moment of childishness.

It was an Arab channel. At first I didn't pay attention to the dialogue or the subtitles. I was keeping an eye on Vinod. But at some point, I started watching. In that story, Tom was an impoverished local and Jerry was an invading foreigner. Tom had a small box in his hand and Jerry was trying to snatch it from him. As he ran away from Jerry, Tom ran into an old friend of his. He shows his friend the box and says, 'Inside this is a small slice of land. It is my ancestral property. They kept it safe for centuries and it has passed down to me. My grandfather gave me all the documents for it before he was killed. But now this invader Jerry says it is his. It is my responsibility to protect my ancestral lands. That is why I am running away from Jerry.'

I watched for a bit. The next cartoon was Ben 10, and the plot was similar. These cartoons were remarkable examples of how to inject religious and national sentiments in children's minds and hearts.

Vinod had left by then. I switched off the television and rushed to Riyaz's room. I was determined not to repeat my mad search. I started in a corner and systematically went through the entire room. The hiding places were few: the suitcases, the desk drawers, the bookshelves, under the bed, the bathroom, the wardrobe. But the book was not in any of those places. Within half an hour I had run out of places to look in. I could not help but be impressed by Riyaz's skills in hiding this book in new places each time. I went back to my room, but I felt restless. Should I admit defeat that easily? The previous two times I had managed to find the book. This time too it was a matter of determination. Back I went and searched again, this time with sharper eyes. Finally, I proved to myself that fortune favours the brave. Finally, I found that book.

Part Seven

Silver Owl

New Faces

I finished most of Sameera's novel in that sitting. All I had left were the final few chapters. The novel was deeply intertwined with the City and its life. Why hadn't Riyaz mentioned it to us? I decided I would ask him about it. Relieved by my decision, I fell asleep.

Daisy's call woke me up. 'I am investigating the disappearance of an international journalist,' she said. 'He came to see us once and never returned. Perumal has been asking after you. I am going to come and pick you up this evening. Same time, same place, same car, same person.' Before I could respond, she had hung up.

I was eager to see Riyaz and ask him about the book. I wavered between Daisy and Riyaz. I called him to see when he would be back. A bit late, he said. I would go to Daisy's first, I decided, then return early to meet Riyaz. I called Daisy.

'I'll get there. You tell me the way to your place.'

'Oh sorry, I don't know how to direct you here. I know how to get to work and return. That's all.' She was as helpless as a child.

'Never mind. I sort of remember it from last time. I'll get there.'

'But make sure you come. If you don't, I might have to kill you.'

'Why, is there some kind of emergency that requires my presence at your house?'

'Oh, will you come only if there's an emergency? Well, sorry to disappoint you, but there's zero emergency. A girl who secretly crushed on you years ago and her jealous husband want to see you. If that appeals to you, come and hang out with us.' She hung up again.

I sat there in shock for a second or two, her words echoing in my unbelieving head. A girl who secretly crushed on you. Was she being flippant or was it truth disguised as an off-the-cuff joke? If the latter, then surely her timing was wrong. She should have said these words fifteen years ago. Had she spoken then, the consequences would have been so different. I considered it.

1. Fifteen years ago, she could not have said this so lightly and easily.
2. Had she said it, I would have been far more delighted than I was now. But I would have still pushed her away.
3. She must have approached me several times to tell me how she felt. But my indifference would have defeated her.
4. In those days, I only had eyes for an illusion called Jasmine. I did not have the eyes to see any others, even if they were more real.

5. Though she didn't know Jasmine, Daisy, with her feminine intuition, must have guessed that I was obsessed with someone else.

6. There was a good time for every declaration. Daisy had just proved that some things needed to be said in time or not at all.

7. And yet, her words did thrill me. Who can deny the pleasure of a confession of love from a woman you thought beautiful?

That evening I had no trouble finding my way to Daisy's home. Though I couldn't have said so when I started out, I knew exactly which landmarks to look out for and where to turn. Is there a bigger GPS than the mind?

Daisy was amazed. She couldn't imagine how a person could memorize a route they had taken only once. 'I come from a land of great sages who could memorize an entire book if they heard it once. Perhaps their seeds scattered around,' I told her proudly, raising my collar in front of her.

'Fake feminists like her don't understand that men have special powers like this.' Perumal laughed as he greeted me.

As I walked inside, I was viewing Daisy through a different lens. But she, on the other hand, did not have any of the tension or anxiety of someone who had shared a huge secret. She was cool and collected and even when our eyes met, her eyes looked into mine as if they had nothing to hide. As far as she was concerned, it seemed to me, she had made a joke and then forgotten all about it. Women are capable of this. Not men. Even the knowledge that someone had loved me once upon a time was enough to rattle me. I was like a drunk hen.

Passion Fruit

There was another guest at Daisy's house that evening. He was looking through Perumal's library when I got there. Perumal introduced him as Father Geevarghese Pachamannil. He was in the City on a three-year deputation, but halfway through it he had taken permission to quit and go home.

My Christian friends had often told me that most priests on deputation would try to extend it by a year. In fact, they called such deputations 'harvest time'.

'I am going to let you in on a little secret,' Perumal said. 'Tonight is also a farewell gathering for Father.'

'I would have declined if you had told me that,' Father said, clearly a bit annoyed. 'These meaningless rituals. I came to the City without any fanfare and I want to leave like that too.'

'Don't worry, Father. It's just the four of us. We'll sit together one last time and chat and break some bread together and feel the love. If we don't give and take from each other, if we don't share our joys and sorrows, then what is the meaning of life? What will we remember about our lives when we reach the end? So, Father, don't think of this as a ritual.'

'See, Pratap, Perumal is not the kind of person given to asking priests home. But Father Geevarghese is different. He is a bit of a renaissance man. He is good at public speaking, writing, art, music, even, would you believe it, magic! He is a master glass painter.' Daisy turned to Father Geeverghese and added, 'We thought you two must meet. Pratap lives in Canada, but we used to be classmates.'

'Always happy to be part of something like this. It's the formalities that I detest. So what brings you here?'

For a minute, I did not know what to say. What was the right answer? A market study? Searching for the love of my life?

'He is writing a novel. He is gathering material for that,' said Daisy before I could respond.

'Please don't display your foolishness to our guests,' Perumal said.

'What else is he doing if not writing a novel?' Daisy asked in all innocence.

'Are all women like this, Father?' Perumal asked. 'Do they simply hear from one ear and let it out from the other?'

'Pratap, what is wrong with what I said?' Daisy asked.

'Father, Mr Pratap and his team are here to collect data for a novelist. My beautiful wife is completely muddled.'

'Really, Pratap? I thought you told me you were writing the novel,' Daisy said, chagrined.

'Why don't you get our guests some juice?' Perumal sent her off.

'I don't want any juice right now,' I said.

'This is not some tetrapack juice full of chemicals. You have tasted nothing like this before. This is passion fruit juice and it comes from our garden here.'

'Perumal, your garden is quite a miracle in this desert city,' Father Geevarghese said. 'I remember this passion fruit vine climbing around a jackfruit tree in front of the convent where I studied. In those days we used to get mangoes and cashew fruits and passion fruits from our garden. Since then I have never come across passion fruit. It had been erased from my memory.'

'A friend sent this to me from Australia. I had a hard time getting it through immigration and customs here. I must have visited the agricultural department at least one hundred times. Now it is climbing around a wild lemon tree in my backyard.'

'Where does passion fruit come from originally?' Father asked.

'I don't know. I imagine the Brazilian forests, like so much else. Anyhow, it is the Portuguese who took it around the world.'

'You have to give credit where it is due. While they were busy colonizing the world, they also played a big role in cultural exchange. Imagine the history behind both a Brazilian and a Malayali loving tapioca. I think the colonial rulers who came afterwards simply didn't know how to get their colonies to eat out of their hands like the Portuguese did.'

Daisy brought the juice and asked if anyone wanted sugar in it.

'No, no,' Perumal cried out. 'If you want to enjoy the real taste of fruit, don't add sugar.'

'Very nice philosophy. But the juice is a little sour, so I'll bring you some sugar.'

'Then why don't you serve us sugar water?'

'Is there a Nobel Prize for Patience? Someone should give that to me for living with this guy,' Daisy retorted.

'I think everyone who is destined to lead a married life probably deserves that particular Nobel.' Father Geevarghese laughed.

'But, Father, what was so wrong about what I said?' Perumal marvelled. 'Did I say anything to annoy her? Nature has given each object its own taste. All I want is that we enjoy that taste, instead of diluting it with artificial stuff.'

'Well, nature also gave us sugar. I didn't invent it. You need to learn that two things can combine to create a third beautiful thing,' Daisy answered back.

'How about we add a tiny bit of sugar to sweeten the juice but not so much that it takes away from the authentic taste of the passion fruit?' I said.

'Good approach. All the problems we encounter in life can be solved easily like this. All you need is a sense of humour,' Father Geevarghese said.

'But Perumal is a perfectionist. Who can achieve one hundred per cent perfection? That is the main issue between us,' Daisy said.

'You know, this reminds me of a movie I once saw. A man was preparing for death and decided to write down ten things he wanted to do before that. He started writing eagerly. One, two, three . . . but by the time he reached number four, he couldn't come up with any more desires. There was nothing left. And that's what all our lives are like. Small, shrivelled lives that cannot come up with even ten things to do. Shouldn't we make the most of these little lives? Be true to life, live in harmony with nature, give back a little to the earth we take so much from – I am stubborn about these few principles of mine. Father, you have known me for a few years – I am against all established religions that are centred around humans. It is these principles that give me the courage to take such a strong stand. What a pity that Daisy has not been able to understand me.'

To change the subject, I asked, 'So what is the one thing that we each would like to see happen before we die?'

'I would go with the Ark of the Covenant,' Father said. 'God gave it to Moses when handing down the Ten Commandments. It is hidden somewhere on this planet. I would like to see it discovered before I die.'

'That's beautiful,' I said. 'What about you, Daisy?'

'I don't have a good answer right now. Why don't I think about it and tell you tomorrow?'

'No, we want to know what you think right now,' I insisted.

'Marriage is the most hypocritical system in the world. I would like to see it shattered before I die,' she said fiercely.

We shuddered.

Before I could turn to Perumal, he jumped in with his answer. 'I want to see aliens visit the earth. I want life to be discovered outside this planet. That will show the Semitic religions how mistaken they are to think that humans are the apex of creation. Whenever I am on a flight, I look down and wonder how the earth looks from space. A cloudy, lifeless mass. I fear that alien life forms have come all the way to the edge of our skies and looked down and decided, no, there cannot be any life down there. How can we convey to them that under those oceans of air, we somehow exist, strange and impossible as our life might seem to them. I worry that like ships that pass at night, we earthlings and aliens keep missing each other.'

The conversation ended there with a phone call for Perumal. That is the tragedy of our times. The ringing of the mobile phone can interrupt and, in fact, destroy the most important of conversations, the funniest punchline, a tender exchange between lovers. It can kill a poem or a story in the middle of its writing. There is no going back to what was before the phone rang. It is high time that cell phones are banned in public places, like smoking and drinking. Daisy got up and went to the kitchen. Father turned to a magazine lying on the table. And I remembered that I had planned on leaving early so I could find Riyaz. As soon as Perumal put the phone down, I got up to leave.

'I have some other work to take care of,' I said. 'But very happy I could meet you, Father. I found out today that priests can talk not only on spiritual matters, but also about passion fruit.' I meant that.

Perumal was surprised. 'What, you are leaving? Daisy, come here. This is not what we planned. We wanted a long evening, full of conversation and eating. Why in such a hurry, Pratap?'

'I have to do some things ...' I repeated, but Daisy scolded me. 'Stop it. Stop playing so hard to get. You are not going anywhere.' She snatched my car keys from my hands like a kid grabbing a piece of cake. Had it been anyone else, I would have lost my temper. But I found myself sitting down obediently. That was how intoxicated I was by that one sentence she had thrown at me in the morning.

'Pratap, I have ulterior motives in asking you to stay,' Perumal said. 'I want you to drop Father off at his parsonage on your way home. That will save me a trip.'

The conversation was resumed, but my heart was not in it. Riyaz must be back by now. I had to see him and ask him about the book, so I kept mentioning that I was in a rush. Daisy quickly got the dinner to the table so I would calm down. Chapatti and salad and vegetable pulao and chicken curry and mutton fry. Father did not eat the mutton. 'I just read a book about goats recently,' he said. 'Since then I have stopped eating mutton.'

'Can literature influence us that much?'

'Oh yes, literature can create miraculous changes in how we see the world, how we behave in it, even what we eat. But since readers are a minority in our society, those changes are invisible.'

A little snippet from my interview with Ahmed Al Qaid came floating back to me just then. Novels and poems tell us only the most ordinary facts about human life and society. Often they are simply elaborations on what we read in the newspaper. But when it is written as news, no one cares. When it takes the form of literature, that's when people react, that's when it hurts them and provokes them. I mentioned this.

'Literature is all that's left for ordinary citizens. What other avenues do they have to respond to society or religion or the establishment? All other avenues are closing one by one. That's why I believe literature will become tomorrow's weapon.'

Though it was one of those conversations that should have gone on all night, we finished dinner and rose quickly because of the constant hints I was dropping. My eagerness to get back and see Riyaz had become almost torture for me.

'I want to see you soon, Pratap,' Perumal said. 'We need to talk.' I guessed that he was also thinking of that book. Daisy accompanied us to the car.

As we shook hands and promised to meet again, her eyes met mine. I knew then that she had not been joking that morning.

God's Question

'There are three guiding lights in my life. The first is the novel *Les Misérables* and the character of Jean Valjean. That book taught me that humans are innately good and that we have to use the goodness within ourselves to find the goodness outside. Secondly, the idea that living a rich life in this poor world is a sin. This has destroyed any desire of mine to accumulate money. And finally, the question that God asked us humans. That question has haunted me all my life. But it became even more relevant, even more intense when I came to the City. For some time, I tried to ignore it. But I can't. The things that happen in the City keep asking me that very question.' This was Father Geevarghese's response when I asked him why he was leaving the City.

Though the cars were moving bumper to bumper in the

usual weekend traffic, I took my eyes off the road to stare at him. I was shocked at finally meeting someone who at least attempted to live by the principles that he talked about and taught.

"'Where is your brother?' That was what God asked. That question must echo in our hearts always, like an eternal thunder. We must not forget that we will each be obliged to answer that question one day. But when we fail to remember it, all this violence in the name of religion and race and caste and ideology will continue. I used to see this question as a theological issue until I arrived here. But these streets changed that. Innocents hunted down. Justice denied again and again. Strongmen ruling the streets. And I was supposed to turn away from all that and preach about love, justice, kindness. Only a hypocrite could do it.

'If I could have thought of this as a Muslim problem, why should a Christian like me worry about this, my people and my church are safe, then I could have had a comfortable life here. There are people who can read the Bible daily and pray for God's grace and not pay attention to what is happening outside their doors to other people. They only care if those injustices are affecting their own lives. I have tried to be one of those people. But I failed. I cannot bear to think that just beyond my own wall, other lives are being destroyed. I could not tolerate the contradiction. So it has been a while since I started wondering if I deserve to be here. Finally I decided to leave. I don't see this as a political problem; I see it as a spiritual problem. But not everyone understands this with the same level of intensity. Father has gone crazy here, they say. And I don't correct them. One should not expect to be understood by more than a handful of people. Let the others have their misconceptions.'

Silence filled the car. I was wondering how I would answer that question – Where is your brother? Could I respond to it with anything except a head bowed in shame? Would I have to secretly examine my hands for my brother's blood? After foaming at the mouth writing articles about dictators and democracies, how could one sit inside KFC eating fried chicken and drinking Pepsi and watching streets full of violence outside its glass windows? I had so many beliefs and values and ideologies. But how did they fit into my lived reality? It was as if my values and my life were on parallel roads that did not meet. In fact, there were two 'me's – the one who thought and the one who lived.

But once again I had found that the entire world had not been corrupted, that there were a few souls who held on to the light of goodness. To live lives of integrity, they were willing to abandon what was considered important in the world. The world had not sunk into darkness completely. God had promised that if there were five good people in Sodom and Gomorrah, those places would be spared. I understood then why God had spared our own world.

After dropping Father off at the parsonage, I sped home. But Riyaz was not back yet. The door of his room remained shut.

The Beginning of the Return

James Hogan called me that night, for the first time since my arrival in the City. He was anxious about when we would return and wanted to know how far we had got in our research. I got the sense that he wasn't completely satisfied with my daily email updates. 'It's not just the amount of time that I am worried about,' he told me. 'I am not convinced that you have gotten to know the City well enough. You are floating on the surface of the City, like a hollow log on water. I doubt that your research has the depth to satisfy our anonymous novelist. He might drop us from future assignments.'

'James, our calculations were wrong. We are not in a place where the conflict is ongoing.' I tried to justify our work. 'This is a city where the protests are over and an authoritarian government is in full sway. There is a limit to what we are allowed to see. Fear has enveloped the City like morning fog. But we have still managed to unearth some experiences that penetrate that fog. And I believe that Edwin, as a representative of the novelist, is perfectly happy with what we are finding. Why don't I discuss our return with him and let you know?'

For the first time since my arrival, I considered the question of returning from the City. I had not achieved what I wanted to, and sadness was hanging over me like a raincloud. After all these days, I had no idea why Jasmine was silent. She knew by now that I was in the City. In every mail I sent her, my phone number was in my signature. Still, she hadn't called. Surely that meant she did not want to see me or talk to me. Then why had she re-entered my life? Why had she offered her friendship? Her messages, her photos, her updates? Like a shooting star, she had made a brief appearance and then disappeared into darkness. Would I have to wait another twelve years for her next appearance?

When I was a child, we kids would play hide-and-seek. It was fun hiding while someone searched high and low for you. The thrill was in finding the best hiding places, in not being found. But then, as the search went on and on, the person seeking got frustrated, the person hiding became anxious to be found, and fear would soon replace the excitement. The person hiding would slowly step out, making themselves available to be found. In fact, we play hide-and-seek so that we can be found. But Jasmine, our game has turned out to be the opposite.

Perhaps the novelty of finding me again had died out. Perhaps, she thought there was nothing more to exchange now that we had caught up on each other's lives. But I, on the other hand, felt like a bunch of firecrackers that had been set alight. If I were to leave the City without meeting her, I would spend the rest of my days hurting for her. I cannot give up on myself like that. Vinod's idea of involving the police was not only dangerous, it was taking forever. The police had not responded. I had to find a new solution before James Hogan's next call. Now it struck me that I had been foolish. I had been behaving as if I had all the time in the world, entire eternities to spend in the City. I had imagined myself smart enough to fool everyone, but I was the biggest fool here.

Through the night I thought of ways and means to find

Jasmine. If only there was a yellow line, like the one leading to the emergency room in the hospital, that would lead me to Jasmine. At some point between my fevered thoughts, I slipped into sleep. But in the middle of the night, I woke up with a start, and immediately, the path to Jasmine lay in front of me, as if it were a clearly marked road on a map. It could not have been clearer if it had been printed on a piece of paper. I had no idea how my mind had put the pieces together while I was sleeping, but this new possibility of seeing Jasmine made me feel buoyant with hope. The name of that possibility was Daisy.

The Ruined Road

I knew that Daisy would do whatever I asked of her. But when I called her the next day, I made up a strange pretext. 'Do not invite me to any more parties,' I said harshly. She was probably taken aback at my about-face. 'I forgive you for yesterday because Father Geevarghese was such a unique character. But had it been anyone else, I would have walked out without any care for your feelings. I am always happy to come and see you or Alex Perumal when you want me to. But if you invite me, please make sure you are alone. I am not asking for any special treatment; it's just that I hate dining and travelling with strangers, so I want to avoid it as much as possible.'

Daisy was full of apologies. 'I was wrong to trap you like that without your permission. Stupid me, trying to create suspense. I'll never do it again. Promise.'

'That's fine, but it's not going to undo how bad I felt yesterday.'

'I know . . . tell me how I can make it up to you.' She was almost crying.

'I have a punishment for you in mind.'

'Punish me. I'll take whatever punishment you want to give me.'

'Really? You'll do anything?'

'If you are the one asking, I might just have to.'

'Are you sure?'

'Sure.'

'Hmm . . . then there is something I need from you,' I said.

'What is it?'

'Never mind . . . not today. I'll tell you another time.'

'Stop stressing me out. If you don't tell me, I am going to think about nothing else all day.'

'But will you agree to do it?' I stretched out the suspense.

'Yes, I will.'

'Without misunderstanding me?'

'I won't misunderstand anything.'

'Never mind. I am not in the mood to talk about it now. Another time.'

'Stop it. You are making me crazy. What is it? Do you want my body?'

'If I ask for it, are you ready to give?'

'Ask and you will find out.'

'I'll have to try that some other time. This is something else. I need your help in finding someone in the City.' I finally came to my problem.

'Who is it? Are you on the trail of some criminal?'

'Yes, it is indeed someone who has committed a major crime. I cannot let her go free any more. Do you remember her? She burned my heart and soul all those years ago when we were in college? Well, I am still burning. She is in the City but hiding from me. I want to see her once before I leave. I know it is cruel to ask you for help. But I don't have any other choice.'

For a moment Daisy was silent, like an animal that is shocked to realize it has been shot. Then she recovered, and without any sign of the hurt she felt, she said, 'Okay, give me the details. Let me see what I can do.'

Without feeling any guilt or shame, I gave Daisy Jasmine's email address. Daisy was the road and Jasmine was the destination. If the road had to be ruined on the way to the destination, so be it.

In Other News

Later that day I got a call from the CID office. They had some questions and wanted me to stop by. I wanted to take Vinod with me, but he was busy. I felt a little uneasy going to the CID office by myself, possibly because Perumal's story was still ringing in my head. Riyaz was still not in his room when I checked and Edwin's phone was busy.

Might as well go alone, I thought. If nothing else, I had my Canadian passport. Surely the embassy and *Toronto Sunday* would take care of me if there was some trouble. Just then

I remembered our driver Faisal. At least he could interpret for me if there were some language issues. But when I called him, he said he was taking Vinod somewhere and then had to buy fish for Abdullah Janahi. As soon as that was done, he said, he would get to me. I lost my temper. 'We didn't hire you for running Abdullah Janahi's market errands. Be here within half an hour, no matter what!' I hung up before he could say anything.

Within fifteen minutes, Faisal screeched into the parking lot. I got into the car. We were both silent. He can ask if he wants to know where we are going, I thought. But he drove aimlessly, as if to say, 'You are the one who should be telling me the destination.' Finally, I accepted defeat and told him to take me to the CID office.

That was all Faisal needed. It was as if hearing my voice unleashed his voice. 'He is the one giving me my wages. That's why I obey him. It's not because I like being his kitchen boy. If you don't like it, you should have looked into it before. It was your responsibility to find out what kind of tasks he is giving me and where he is asking me to go. But you didn't do that and now you are angry with me.' He tossed the ball into my court.

'I'll look into that,' I said curtly.

Then, perhaps wanting to get on my good side, or perhaps out of sheer resentment, he unwrapped his bundle of complaints against Abdullah Janahi.

'He makes me do all his household shopping. I am the one who takes his kids to school. When his wife needs to go to the beauty parlour, she calls me. You are the ones spending money, but you have no idea. Do you even notice whether he comes to work every day and how little time he spends in the office? Even if he is in the office, what does he do – drink sulaimani tea and eat melon seeds. His ear is always pressed to his phone. Do you know what he is doing? He is conducting his real estate business.' Faisal was hot with rage.

'But that is none of my business. Abdullah Janahi is not a full-time salaried staff member in our office. We pay him a small fee in return for administrative assistance. So what he does with his time when he is not working for us does not concern us.'

'Pratap sahib, here's something you don't know,' Faisal said. 'He owns our office building. He rented an office to you in his building and now he sits in the office you rented and conducts his business. That's how sneaky he is.'

I sat up and paid attention. When Abdullah Janahi insisted that we rent an office in that building, I had not guessed that he had a vested interest.

'Does he really have enough money to own that building?' I said, still not believing Faisal completely. I was remembering Abdullah's dilapidated car and his primitive mobile phone and his old shoes and his even more old-fashioned ways.

'He is such a Scrooge that you won't think it. But he used to have a government job and the real estate business on the side. You are surprised he owns one building? He owns fourteen such buildings.'

'Really? He used to have a government job?'

'Yes.'

'And what happened to it?' If a barometer could measure my curiosity, it would have been off the charts.

'He played at protesting. They fired him. He has appealed the decision though and they might take him back.'

'What kind of job did he have?'

'He used to be the head of maintenance at the local radio station.'

'At the radio station?'

'Yes, why? Do you know someone who works there?'

'No, no. I just didn't guess that was his background.' I evaded the question.

But my real reason was different. The book that I had stolen from Riyaz's room also mentioned an Abdullah Janahi who worked at the radio station. If it was indeed based on a true story, could that Abdullah and this Abdullah be the same? Surely, that coincidence, along with Perumal's story, meant that the novel I had read was indeed the story of the City. Did Abdullah Janahi know some of the characters in that novel? Then maybe he knew what happened to them. And maybe he also knew the sordid intrigues that surrounded the book.

I felt as if I had picked up a pot of panic and poured it over my head. Cold fear washed over me.

Some Important Questions

Faisal refused to come with me to the CID office. 'I will come with you where you want, but not there.' When I asked why, he simply said, 'No one who knows the history of this country would go to the CID office. Half the people who have gone there have not returned.'

I was extremely worried. The case that Vinod and I had registered was so obviously a false case. What a stupid move that had been. I comforted myself that all I had asked for was to find the person behind the email and gathered the courage to go inside.

Once there, they sent me running around. What complaint? About who? Who called you? When did they call you? Go there. Ask here. Finally I found a policeman who listened to me and took me to the right officer.

'Please wait,' the officer said. 'I'll call you.'

Perhaps, like Perumal, I, too, was destined for an endless waiting game. I should never have come, I thought. At the same time, I also knew that if a door to Jasmine opened up because of this, even this waiting would be worth it. My days in the City were numbered. James Hogan might call me any minute. I would have to spell out a return date then. I had still not discussed this with Edwin. I had to find Jasmine before all that.

Luckily my wait was not very long. The officer invited me inside. We walked through the long, dark corridors that Perumal had described. We arrived in a room with nothing but a bench and a desk, just as Perumal had described. I listened for screams but did not hear anything. Still, fear crawled all over my body. Were they going to question me and torture me? I sat there waiting for the inevitable. The atmosphere in the room was enough to convince an innocent person that he was guilty.

The police officer arrived a few minutes later. I had been preparing myself to sit on the floor. But he did not ask me to stand up or sit on the floor. Instead, he placed my file on the table. Unfortunately, this case could not be accepted for investigation by the police, he said.

'Why couldn't you have told me this over the phone?' I asked, summoning a tiny spark of courage.

'We needed you here,' he said.

'No, you did not. Your childish explanations are of no use to me,' I responded.

'We wanted to see you, but not regarding this case. We have some other important questions for you.'

'Go ahead, please.' I said.

'Pratap Kizakkedathu Vittil Manoharan, correct?'

'More or less. The pronunciation is wrong.'

He ignored me. 'You are an Indian with Canadian citizenship, correct?'

'Yes.'

'You are on a tourist visa, but not a tourist.'

'Yes, I am here for a market study.'

'You work for a newspaper in Canada, right?'

'No, it's actually a weekly.'

'Either way, you are here for journalism?'

'No, this is a completely different project,' I said.

'Please explain.'

'Some company is studying the market for their products here.'

'Which company and what is the product?'

'I don't know.'

'Usually journalists don't do market studies. So why are you here?'

'I don't know why we were chosen. They want to know about the social conditions, living standards, government stability, the way money moves here . . . and not just economic facts. Perhaps they thought journalists were better at this kind of investigation.'

'We are confident that our people have high living standards and security. Anyone doing a market study here would see that easily. We have no doubt that their results will be positive. Still, out of curiosity, what are your findings, Mr Pratap?'

'Other than some difficulties with financial flow, I found nothing of concern. I have no complaints,' I said.

'That is not a domestic issue. We are also affected by the worldwide financial crisis. Give them a good report,' he said.

'Certainly.'

'So do you also write book reviews at the weekly?'

'Sometimes,' I said. It was a lie. I had never done any reviewing. But I felt a bit embarrassed to admit that.

'You must be getting books from around the world then.'

'Yes, but they don't come to me directly. The office receives them.'

'So do you read them and keep them or do you return them to the office?'

'We are supposed to bring them back to the office. But if I like a book, I keep it at home.'

'And if you really like it, you'll send it to friends, right?'

'Yes,' I said, and just as I uttered that word, everything

fell into place in my mind, as if illuminated by lightning. Perumal and his story to the police. Is that where he was leading me? Had I just blithely walked into his trap? I broke into a sweat.

At that moment, we heard a scream from the next room. Even though I had been listening for it, it sent shock waves through me.

'Oh, just ignore that. That is just someone who does not speak the truth.' The police officer's voice had changed. 'Tell me, who are your friends in the City?'

'No one in particular.'

'No one at all?'

'No.'

'And this email address is yours?'

'Yes.'

'Can you vouch that no one from the City has contacted you at this email address?'

'I cannot. In fact, my complaint is about someone who keeps writing to me at this address. But you refuse to register a case.'

'Do you send books to this unknown person?'

'No.'

'Are you sure?'

'Surely I would know their mailing address then? And I would know who they are. Why would I come to you then?'

I thought my questions would hit the mark, but he was far too well trained in the art of police interrogation.

Without even a moment's hesitation, he fired back, 'So what is the relationship between you and Perumal?'

'He is my friend's husband.'

'How many books have you sent him so far?'

'I can't remember. He is a voracious reader. So whenever I see a book that I know he won't find here, I send it to him.'

That was the best I could do in that moment. I knew that if I was not careful, Perumal and I would both be trapped.

'Then why did you tell us that you don't have any literary friends in this city?'

'He is not just some literary acquaintance. He is one of my best friends.'

'So you made a best friend out of your ex-girlfriend's husband. Or would it be more accurate to say your secret girlfriend's husband?'

'What makes you think that?'

'It's a universal truth. The girlfriend's husband is a man's best friend. And that idiot has no idea.' He laughed. 'And catering to his weakness for books means you can keep up your friendship and your romance.'

'Thanks for broadening my horizons. But that's not the nature of our relationship.'

'Where did you get hold of that book?'

'What book?'

'If you are such good friends, I am sure you have already talked about that book.'

'Oh I see. He did mention that the police questioned him about some banned book. Is that the one you mean?'

'Yes, that's the one. *A Spring Without Fragrance*. How did you find it?'

'Actually I don't remember this book so well, even though

Perumal talked about it. Probably came to our office as a review copy. If I am remembering right, I abandoned it after reading the first fifty pages. I must have sent it to Perumal since it was about a country in this region. Are all banned books that boring?'

'How would I know? I don't waste time reading.'

'Sir, why was that book banned here?'

'It contains a few sentences that malign this country. I don't know what exactly since I haven't read it.'

'Of course. What would be the point of banning the book and then giving it to you to read. But, sir, help me understand something. So what if there are some sentences that malign the country? Is the country's self-esteem so low that a few sentences can hurt it so much? What about all the websites and blogs and Facebook status updates that speak against the country? Shouldn't they all be banned too?'

'Mr Pratap, this is not a question befitting a journalist like you. You know the real reason. Books are sacred. The words in them belong to God. They will live forever. So if a book contains falsehoods, we have to assume it is satanic. It is the duty of everyone who loves truth to destroy such a book. And that's what we are going to do to this book.'

'But it sounds as if the book has already been read by a number of people. What can you do to those readers? Are you going to kill them?'

'We have ways of silencing those readers.'

'Really?'

'Yes, and clearly we are succeeding because there isn't a single sentence on the Internet about that book.'

'There's still time for that.'

'We need your help figuring out who sent the book to your office.'

'That's impossible to find out. We get books from around the world. There's no way to trace who is sending what.'

'How many copies of that book do you have at your office?'

'None, I am sure. We usually get only one review copy.'

'Thank you very much. We apologize for inconveniencing you. But this is a question of our country's honour.' He stood up and so did I.

Packing Up

Faisal was waiting for me outside. 'I was really scared. I had my foot on the pedal all this time,' he said as we drove home.

'Why? Why are you so scared of that office? Have you had any bitter experiences there?'

'Do we learn to fear a snake after it bites us? No, we know it is lethal, we have heard what it can do. The CID office is like that. I have heard so many stories from people in my family, in my village . . . Innocents who have been taken away for questioning and then they never came back. No explanations about what happened to them. Can you imagine that happening in your country – a citizen goes missing without any reason? It would quickly turn into a political issue. I have even read about governments that came tumbling down because of a single missing person. But here if a person is missing, it is the end of the story. And this office is at the heart of all this. There isn't another place in the City that I hate and fear as much.'

I could understand that explanation. What would be the point of saying that a snake was a harmless creature that only attacked humans when it needed to defend itself? When fear was this deeply rooted, it was impossible to dislodge it.

We returned to the office. Edwin and Vinod were present, not to mention Abdullah Janahi, chewing melon seeds. As soon as he saw Faisal, he started scolding him in Arabic. Faisal yelled back. I tried to use the bits and pieces of Arabic I had picked up in the last few weeks to understand their conversation, but it seemed as if they were talking in some other language. Clearly it was about the errands that Faisal had left undone in the morning. He walked out in a huff.

I told Vinod that the CID office had declined to take up my case. I did not tell him the rest of the events.

'Well, that firecracker fizzled out the minute you changed the complaint,' he said. 'If only you had taken my advice.'

'Never mind, Vinod. We can figure out another solution.'

'Let's talk more this evening. I haven't given up.' He sounded as if this was his problem.

I approached Edwin's table. 'We need to talk urgently.'

'Tell me, I am listening,' he said without moving his eyes from the computer screen.

'James Hogan called. He wants us to wrap up here and return as soon as possible.'

'Is that so? I was thinking along similar lines. But I'd like to stay for a few more days. At least until Asmo's next vacation.'

'Where is Riyaz?'

'No idea. Haven't seen him for a couple of days. I thought he was on some assignment with you.'

'Haven't I told you many times that he has some secret activities of his own?' Vinod interrupted us. 'You should be reining him in when he goes off gallivanting without doing his work here. I am sure he will get us into trouble otherwise.'

'That's not how I see it. He always struck me as responsible and hard-working,' Edwin replied.

'Hard work! That is so twentieth century. We are now in the era of smart work,' Vinod said.

'Yes, indeed. And smart work is all about conning the people you work with, whereas honesty was the hallmark of the era of hard work. So you see, Riyaz will have the honesty of that bygone era.'

The conversation ended there. However, I couldn't help but wonder where Riyaz had disappeared. And, despite myself, Vinod's words kept ringing in my head. Then I remembered what Faisal had told me in the morning and turned to Abdullah Janahi.

'Faisal was with me all morning. Didn't he tell you that? Then why were you scolding him?' I put on a stern face.

'Mr Pratap, I was not scolding him for taking you around. But he didn't take care of some other jobs he was supposed to . . .' he replied between mouthfuls of melon seeds.

'What are these other jobs that we don't know anything about? Your household errands?'

For a moment, he was stunned by my question. Then he recovered.

'Yes, sometimes I send him out on my household errands. But only when there is no other work in the office. After all, we pay him for a full day's work. You don't know drivers in the City. If you let them sit idle, they make all kinds of mischief. If there is no work in the morning, I just send them to find out the prices of diesel and petrol.'

We laughed.

'But today, we weren't talking of errands. Muharram begins tomorrow and he said he wanted to take time off from work. We were arguing about that.'

'What if he doesn't turn up for work tomorrow?'

'No big deal. I haven't paid him yet for this month. Anyway, we can get hundreds of drivers in his place.'

'How much time does he want to take off?'

'There are forty days of rituals for Muharram. Ten of those days are special, and of those three are extremely important. I told him he could have the three days off, but he wants all ten days off.'

'Oh, there's no way we can give him ten days off. They are already telling us it's time to return. Every single hour from now on is precious. We absolutely need a driver around.'

'That's what I told him, and he went off in a huff. But don't worry, how far can he go? He'll be back soon with his tail between his legs.'

'What language were you talking in? It didn't sound like Arabic,' Edwin asked, still at his computer.

'We spoke in Farsi. That's how Shias in the City communicate with each other.'

'So are you also Shia?'

'I used to be. But then I fell in love with a Sunni woman and married her. So now I have become Sunni.'

'Is it that easy to convert between Sunni and Shia? I didn't know that. All these years I thought these sects were something you are born into, like caste in India.' Edwin was so excited he got up from his computer and came up to Abdullah.

'Yes, of course you can convert. After all, they are just belief systems. It's like a Catholic becoming a Protestant,' Abdullah enlightened him.

'I remember I was so perplexed when I read about Sunni terrorists exploding bombs in Shia territories in Pakistan. I was sitting there with my mouth open till a colleague explained that there were all these sects within Islam,' Vinod said.

'So do Sunnis not observe Muharram?' I asked.

'Well, Muharram is the name of a month in the Muslim calendar. Just like the fasting month is called Ramadan, the rituals that take place in the month of Muharram also became known by the name of the month. In fact, the actual name is Ashura. And it is observed only by Shias.'

'I saw an Ashura procession once when I was living in Hyderabad. It is quite a spectacle,' Vinod said.

'That's as far as most non-Shias have gotten,' Abdullah added. 'If you really want to see Ashura rituals, you have to go to one of the Shia villages deep inside the country. Over the course of the month, each village will have its own matam for Ashura.

'What's a matam?'

'It's the ceremonial mourning. The villages take it very seriously.'

'I have an idea,' Edwin said. 'Let Faisal take all the days off he needs. But on one condition – he should take us to his village so we can see the ceremonies.'

'Will they let us do that? I don't think so,' Vinod said. 'Wouldn't they be suspicious of a bunch of strangers who turn up to see their ceremonies? That's one of the problems with religion everywhere. Too suspicious of others.'

'Well, there's a good reason for that,' Edwin said. 'Today, religious celebrations and festivals are major bomb targets. Look at Iraq and Syria and Lebanon and Pakistan. So, of course, people get suspicious when they see strangers.'

'Well, you don't have to worry about that here,' said Abdullah. 'We have the world's most peaceful Ashura. Anyone can visit. Instead of suspicion, you will be welcomed with open arms.'

'Call Faisal then so we can talk to him about it.'

Faisal arrived within five minutes, almost as if he had been waiting for our call. He was very excited by our idea. 'Just say when. I'll make sure you get to see everything,' he assured us.

Just then Riyaz walked into the office. He looked exhausted.

'What happened to you, Riyaz? Where have you been the last couple of days?' I asked.

'I was with a friend. And my phone was out of battery.'

'You look very tired. Are you sick?'

'I need to go home. I got a call from my family. Baba is sick.'

'Of course. See if you can get a ticket to leave today if possible. The project is almost ending anyway and we are about to start packing up. If something important comes up, we'll call you. Otherwise, we'll see you in the next city,' Edwin said.

Riyaz nodded. Abdullah booked his flight and gave him some money for his expenses. He was to report to the airport within two hours.

'Let me go pack up then.' Riyaz hurried off.

I offered to take him home and then drop him off at the airport, but he refused. 'Faisal will take me,' he said.

As I watched him leave, I felt a frisson of longing for the book that was going to leave the country with him. Even in that last minute, I could have asked him for it. But he was in such a rush. We didn't even have time to say a real goodbye. This was not how I had anticipated our group's farewell. I had imagined a party on our balcony with Asmo and Priyanka and Biju and Daisy and Perumal, a joyful final gathering.

Then an unwanted thought snuck in. Had Riyaz told us the truth? Where had he disappeared for these last two days? If his phone was out of battery, how did he get the call from home about his father being sick? Was that a pretext for leaving the City suddenly? Perhaps Vinod's theories about Riyaz were not that far-fetched?

Matam Al Gazab

We did go to Faisal's village to watch the Ashura ceremonies. I asked Abdullah Janahi to accompany us there, just in case. As we stood on the balcony waiting for Faisal to pick us up, I had a moment alone with Abdullah and I took the opportunity to find out more about what Faisal had told me of him.

'What did you do before this job?'

'For a long time, I was an auto mechanic. Then I worked in security. After that I was an electrical contractor. I started a real estate business around then. Alongside that I started a clearing agency, you know, to help people with government records and documents. The travel agency came after that. And somewhere in between all that, I also got a job as the head of the maintenance department at the radio station. So there you have it, the things I did to make a living.'

'Why do you keep moving from one thing to another? Wouldn't it be better to be consistent within one career?'

'But I am not moving from one career to another. I am merely adding to the existing ones. In fact, I still have most of the jobs I mentioned. Maybe it is better to think of me as the chairman of a group of companies!'

I could not tell if he was being sarcastic or if he was genuinely proud.

'What about the radio station job? Do you still have it?'

'No, that one is gone. Because I didn't show enough support to the government here during the protests. But I have appealed the decision. Who knows, they might give me my job back. But I thought, why waste time. Might as well work for you till then,' he said.

'Did you know a girl called Sameera there? She worked in the Hindi station.'

'How do you all know her? Riyaz was also asking me about her.'

I didn't know what to say for a minute. Would I have to tell him about the book? But then that other me, the one that knew how to steal books and lie effortlessly, spoke.

'I heard that she is a famous radio jockey in the City. Even those who don't listen to Hindi music seem to love her. So I was curious if you ever encountered her. You know how it is. Commoners like me are curious not only about celebrities but even about those who might know celebrities.'

'My friend, you have no idea. There are twenty-one radio stations in that complex. So there must have been hundreds of jockeys there. Only outsiders think jockeys are a big deal. For us, they were ordinary workers. I never noticed any of them. In fact, let me tell you a secret. They might have good voices, but these radio jockey girls are usually ugly as hell. They reminded me of dry dates. Best not to see those faces.'

Faisal had reached by then and our conversation ended there. The two of us went downstairs along with Edwin and Vinod. Faisal had exchanged his usual bright colours for an all-black attire. The sound of a dirge filled the car and a melancholy mood permeated it. But on his face I saw the excitement of someone eagerly awaiting guests.

On the way, we saw some men constructing something right in the middle of the street. Faisal stopped the car and talked to them. 'Did you see that?' he asked us. 'That was the dargah of a famous Shia scholar, Imam Sadiq. Whenever there is a problem in the City, the government takes its revenge on the Shias by razing it down. In my own memory, this is the fourth or fifth time.'

'They pulled it down because it's in the middle of the road, obstructing traffic. Not because they want revenge,' Abdullah muttered from the back seat.

'This dargah is a very old one. In fact, it was the trail to the dargah that the government widened and made into a road. They could have routed the road in such a way that the dargah was not affected. But they planned this so they have a handy excuse to destroy it.'

'If they wanted to destroy it, they could have done it several years ago,' Abdullah said.

'Well, this animosity towards dargahs is a very recent thing, it only started after Wahabbism became popular among Sunnis. Till then, dargahs did not pose any problems to anyone. But the Wahabbis have even destroyed the house and tomb of Prophet Muhammad, peace be upon him. They did not preserve it even as a historic monument. So what can you expect from them when it comes to a small dargah like this one? They will bulldoze it. And we will rebuild it. As long as there is even one of us, we will rebuild it,' Faisal said.

Abdullah was about to retort to that but I stopped him.

As soon as we entered Faisal's village, we could see the signs of Ashura. Black flags lined the street. Black banners on buildings. Portraits of the Shia imams. Pole tents for street gatherings. And, everywhere, men and women in black. A procession was coming towards us and we parked on the side to let it pass. It seemed almost like a dark flood

flowing towards us. But right in the middle was a riderless
white horse. Songs of lament sounded throughout and the
procession was moving to its rhythm. In the middle of the
song, everyone would pause for a moment. Then the drum
would sound loudly. Everyone would beat their chests. They
would take the next step. Then the drumbeat. The beating
of the chest. The people in the back of the procession were
beating themselves on their heads and backs with heavy iron
chains. Some of them even had swords with which they were
hitting their foreheads. Blood flowed from their wounds. But
it seemed to me that those wounds were giving them not
pain, but ecstasy.

'That was Matam Ben Rajab's procession,' Faisal said.

That night we visited several villages and matams. Matam
Ben Rajab, Matam Al Gazab, Matam Al Ajam, which was
populated by people of Iranian descent. When we arrived at
this last one, people were greeting guests in the street and
distributing water. 'Drink the water and curse the Yazid,'
one of them told me as he offered water. I asked Faisal what
that meant.

'That's a common saying here. Yazid is Yazid Al Muawiya,
who trapped our beloved Imam Hussein and his followers in
Karbala, and forced them to die of thirst. With every drop
of water we drink, we remember how the Prophet's own
grandson must have longed for water and we curse that brute.'

In Matam Al Gazab, an imam was making a speech just
as we walked in. He switched to English, perhaps because
of us. Hussein was beheaded just as John the Baptist was

beheaded, he reminded the audience. He compared their lives and deaths.

Elsewhere, on a stage adjoining the village mosque, actors were performing what seemed to me a mythological drama. People wearing red and people wearing green were arguing with each other onstage. In the audience, women and children were responding emotionally and intensely, as if what they were seeing was a real event. A wedding took place onstage and then the bridegroom was killed by the other group. Another character emerged with a baby in his arms. An arrow struck the baby. As the father cried, the audience joined in. Two enemy characters came onstage to say their piece, and a woman who was watching stood up and cursed them. The audience was not merely watching a drama, they were reliving those incidents. But without knowing the story, it was impossible for me to understand what was going on.

Part Eight

The City of Jihadis

Guilty

The next day, Perumal called me. 'I want to talk to you in confidence. Tell me a time and place that works for you.'

'I am not doing anything this evening. You choose the place. I'll get there.'

'There's a restaurant called Caesars on Seaport Road, where you live. What about meeting there at 5 p.m.?'

'I'll be there,' I said.

'One more thing. Daisy should not know about us meeting.'

'Okay, I won't tell her.'

I knew he wanted to meet about that book. But it had sailed across the seas many days ago. Perumal would be disappointed to hear that. I, too, was disappointed. What bad luck that I could not get hold of it again. Some objects of desire will always elude us. Others fall into our laps even when we are not looking. I thought of the many alleys I had walked in the City, the roads I had driven on, the malls I had wandered through. It seemed to me that everyone living in the City must have passed before my eyes. Everyone except who I was looking for. So it was with this book. Perumal, you and I are both unfortunates. How close I had come to the book, and yet it had slipped away.

Caesars restaurant was not that far from our apartment. I reached there well in advance. Though it was an Indian restaurant, there were several non-Indian patrons.

I leafed through the magazines lying on the table while waiting. Most of them were glossy lifestyle magazines and promotional publications filled with ads. But among them was a Malayalam magazine. It was the annual magazine of an Islamic organization in the City. It was titled *Glimmer of Spring* and was dedicated to the Arab Spring. The articles in it praised the Arab Spring as an Islamic resistance after centuries of oppression by faithless rulers. According to the magazine, the victory of Islamic political parties in some countries where elections had taken place was a major win for Islam itself. It also scoffed at attempts to bring the Arab Spring ideologically in alignment with communism or Western democracy. But what really struck me was the magazine's firm position that while the revolutions elsewhere represented genuine Islamic resistance, the protests that had taken place in the City were reactionary. While rulers in other countries who had been in power for more than forty years were cruel dictators, here in the City those long decades were an era of stable government that had established a strong foundation for progress. Only reactionaries who had strayed from Islam's straight path would want to protest against a compassionate ruler such as His Majesty.

I couldn't help but laugh. We Malayalis. Like sure-footed cats, wherever we go, we know how to land on our feet.

Perumal arrived soon. After we ordered coffee, I showed him the magazine.

'Amazing how people can twist their tongues and say two completely different things in the same breath. They also know how to interpret situations according to convenience. Most of the expats here would like to see history rewritten, as long as it does not affect their cushy lives in any way. There are plenty of people here who make big speeches about international politics and world democracy, but their tongues are tied when it comes to the situation here. Playing football without the ball! That's what it is. They can run fast and head off opponents, but without a ball, what's the point?'

'So what did you want to see me about?'

'What do you think it is about?'

'You are anxious about that book, right? Well, I am sad to say there is no hope. I asked my friends in Canada and made Edwin ask his friends in London and Riyaz ask his friends in Pakistan . . . But no luck. I am sorry.' Never mind that I had read most of the book. I lied through my teeth. In fact, a part of me wondered how I had got so good at lying, despite my lack of experience in it previously. And that too for no special gain.

'I know, I know. That is not the sort of book you can find easily. The government and the police in this country are on its track. So I don't even bother thinking about that book any more. Hopefully, some day, somewhere I'll come across it again. But I wanted to see you today about something else. Something far more important.'

Perumal was silent for a minute. Then he took my hand suddenly. 'Pratap, please don't ruin my life.'

I was perplexed. 'What do you mean? How would I ruin your life?'

'Daisy is a different person from the moment she learned of your arrival in the City. It is true, Pratap. She has found a strange, new courage. She argues with me often, mocks me like she has never done before. Finds flaws in my behaviour. She has started doing all kinds of things independently. The other day, she asked to manage her salary herself. Now she wants her ATM card back. She used to joke very occasionally about divorcing me, but now she brings it up at least three times a week. Where did she find all this courage? I have thought a lot about it, and I see only one answer. You, Pratap. Her lover's presence has inspired her. All this while she thought she was alone in life, but now she has someone. This is dangerous. She will see more and more flaws in me. I will become a piece of trash in her eyes. She will run away with you. Fear, disgust and shame: a woman who has lost these three things is a woman to be feared. Such a woman is capable of anything.'

His hand felt warm in my mine. 'Please, Pratap. I don't have anyone else. I am an orphan. If Daisy leaves me, I will die. Only you can help me. I am helpless.'

I had no idea how to respond. 'Perumal, this is all in your imagination. There is nothing between us. There was nothing even when we were students together, much less now. Besides, in those days, I was deeply in love with another woman. Daisy was just a friend,' I stammered.

'Perhaps for you. But for Daisy, I am sure it was different. Have you noticed what she has been sharing on Facebook lately? They are all quotes and pictures about undying love and lost dreams and the return of a lover. Facebook is like a mirror to our heart these days. She loves you secretly. All these years, that love was lying low. She may have never spoken of it to you. But the moment she saw you again, it resurrected. You may not understand it, but I do. I have been living with her all these years. She is obsessed with you. The way her eyes gleam when your name comes up, the lightness in her step when you are on your way to us . . . I don't need any other proof.'

'Perumal, you must not suspect Daisy like this. She is a good wife. The mother of your daughter. Even if she did have some dream like that once upon a time, she has forgotten it completely by now. Each moment, aren't we all becoming different people as life takes us forward? Remembering old dreams will only embarrass us now.'

'Then you have failed at understanding Daisy. Perhaps the same mistake you made long ago. You have always been on her mind.'

'What do you want me to do, Perumal? Should I not see her or call her? Fine. From now on, I won't. There will be no more friendship between us. I apologize for coming to visit you.'

'Pratap, I didn't bring this up to hurt you. And maybe you are innocent in this matter. But given her current state, simply not calling her or not seeing her is not going to help. You have to leave this city forever.'

'That's actually going to happen. Our project is in its last phase. We will be leaving soon.'

'Oh, very good. The sooner the better.'

'Well, obviously I cannot simply abandon the job I was given.' I was irritated and I showed it.

'Pratap, I hope you won't misunderstand me. I have no quarrel with you. I respect you and I know that you have no part in all this. It's all Daisy. In fact, even if you leave, she is not going to calm down. I know her. She will keep contacting you. These social networks are such dangerous places. They are like devils whispering in women's ears that there is a universe of happiness waiting for them beyond their husband. Remember what she said that day? That the family is the worst system in the world? And it must be destroyed? What does that mean? She wants to leave me, what else? But you are an intelligent man. You are my friend. You must not respond to her. Don't fall into her trap. Promise me.'

'Perumal, let me ask you something. How long do you think you can keep your wife in a cage? If she really wants to leave, she will leave one day.'

'A cage? Of course not. Daisy can come and go as she pleases. She has every freedom. I only want to separate her from you. Because right now she is on fire for you. Whatever you ask, she will give you. But that is because you are a presence in this city; you are near her. Once you leave, that fire will slowly die out. Eventually, if you do not communicate with her at all, she will start wondering if all this was an illusion. Then, in two or three months, her old life will be back on track. She will realize that there is no world beyond me. That is all I need.'

Pity for Perumal surged inside me. Oh, the many ways in which a man could be reduced to helplessness.

'Don't worry, Perumal. I didn't come to live here. Go in peace.'

'One more thing. Daisy must never know of our meeting and this conversation.'

'Okay, I will never tell Daisy about this.'

Perumal left, coffee undrunk. I watched him go, his tired gait, and sat there thinking. One man, so many faces.

Two Electricians

Edwin spent that evening in our apartment after several days. Vinod too was around for a change. We were excited to reunite on our balcony. But there was a Riyaz-shaped hole in our evening. If only he too had been there, with his gentle presence and delicious snacks. Some people become precious to us in their absence, even if until then their fate was to be mocked or suspected or neglected.

'I wonder what's up with Riyaz,' I said.

'Remember my bet? We are never going to hear from him again. Don't waste your concern on him.' That was Vinod, of course.

'Perhaps you are right, but what if he's simply too busy with his father in the hospital? Wouldn't he want us to check in on him?'

'But he didn't even give us his number before he vanished. What a con man. Let it go.'

'If he hasn't given it to us, we must find it. What kind of investigative journalists are we otherwise? Pratap, call *Toronto Sunday* and ask them to look up his résumé. Surely it should have a contact number for him,' Edwin proposed.

I called our office human resources then and there. My friend Stella Diamond, a Honduran woman, picked up the phone. 'Pratap! Long time no hear. I thought you must have married some Arab beauty and settled down there.'

It was a bit of work, but she was able to find Riyaz's number in five minutes.

'That was simple, wasn't it? Where there's a will, there's a way. In fact, many ways,' Edwin said.

I called the Pakistan number she had given me. 'This number does not exist.'

'That's sad. I wish we knew how his father is doing,' I said. The conversation turned to our fathers. Vinod's story about his father was the saddest. He died in an accident when he was thirty-five. It was a death without any dignity. He was at an amusement park and the basket of the roller coaster he was riding broke and fell off. It was probably the first amusement park death in the history of India. Strangely enough, up until then his life had been a very smooth ride. He was the son of a district court judge in Nagpur. He went to good schools, entered government service at the age of twenty-two, and married the daughter of the wealthiest businessman in the City. She was a great beauty, and by the fifth year of their marriage they had two adorable children. Then came the roller-coaster death. 'Was my father blessed by fortune or a deeply unlucky man?' Vinod asked.

'My own father struggled throughout his life,' I told them. 'His childhood was very drab, as far as I can understand. He got a paltry education, and his life was a battle to make ends meet. But his children did well, and in his old age he is content. His son studied well and reached a position that he could not have dreamed of. His daughter is a happily married teacher. His wife is alive and healthy enough to take care of him. Beautiful, brilliant grandchildren. Unlike in his youth, he lives in a good house and has enough for his needs. Above all, he has wonderful health in his old age. Even at seventy he does not need to trek to pharmacies with doctors' prescriptions or wait in medical labs for blood tests. He drinks his daily tea with two spoons of sugar. He can eat all the laddoos he wants without his wife getting worried. Milk, salt, a fried egg for breakfast – no problems there. No stomach aches. Isn't he a lucky man? I think the measure of a lucky man is not how he lived his youth, but how he spends his old age.'

'My father did nothing remarkable other than cause the birth of two sons. But he must be the first person to die in an amusement park accident. Shouldn't that earn him a place in history? In fact, I am trying to get Papa's death recorded in the *Guinness World Records* or the *Limca Book of Records*. I want him to be known forever,' Vinod said seriously.

Edwin was completely uninterested in our conversation. He changed the topic. 'I came over because I have something urgent to discuss with you. We have an important assignment for tomorrow. But I won't be able to do it. Do you remember going to see Khalil Mohammed – he was in the hospital on a protest fast?'

'Yes, I went with Riyaz. Vinod was not there,' I said.

'I, too, went to see him after hearing what you had to say about him. He arranged for me to see someone. In fact, he had to go to a great deal of trouble to arrange this. We must make use of this opportunity,' Edwin said.

'Who is this?' Vinod and I asked simultaneously.

'This is extremely confidential. She is a European woman who used to be very close to the royal family. But now she's under house arrest.'

'Shouldn't you come with us then?'

'Impossible. They won't allow any Westerners or locals. Nothing must be recorded. No unnecessary questions. She said yes only after I agreed to all these conditions.'

'What's the big deal with this auntie anyway? Don't worry, we'll take care of her,' Vinod said.

'But you will have to take some risks . . .'

'What do you mean?'

'You cannot walk in there as journalists. So you are going to be disguised as two electricians. She is surrounded by spies. If they smell anything fishy, she and you will end up in prison. Don't worry. Tomorrow morning, you will wait in front of the hospital. Khalil Mohammed has made all the arrangements. You will receive instructions as and when you need them,' Edwin said. Then he added, 'Pratap, you will have that pen of yours with you, right? It might be worthwhile to ignore one of the conditions.'

'Done.'

The next day, by 9 a.m., we were in front of the hospital.

After some time a pickup truck stopped in front of us. The driver, a Sardarji, leaned out of the window.

'Are you the two electricians Khalil sahib mentioned?'

'Yes.'

'Get in.'

The radio was playing very loud music, and the Sardarji was yelling at someone on the phone even more loudly. All this was punctuated by angry blows at the steering wheel and dashboard. A few times, he even flung his phone away in rage and then rummaged for it so he could yell into it again. We narrowly avoided a couple of dangerous accidents.

'Kya ho gaya, bhai sahib? Kuch tension mein hain kya?' Vinod asked.

'I sent my chutiya son to school and this is what he does. He is in twelfth standard in the Indian school. Now he says he is in love! With a girl in the Pakistan school, no less. Both of them have been cutting classes and wandering around the City. I had no idea. Here I am running around trying to make ends meet, and he is immersed in his little romance with his little girlfriend. Her family found them somewhere coochie-cooing yesterday. And they have a lot of police influence. So now he is in prison. They must have beaten the dust out of him by now. What can I do? He's my flesh and blood after all. So I am trying to get him out before they make a corpse out of him.'

He went back to yelling and cursing on the phone. In between, we stopped at a couple of construction sites and he offloaded building materials. After driving some more, he dropped us off in front of an electrical company and rushed off to the police station.

An office boy escorted us inside and asked us to sit in the conference room. Despite the name, it was just a small table and three chairs surrounded by switchboards and wires and catalogues and files and drafting paper and whatnot. We sat there drinking tea. Eventually, a very well-dressed, dignified man came and took us to another office. From the photos and decoration in that office, I assumed he was the owner of the company.

'I am doing this only because Khalil asked. That house is completely under the police eye. You must be very careful. You must not give rise to even the slightest hint of suspicion. If anything happens, that is the end of my business. But I am doing this anyway because I want the world to know what is going on in this country. Do you have passport-size photos on you?'

I had one in my wallet but Vinod didn't. He was sent to a nearby studio to get instant photos. After that, we were issued identity cards with our photos and new names. I was Kallambandil Pavithran Sukumaran and Vinod was Laburam Boppara.

'Remember to use these names till you return,' the owner said and asked us to leave our phones with him. We were given two old phones and made to memorize their numbers. Then he gave us some tools: pliers, cutters, screwdrivers, testers, clamp meters. Finally, we put on blue overalls. That's when we turned into electricians. I began realizing the gravity of what we were undertaking, and felt a tiny prick of fear.

'You are journalists. You know how to be careful. But do not take the liberties that you would take in your countries. The police here are like foxhounds greedily waiting for the hunt,' he reminded us one last time as we set off.

Another driver took us in his pickup truck.

'You know how CID officers in movies have a stupid sidekick along with them? You look like that,' Vinod mocked me.

'Well, now you know that sometimes movies imitate life, sometimes life imitates movies,' I retorted.

'We have arrived,' the driver announced. A chill went up my spine.

Water House

As soon as we approached the gate, a car sped towards us and stopped next to us. A man leaned out and showed us his identity card. 'I am from the interiors ministry.' He questioned us, examined our identity cards, and took down our phone numbers. He didn't seem entirely convinced by us, but eventually allowed us to enter.

The house itself was quite a sight. A big fountain was the first thing we saw. Small streams ran up and down the spacious gardens, towards a pond set in a lawn on the right side of the house. The water from the pond fell gracefully over a pile of rocks and flowed again through the garden. We had to walk over two bridges to get to the veranda of the house. But even then the magic of the water was not done. One of the streams ran through the living room itself and the couch and coffee table and chairs were on a bridge hanging over the water. Water dripped down the walls and flowed through tiny canals and fell into the stream. The floor was mud. Flowering plants grew on the banks of the stream and cacti were arranged along the glass wall.

However, mould and algae were also rampant. The beautiful living room seemed abandoned.

We waited there. Eventually, a European woman, of about forty years, came down to see us. She had an elegant face but melancholy had taken over her features. Her hair was grey and uncared for.

Silently she took us upstairs and showed us some electric appliances that needed repair. I began fearing that she had mistaken us to be real electricians.

'Khalil Mohammed sent us here,' Vinod told her in a soft voice.

'I know. But we cannot trust even a pillar in this house. Please pretend to repair this and we can talk.'

I started examining a table lamp, while whispering to her that I was a reporter from *Toronto Sunday*. I left out the anonymous bestselling novelist and his research mission. We were planning to do a feature on sixty different lives in the Middle East, I told her.

She started her story without a preface. 'My husband Yasser Al Waleed used to be a high-ranking military official. He was part of His Majesty's inner circle. He and I met and fell in love when he was on a trip to Europe. In those days, I was studying medicine. Most Arab men forget such encounters when they finish their European trips. But not only did he continue to love me, as soon as I finished studying he married me against the wishes of his conservative family. His Majesty supported him and even gave me a well-paying job in the hospital. We lived fourteen long years in this country. Then misfortune struck.

'Every now and then, His Majesty would invite his trusted generals and commanders for a big banquet. While everyone was eating, he would say, "There is a traitor among you and I have poisoned his food." Then he would examine each face, each gesture for any unease. Whose face had suddenly gone grey? Who was hesitating to bring food into his mouth? Whose hands were trembling? If he found anyone's movements suspicious, the next day that person would find himself in jail. During one such banquet, His Majesty found my husband suspicious. My husband had no idea, and even when he reached his office the next day he suspected nothing, because his conscience was clear. The office boy approached him and gave him a broom. "We have received orders from high above that you are to sweep the entire office," he said. My husband understood his fate then and there. But his pride would not allow him to acknowledge it. Every morning he would go to work. He was ordered to sweep the office, clean the toilets, wash the dishes in the kitchens. He did it. He took every insult that came his way. But after he finished his tasks, he would be taken to the prison and beaten up, given electric shocks. They would let him go at the end of each day when he was almost dead. He would come home exhausted, but he never uttered a word to me. Several times he met His

Majesty and explained that he was innocent, but to no avail. Finally, one day, he reached his limit. He had walked out of home to drive to work, but he came back inside, took his pistol and shot himself in the forehead. I found out the whole story from a letter he had written before he died. In the letter he also asked me to be on guard and to never ever indicate that he had told me anything.

'The day after he died, a messenger from His Majesty came over. He gave us a small padded envelope. There was a note in it, "For the safekeeping of secrets." There was only one other thing in the envelope – a bullet. It sent me reeling in fear. My children. I had to keep them safe. I did not tell anyone about the message.

'I told people that my husband had committed suicide because of family problems. They had isolated him for marrying a foreign woman. Neither I nor my children were allowed to meet them. Once they heard that he had committed suicide because of family troubles, their hatred towards me only intensified.

'I could understand that. But what puzzles me is that His Majesty was not satisfied with driving my husband to death. I was fired for silly made-up reasons. The government scholarship that my son was receiving for his education in a foreign country suddenly ceased. Days of poverty followed, days of emptiness. For the first time I learned the importance of money. My son waited tables abroad to finish his education. I tried to leave for Europe with my other children. That was when I was put under house arrest. I know now that he will never let me leave the City. All these years I have been hiding these circumstances from everyone. Partly out of fear and partly out of shame. But now I worry that my end is being plotted. So I need to talk.'

'What makes you think that death is nigh?' I asked.

'Perhaps because I know more secrets about him than my husband knew. Remember I said I worked in the hospital? Do you know what my job there was? Reconstructive work on the vaginas and anuses of boys and girls who had been subjected to his outlandish sexual assaults. He was especially fond of children. In fact, he visited schools and colleges so that he could choose his prey. If he liked a child, he would pat his or her back – that was a signal for his lackeys. It was their job to get the child from its parents, often by force. It was our job at the hospital to inspect the child and ensure that he or she was free of sexual diseases. Then it was the poor child's job to slake his lust, his cruel kinks. He even had a secret room in the palace that he fondly called the rape chamber. Thousands of maimed children came my way from the rape chambers. His hobby was biting off nipples and penises. So many children died and were buried secretly in the desert. The ones who survived were sent home with an envelope of money and a single bullet. You might well ask why I did not speak out before. But to fall in with a ruler such as this one is the same as joining the mafia. There was no escape for me. They would have easily hunted me down anywhere in the world and punished me if I betrayed him. People are not loyal to him because they love him or approve of his actions; they are simply trying to stay alive. All underground criminal networks work in the same way – but some come to power while others stay underground.'

She paused there. We stood there silently. We had arrived at her house with hundreds of questions. But now our tongues were tied.

'You must write about this. The world needs to know. Do not think about what might happen to me. Now I know why some people turn themselves into suicide bombers. I will happily sacrifice myself if that means he will also be destroyed.'

In the car after we left her home, Vinod and I could barely speak to each other. We sat in a cloud of fear. When the driver returned our phones, I saw that I had missed three calls from an unfamiliar number. I called back.

'This is Jahangir,' the person at the other end said. I didn't recognize him at first. 'I am Riyaz's friend, remember? We went to the hospital together to meet Doctor Mamu.'

'Oh yes, I remember now. What's new?'

'I am calling about an urgent matter,' he said in a strained voice. 'Cannot speak on the phone. Can I come to your place right away?'

'I'll be there in half an hour. But what is this about?'

'Our friend Riyaz is in jail.' And then he hung up.

Examinations

We rushed home as if our tails were on fire. Along the way, I called Edwin and told him there was an emergency and he was to meet us at the flat. He was at the door when we walked in.

'How many times did I tell you to be careful? What happened? What did you do?' he said, imagining that our assignment had somehow gone wrong and we were in trouble.

'It's not that.' I pulled him inside.

'Haven't I always said we can't trust him? And now this?' Vinod started yelling angrily as soon as we were inside.

'Can someone explain what's going on?' Edwin was about to explode.

'He is inside,' Vinod said.

'Who?'

'Taliban!'

'Riyaz Malik?'

'Yes.'

'Inside meaning what?'

'Inside meaning inside jail. Where else?'

Edwin's eyes were about to fall out of their sockets.

'He is right. Riyaz's friend Jahangir called me on the way,' I said. 'He hung up without telling me anything more, but he's on his way here.'

'God knows what trouble he has gotten all of us into,' Vinod said.

But Edwin cooled down quickly. 'So what if he's in jail? Let's be calm and find out more. Where is he in jail? Here or in Pakistan? When did all this happen? Let's wait for Jahangir.'

We waited for another ten minutes, Vinod getting more and more impatient with each passing minute. 'Where the hell is he? Pratap, call him.'

'Please. He said he's on his way. Let's just wait patiently.'

'Riyaz must be imprisoned in Pakistan. If he were here, then we would be in trouble. But that can't be,' Vinod tried to console himself.

'Why should we panic? We haven't done anything wrong,' Edwin said.

'Really? Is it only guilty people who get arrested? What if he has implicated us in some crime? I made it clear I didn't like him. What if he has decided to take revenge on me for that?' Vinod was almost delirious by then. I had no idea he had such little nerve. How fierce he used to be when there was no trouble, and now at a time when he needed it, all that ferocity had been abandoned. He was nothing more than an adult male baby.

'It's no big deal for a journalist to be imprisoned. In fact, we should admire his resolve if it happened in the course of his work,' Edwin shot back.

'I for one can do without that dubious honour. Have you forgotten all the horror stories we have heard of jails here?' Vinod sulked. What use was it expecting valour or ethics from him, I reflected. He was a man whose mission was to enjoy the sensuous pleasures of life.

The doorbell rang. Vinod opened the door. But it was not Jahangir. Four strangers stepped into the room. We were stunned.

'We are from the CID office.' They showed us their IDs. 'We need to search your flat.'

We stared at each other in consternation.

'We are not conducting any secret operations here. We

have the visas and other legal documents required to be in this country. What's the basis of this search?' Edwin said.

'Don't worry, this is a standard procedure. We are authorized by the government to inspect the residences of those who are here on extended tourist visas. Please cooperate with us. Switch off your cell phones and hand them over. Then please open all cupboards and suitcases and bags. Switch on your laptops and log in. And then wait in your living room while we conduct the examination. We will leave as soon as we finish our assignment.'

'This might be your assignment, but this is also a huge invasion of our privacy. Our bags and computers might contain things we want to keep confidential. It is not possible to share everything with you.' I found my voice.

'My friend, you are educated, you are journalists, you know the way the world works. What is this privacy you speak of? No one living today has any privacy that is not limited by the government and its laws. Your bedroom and even your bathroom fall within those limits.'

Edwin was about to respond to that, but the other officer lifted his hand to deter him. 'We do not have the time to argue with you. Please do as we have asked.' His voice was stern and rang with finality.

Vinod and I went to our rooms, laid bare our lives and came back to sit on the living room couch. The officers began their inspection. Every now and then Vinod would shoot me and Edwin an accusing glance, but we ignored him.

'What on earth do these guys hope to find here?' Edwin

was so mystified by the search that he found it funny. Vinod on the other hand was convinced that Jahangir had lied about us and put the police on our track. I, alone, knew what they were searching for. The book that Riyaz had had in his possession. So they had not found it on him even after they imprisoned him. Now they were looking for it here. So that meant Riyaz might not have taken it with him. Had he given it to someone else for safekeeping? Jahangir? Was that why he didn't want to talk on the phone? Had the police bugged that conversation and taken him into custody as well? Were we next?

Questions and more questions, none of them with answers, flowed through my mind like a heavy, muddy river. Unable to share those questions aloud with anyone, the river grew more and more sluggish.

Jahangir

Finally, the CID officers left. They had found nothing, and their faces said it. But they did not ask us any questions. I started feeling that it was dangerous to keep from my colleagues what I knew about Riyaz and the book. I had been called in for questioning already and clearly I was precariously close to becoming a suspect myself. Today's raid proved that they were expanding the circle of suspicion. Edwin and Vinod must know. Perhaps they could analyse the situation better than I could. Perhaps they too had secrets to share and together we could piece together the jigsaw puzzle. I was almost ready to tell all when we heard a knock on the door, an urgent knock. There was surprise on Edwin's face and panic on Vinod's. They refused to open the door. Then the bell started ringing. It was a long, moaning ring. But they continued to stand there like statues. I got up and opened the door.

It was Jahangir, his face wrinkled with fear. He was panting.

'I had just reached downstairs when I saw the CID officers arrive. So I waited till they left.'

'How do you know they were from the CID?' Vinod asked.

'I know them well. Two of them are from my country,' he answered.

'What happened to Riyaz?' Edwin asked.

'No idea. A policeman friend of mine called me secretly from the jail and told me. He was arrested at the airport.'

'What did he say the case was?'

'He has no way of knowing. In fact, Riyaz himself probably does not know. But you all are so influential. Surely you know someone who can at least tell us what is going on,' he pleaded.

'Riyaz was missing for a couple of days before he left. Do you have any idea where he was?' I asked.

'No. I have not seen him since that time we were all together. He called me on the way to the airport and told me he was going home urgently and would call from there.'

'He told us his father was sick. Can we check that somehow? How about we call his house?'

Jahangir fell silent.

'Don't you know his number back home? Or maybe you know a common friend? Come on, let's call,' Edwin said.

'There is no way that news can be true,' Jahangir said. 'I know, because his father died five years ago.'

'See? You hear that? Did anyone believe me? Now we know his true colours. He's a con man. A con man. Now we will all be in trouble.' Vinod became hysterical.

'Mr Vinod, calm down,' Edwin said. 'If all this is true, we are already in trouble. So let's think carefully about how to deal with this.'

'What did the CID officers ask you?' Jahangir said.

'They didn't ask us anything. They examined the entire apartment but found nothing that can be used against us.'

'Has Riyaz ever mentioned anything that might be of interest to them?' Jahangir asked.

The answer was yes, but my tongue said no. Somehow I couldn't bring myself to believe Jahangir. My instinct warned me not to share the secret about the book with him.

'Who can we call to find out what's going on?' Jahangir asked.

'We don't know too many people in the City. What about Doctor Mamu? Isn't he close to the administration? He might be able to help.'

'I was thinking of him too. But he seems so innocent. Will he use his influence for us?'

'Please. Forget all this finding out business. What we need to do is escape from the City.' That was Vinod.

'What kind of escape is it if one of us is left behind? How will we live with ourselves if we abandon a friend in his time of need?' I asked.

'Blah blah blah. Your dialogue would be great in a fourth-rate novel or cheap movie. But this is life. I don't feel the need to pay a price for someone else's crime. And that too a Taliban!' Vinod was filled with scorn from head to toe.

'We are going round and round the same topic. Let's stop debating. Right now we need to take a deep breath and think this through carefully. The solutions will reveal themselves. Let's each be alone for a moment. Jahangir, you should leave for now. We will try and find more information and will let you know as soon as we do,' Edwin said.

I have always noticed this. When there is a problem and everyone is in shock, one person in the group will emerge as a natural leader. While the others are yelling angrily, the leader will look for and find the middle path. If a bunch of men are ganging up on a woman, one of them will suddenly find his integrity and will stop the others. Edwin, too, was having a moment like that. But for him, our muddled conversation would have ended up harming our friendships.

Jahangir left and Vinod, sulking, went to his room. Edwin returned to his flat. I was left alone.

Mail

Sleep would not come, no matter what I tried. What kept waking me up every time I shut my eyes was not fear that we were in danger; it was sadness that someone we trusted so much had tricked us so humiliatingly. I had never been betrayed like that and I had never imagined that I would be betrayed. Yet, Riyaz, who I had been so fond of, had done exactly that. I had defended him whenever Vinod took his suspicions out for an airing. It wasn't because I enjoyed playing the devil's advocate; it was because I truly believed that Riyaz was a good human being. Finally, when I was sick of the emptiness these thoughts brought in their wake, I got up, made a black coffee for myself, and switched on my computer.

When we are lonely, when we are troubled, is when those we have loved and lost return to our memories. It had been days since I had checked my email or Facebook. I had lost touch with almost everyone in my life. Except, of course, my family. Shanti would call every day. She was lonely, she told me. Tired of single-handedly managing the family and her work in the hospital. Worried that I was in danger in this Arab land of war and terror. The children would snatch the phone from her to register their own complaints and demands. 'Enough, Papa, just come back,' they would whine. It was, in fact, these grievances and entreaties that kept me alive, moored to the life I lived before the City. More than 150 emails greeted me when I opened my inbox. Most of them were promotional mails and invitations to random social networks. I hit select all on a couple of pages and deleted them. Luckily, just before I did that to the third page, I caught sight of Jasmine's email.

It had been a while since she sent it. I clicked on it urgently and hungrily, like a man about to starve to death.

Pratap,

Do you know how many times I have read the emails you sent me from the City? I have lost count. I don't just read them. Sometimes like a kid in fourth grade practising cursive writing, I copy them. Not once, but a hundred times. I know by heart each sentence, each word in every sentence, each inflection in every word. I know the blackness of the letters. Now you know how dear your letters are to me. I could recite those letters in my sleep, as if they were Bible verses.

Perhaps you are wondering why I didn't reply to those letters then. I am afraid of men, of proximity to men. You will ask why. But that's what my life has taught me. When you were far away from me, I felt secure. I felt confident enough to talk to you openly. But knowing that you are in this city makes me afraid. Yes, I do know that the friend who has arrived in this city is none other than you. Trust me – I am not afraid of you, I am afraid of myself.

This new era and its technological advancements and the infinite possibilities they have opened up have brought us back into each other's orbit. Without Facebook, it would have taken a lot of hard work. You would have had to track down my mailing address or my phone number. Perhaps this new chapter in our relationship would not have happened at all if we lived in a different time.

Perhaps more old-fashioned people, trapped in yesterday's mores, might consider me a loose woman. I don't give a damn. I don't consider it a sin to share this emotionally fulfilling friendship with you even though

I am married to another man. If it is indeed a crime, then I am not the only one that is guilty. Yesterday when I was lying in bed with my husband, I thought to myself, lying next to me, he is so far away. You, on the other hand, might be far away in physical distance, yet you are so close to my heart. Is it the body or the heart that decides what is near and what is far?

Till yesterday, I was a prisoner of loneliness. But then I found you and was no longer alone, no longer in prison. I found myself again. It seemed as if a pole star, however far away, was shining just for me. Someone somewhere is thinking about me, worrying about me, praying for me. The confidence I gained from that thought is no small thing. It gives me energy and life. Like a beating heart, the dream of you ticks inside me. I talk to that dream of you throughout the day. If I am buying a new dress for myself, I ask you, do you like it? When I am eating something sweet, I ask you, do you want to share this with me? I'll take selfies just for you. I see you more than you see me. You live within me more than I live within you.

Pratap, I do not concern myself with where you are. I hope to continue our friendship through email. If my messages don't bother you, let's continue to meet in this invisible city called the Internet. Surely we who know each other so fully don't need physical proximity to sustain our friendship. What would we gain by meeting in real life? Aren't we tied to each other by underground webs that go deeper? I promise you that when I die, your name will be written in every molecule of my body.

Please do write. I am waiting for your sentences.

With love,

Jasmine.

NB: Please do credit me with enough female intuition to understand that those other emails I am getting from a so-called old classmate are coming from a fake ID of yours (or some benami you delegated it to. Abandon that attempt. You will not win.)

I burst out laughing. How easily a clever woman could see through the antics of an anxious, eager man. I did not know till then that this was how Daisy was fighting my battle for me. It was certainly worth trying. If a stranger suddenly appears out of the blue and says, 'Remember me? We used to be classmates,' few of us can say, 'No, go away.' If they start reciting any names or incidents from that long-gone era, even if they are made up, we will definitely believe them. We will convince ourselves, yes, we used to be classmates. Yet Jasmine had resisted Daisy's little trap.

I had to inform Daisy so that she did not embarrass herself any more. I had to flout Perumal's condition of no contact at least this one time. So I wrote her an email. 'Having realized the unfeasibility of the mission I gave you, I am discharging you with full honour from it.' She must have been online because within five minutes she sent me a Google Hangouts chat. 'What's up? Any problems? I am almost at the finish line! Positive that I can get her details. Be patient!'

Poor Daisy. Her words were full of such innocent

excitement. She had no idea that her little trick had been completely exposed.

'Impossible to find people on social networks using that "old classmates" trick. We will have to come up with something else.'

'Really? Has she found out? How?'

'When a woman is on the alert, her eyes are like an X-ray machine. Everything she sees will be ruthlessly examined. And Jasmine has always had a gift for that.'

'I did my best for you. Sad to know I failed. Forgive me.'

'No need for an apology. I am the one who has failed. Why am I chasing someone who has no desire to see me? After all, this chase could easily end in one email from her. There's a lesson in this for me. Unrequited love is just a series of humiliations. Anyway, that chapter is closed.'

'How do you know she found out? Did she contact you?'

'She emailed me after a long time and mentioned this. Don't worry. I'll tell her that the fake ID was mine.'

'Does she know you are in the City?'

'I thought she didn't. But now I have a feeling that not only does she know, she has been surveying me secretly. Maybe from across the street, or from the roof of a building, or from behind a wall . . .'

'Why do we love people knowing they will never be able to give us what we seek from them?'

'I, too, have wondered exactly that. I am certainly not seeking something from Jasmine because something is missing in my marriage with Shanti. I don't want anything from her. But when I hear her name, my heart skips a beat.

When her face comes into my memory, my heart sobs a little. When I remember the moments I spent with her, I feel joyful. And as time passes, instead of fading, these memories grow stronger.'

'I don't know if I should bring this up in your current mood, but did you ever know that's how I felt towards you?'

'Where is Perumal?' I tried to change the subject.

'He is reading in his library. I am in bed.'

'There is a contract between Perumal and me. He does not want me to ever see you again or talk to you. It would be dishonourable to break that contract. I only got in touch because of Jasmine's email.'

'I know all about that contract. Perumal told me the day he saw you.'

'Really? But he told me you must never know of it.'

'See, that's the Perumal you don't understand. He is always two steps ahead. He knows that you will do exactly what you did just now and tell me about this contract. And he does not want his love or integrity questioned by me when that happens. So, of course, he told me about the contract himself. See how beautifully he undercut the surprise and anger I would have felt when you told me about this contract? It will be quite a while before you catch up with Perumal's astuteness.'

'Amazing, I give it to you. Perumal is supremely intelligent. He deserves you.'

'So stop changing the subject and answer my question.'

'No, I never had an inkling about your feelings. In fact, I don't remember you ever expressing them till that last meeting of ours.'

'That's like shutting the door and complaining about the lack of a breeze. Why don't you stop hiding behind the door? Come out on to the path of love. You will feel the breeze!'

'That door was Jasmine. All the breezes in my life hit that door and bounced off.'

'Yes, I know. But even after knowing that you have signed off your heart to Jasmine, I still can't get over you. It's as if I were a little puppy dog that keeps crawling back to its owner shamelessly even after it was kicked out of home. We all have a dog like that in our hearts.'

'Yes, we do, but maybe it's not that the dog is shameless but that it has a lot of love to give.'

'Our conversation is getting too literary. I didn't realize until now that people in life sometimes talk like people in novels.'

'I have met people who speak much more dramatically than characters in a play.'

'You were talking about leaving soon. What's going on with your novel?'

'You silly woman. How many times have I told you I am not the one writing the novel, but you keep asking me about my novel each time we talk.'

'I know, I know. But I have a feeling that some day you will write a novel. Maybe it is just my fantasy. In that case, I'll also fantasize that it will be dedicated to "a girl who loved me as if I were God".'

'Daisy, did you really like me that much?'

'If you still don't understand the ocean within me, then that is my failure.'

'How does this ocean manage to hide all its waves and appear so calm?'

She signed out without responding.

Headlines

I woke up in the morning to Jahangir's phone call. I had gone to bed very late. After Daisy left Gchat, Shanti appeared on Viber, so I chatted with her and the kids into the night. She knew all about Riyaz. On our daily calls, I would tell her about the little and big incidents of the day. This is one of the problems with the cell phone. We share our news with family and friends instantly. As a result, when we reunite with them after several days, there is nothing new to say. Before mobile phones, there was something festive about catching up with friends and family after a long trip. It was a special moment for both the traveller and the ones waiting at home. That era is now gone forever.

When the phone rang I was asleep, in the throes of an excellent nightmare. In fact, the ringing of the phone sounded like that nightmare's background music. But somehow I crossed over into consciousness and answered the phone.

It took me a minute to figure out the caller was Jahangir. 'Have you seen the newspaper today?' he asked.

'Newspaper? I haven't even gotten out of bed and you are asking me about the newspaper. What's the big deal?' I asked.

'There's a piece about Riyaz. You better read it.'

'What news?'

'I won't tell you. Just read the paper.'

'It's not as easy as you think to get hold of the newspaper. I'll have to go to a store. Please stop your ridiculous suspense and tell me what's going on.' I was annoyed by then.

'This is not something to be discussed on the phone. You have Internet access, right? Just find the news online. I'll call later.' He hung up, as usual leaving the secret hanging in the air.

I could not go back to sleep. Without even washing my face, I picked up the phone and found the online version of the national newspaper. I scrolled through it. On the fourth page, I found the news item Jahangir was referring to. Terrorist Under Arrest for Suicide Bombing Plots.

Riyaz's photo was underneath the headline. Typical of the country's newspapers when publishing photos of thieves and prostitutes and murderers, they had printed a black line over his eyes. Heart racing, I read the article.

The police have arrested a major terrorist who is part of an international gang that traffics in suicide bombers. Asian in ethnicity, the terrorist was apprehended at the airport on the way back to his country after meetings with insurgent groups about bringing suicide bombers to the City. He is suspected to be behind the five bombings that took place in the City last month. The terrorist has admitted that he received training from the secret services of Iran as well as Syria's Hizbollah. He sources suicide bombers from different parts of Asia. Three SIM cards, two laptops, several documents, foreign currencies and traveller's cheques were found on the terrorist. He is believed to be a small link in an international mafia. The police have not provided additional information.

The news hit me like lightning. I fell back into bed, and stared into space, till the very meaninglessness of my action jerked me back to reality. I went to Vinod's room but he was sleeping. I stood at his door wondering whether to wake him up or not. I could picture his reaction – he would grow even more hysterical and start yelling about how his suspicions had been proved right. That would be yet another meaningless action. I left the apartment and went to Edwin's place. He was already up and when he opened the door, I simply handed over my phone. The puzzled expression on his face changed to horror as he read. We sat inside his apartment for a bit, too overwhelmed to talk, simply reading the article again and again.

After a minute, Edwin spoke. 'Please inform James Hogan immediately. I'll write to our author as well. We have postponed our return far too long.'

'Should we wait around at all, Edwin? We have been completely cheated. Can you imagine what someone like that would have told the police about us? As Vinod says, we are in big trouble.'

'Even now . . . even after reading this news, I can't bring myself to suspect Riyaz,' Edwin replied. 'We know all about the trustworthiness of police reports and newspaper articles. But I do think Riyaz was not just a journalist; his goal in coming here was something else. Our assignment was just an excuse for him to get here. I want to find out what the real reason was,' Edwin said.

'What makes you say that?'

'Do you remember that time when the foreign minister was visiting the British Club and then the Indian Club on his community bonding mission? I attended the reception at the British Club while you and Vinod went to the Indian Club. When I returned to the office, there was no one there. I ordered some food and then I remembered that I hadn't checked my mail in a few days. Instead of running down to get my laptop from the car, I thought I would just use a laptop that was lying on the table. It belonged to one of you and was switched on, so I thought it was no big deal. I clicked on the mouse, and the Gmail account that lit up on the screen had not been signed out. I was mystified when I saw the username – Sherlock Holmes. Well, that intrigued me, so I clicked on the inbox. Every single mail in that inbox came from the same ID. And that ID was strange too – Anne Frank.

'I assumed it was a fake ID that one of you created for a girlfriend. Vinod, I guessed. It seemed like just his kind of mischief. But now I was not just intrigued, I was also a bit piqued. So I read a couple of emails. But alas, none of them were in English, though the script was Roman. So I guessed that it was one of your languages, maybe Hindi or Urdu or some other regional language. I forwarded a few emails to my own ID and deleted any clues about the forwarding. Then I left the laptop right there and sat there reading a magazine. I wanted to confirm that the laptop was Vinod's.

'One by one, you all started returning. That's when I realized that the laptop was not Vinod's; it belonged to Riyaz.'

The Face of Truth

'So I decided to investigate the connection between Riyaz, Sherlock Holmes and Anne Frank,' Edwin continued the story. 'That evening I bought second-hand copies of a couple of Sherlock Holmes novels and went to Riyaz's room. He was reading, and as soon as I walked in he slipped the book under the pillow.

"Oh, did I interrupt some serious reading?" I asked.

"Indeed. It's a notorious Urdu porn novel. You can't get hold of it in Pakistan, so I borrowed it from a friend here. Thought I might as well find out what's so bad about it."

'But I knew immediately that he was lying. I had seen the back cover of the book and it was in English. I didn't ask about it though. Instead I offered him the Sherlock Holmes novels and said, "I just finished reading these and thought you might be interested. Do you have any detective novels lying around?"

'His face blanched. Then he recovered and took the books from me.'

"Sherlock Holmes is one of my favourites. I'll take these."

'He gave me a couple of other detective novels to borrow. I felt sure then that he was hiding something.

'Then there was another day when Vinod and I went to a dinner hosted by the home ministry. We met lots of other media people, including one person from your part of India. I forget his name. But from his conversation I understood that he used to work in the radio station here with John Maschinas. You remember Maschinas, right? He was the one who put us in touch with the poet Ahmed Al Qaid. So I told him about our project and asked him to share anything that might be useful. And he said, "But I already talked to one of your colleagues." I thought it must be you, Pratap, but then he went on to say it was a Pakistani guy. That had to be Riyaz. But what was really surprising to me was that Riyaz had apparently told him he was referred by Maschinas, which was impossible because I had never told Riyaz about Maschinas. So how did he know? Maybe he picked up on the name when we talked about meeting Ahmed Al Qaid. But in any case, why did Riyaz go visit this radio guy? And why didn't he report it back to us? Clearly there were secrets swirling around Riyaz. So I went to Riyaz and asked him if he knew any radio people we could get in touch with. And Riyaz said, no, he didn't know any radio people!'

'Edwin, why did you keep all this from the rest of us? How could you continue to keep him around? Didn't the rest of us have the right to know what was going on?'

'Yes,' Edwin said. 'But there was one more incident. You remember he had not been around for a couple of days before he left? But around midnight the night before he left, he came to see me. He looked exhausted and unhappy. "Edwin, I have to leave the City urgently. Tomorrow when I bring it up, please don't oppose it. And, in fact, please convince Pratap and Vinod and Abdullah Janahi. I know you have some suspicions about me. You are right. I did have secret reasons for coming to the City. And I have held some secret meetings here. I cannot tell you anything more. But I promise you that it has nothing to do with any of you and will not affect your work here in any way. After the situation has improved, I'll tell you everything. Until then, forgive me. I apologize for all the inconvenience I am going to cause you." As he was leaving, he turned around and added, "Please don't discuss this with anyone else till I have left." Then he took my hand and kissed it.

'Pratap, I am convinced that Riyaz is innocent; he is an honest man. That is why I did not share all this with any of you. Even now, I believe in him. His face was the face of one who spoke the truth. Be it anywhere in the world, truth reveals itself on a person's face.'

Assumptions

And thus it was that Edwin opened the door to the answers I had been chasing for many days. I realized that it was time for us to share the pieces of the Riyaz jigsaw puzzle each of us had been carrying around, and put together a true portrait of him. Edwin brewed some coffee and as we sat down with it, the African scent of the beans rose in the steam between us. I told him about coming across *A Spring Without Fragrance* in Riyaz's room, about losing track of it and hunting for it everywhere, about Alex Perumal's strange encounter with the book, and about being questioned by the police.

'Unbelievable!' Edwin said.

'It's all true,' I said. 'If this were fiction, it would be considered surreal. But this is our life, and it's all real.'

'So what can we figure out if we put together what we both know?'

'A girl called Sameera Parvin wrote a novel. It was banned in this country. Despite that, somehow Ismael got hold of it and passed it on to Perumal. Riyaz also had a copy of that book. He was determined to hide it and had no intention of showing it or discussing it with anyone. Could it be that he was in the City in connection with that book? Maybe he was trying to find someone mentioned in the book? But looks like he didn't. In the meantime, something terrible happened and Riyaz was captured by the police when he was attempting to return to his country. What do you think?'

'Except for the last couple of sentences, I agree. The last bit is simply what we are assuming. We don't know for sure.'

'Fine. But as someone who read at least part of that book, let me tell you this. The book specifically says that John Maschinas worked for the radio. So for Riyaz, who was familiar with the entire book, it was an easy thing to use Maschinas as a reference to talk to anyone at the radio station.'

'What is the book about?'

'It's about Sameera Parvin, a radio jockey who lived in the City. The book is basically her love story and her experience of the protests that took place here.'

'What is so controversial about all that? Why was it banned?'

'I saw nothing controversial in it. Of course, different

readers interpret the book differently. Religious and nationalist fanatics might feel that each and every word in that book is taunting them. And there is plenty in the book to keep them up at night. The government itself might be innocent – after all, the ruling classes tend not to read. But there are always interlopers, pimping their outrage. Anyway, we can ignore them. What we need to focus on is the relationship between the book and Riyaz.'

'Looks like we can safely make some assumptions now. Riyaz came to the City in search of Sameera. If we can figure out why the police arrested him, we can also figure out the connection between him and the book. But there is only one way to do that: we have to find Sameera. Let's follow Riyaz's footsteps.'

'If we do that, we can expect to follow them all the way to jail,' I said.

'But he was our colleague. We have journalism in our blood – can we simply abandon a fellow journalist knowing what is at stake? We are all in this together.'

'I am with you. What about the brave comrade who is currently asleep in my apartment? From day one, he has had nothing but ill will towards Riyaz. He will probably hit the roof when he reads this news.'

'Leave Vinod to me. I'll take care of him. But, Pratap, you need to call James Hogan and update him. It must not seem like we took these decisions independently.'

I calculated the difference in time zones and figured that James must have just finished his naked strolling and would be getting ready to sleep.

'With certain kinds of news, it is best to call people at a bad time rather than wait for a good time. You will convey the gravity of the matter better,' Edwin said.

With this excellent advice to back me up, I called James Hogan right away. At the end of several long rings, he picked up the phone in a half-awake voice.

'Very good,' he said. 'I was wondering what on earth you were doing all these days. But now that someone has been arrested, I feel much better. Now your job is to find out why he was arrested. Be bold! Seize the opportunity! Now you have an opportunity to be real journalists!'

What a bizarre response. Edwin said, 'Perhaps Mr Hogan did not understand what happened to Riyaz. Never mind. He has given us the green signal to stay on. Let us take him at his word and show our mettle as journalists.'

The Lost Ship

When a ship loses its way, the last people to know are the ones sailing in it. This also applies to the ships of faith, politics and government. In fact, even our daily life is a kind of ship. Until then, we were under the impression that our lives in the City were moving along normally. But the incidents of the next two hours showed us that unknown to ourselves, our lives had tangled up in enormous knots.

As Edwin and I were planning our next steps, Vinod woke up and joined us.

'We need to talk to you,' Edwin told him. 'But you have to keep your cool. What I am about to say is important and we need to think through it very strategically, not emotionally. The three of us need to use the best of our observational, investigational and analytical skills to solve this problem.' Then he told Vinod about everything that had happened.

'I am going to call Priyanka,' Vinod said when Edwin was done. I had expected an explosion, but he was very calm.

'Why?'

'There are four possibilities in front of every writer,' Vinod said in an authoritative voice I had never heard from him before. 'The first is to create a plot and characters completely from imagination. The second is to take the plot and characters from real life. The third is to put very real characters into a purely imagined plot. And the fourth, of course, is to put completely imagined characters into a real-life plot. Now which of these does Sameera and her novel fall into? That's what we have to figure out. Since Priyanka works at a radio station, she might be able to shed some light on this.'

'I have already talked about this with Priyanka, the radio station director Rajeevan, and Abdullah Janahi. All three paths led nowhere. But I have established that Sameera is indeed real. Many people, including my friend Bijumon, have confirmed that.'

'Okay, let's look at other ways to find her. Edwin, you still have the Sherlock Holmes and Anne Frank emails, right? The first thing to do is look through them carefully. We should also call Jahangir and get whatever information we can get from him. And let's cast a wide net around the City for this radio jockey. Finally, we have to hunt down that book.'

'It's easy enough to look through those emails I sneaked out of Riyaz's account,' Edwin said.

'We should start with the most difficult solution,' Vinod said.

'Well, that would be hunting down the book. We definitely don't have time for that.'

'No need to waste time arguing about this. Let's start with what is easy,' I said.

Edwin had found the emails on his phone by then. 'Take a look . . . maybe one of you might be able to read this.'

Irbzh, R wlm'g sld zoo gsvhv szkkvmvw. R glow srn mlg gl kozm z girk gl gsrh xrgb. R pmvd rg dlfow yv wzmtvilfh. Sv rtmlivw nv. Mld dv nfhg urmw z dzb gl hzev srn. Lmob blf xzm wl gszg. Kovzhv hzev lfi Qzevw.

I could not make head or tail of it. Certainly, it was not Hindi or Urdu. Maybe it was some other Pakistani language, such as Pashtun? I passed Edwin's mobile to Vinod, but he too shook his head helplessly after reading it.

Edwin opened another email for us to read. That, too, was beyond comprehension.

'All the rest are the same. I guess there is no point looking at them.' Edwin was disappointed.

'Time to move on,' Vinod said.

'So, call Jahangir? He must know something.'

'Somehow I don't trust Jahangir fully,' I told them. 'Let's

figure out some other way to make him talk. Besides, no one should find out that we know about the book.'

'So all our ideas have fizzled out. What are we to do now?'

'What else can we do. Let's wait for something to turn up.'

We came back to our apartment for breakfast. I was toasting bread and scrambling eggs when Bijumon called. Then Priyanka called. Then Asmo. 'What's going on?' They wanted to know. 'Is the news true? Did the police question you as well? Be careful. You need to leave as soon as possible.' Advice poured in.

We were sitting down to eat when Abdullah Janahi arrived like a storm. I don't know what he was expecting of us but seeing us sitting around calmly eating breakfast threw him into a frenzy.

'What do you think you are doing?' he asked.

'Eating eggs. Would you like one?' Vinod teased him.

'This is not the time for jokes. Your co-worker is in the news. Soon you will find yourself in trouble as well.'

'So we can't have breakfast? That will get us out of trouble?' Edwin asked.

Abdullah ignored him. 'Do you know where I have been? I went to see a couple of newspaper guys who have connections in the government. I also met a member of the royal family who can usually fix things if you give him enough money. I went to the CID office to get more information. I have been running around all morning. And you? You have no idea what jails are like here. Journalists and murderers and drug dealers are all the same there. They will treat you like animals. Those wolves . . .'

Abdullah stomped his feet. We quit teasing him.

'What do you think we should be doing?' I asked him.

'Go fall at the feet of someone with influence and make sure we don't get into trouble as well. And then try to save that poor guy. Sitting here eating your eggs and toast won't help anyone.'

'But Abdullah, we don't know anyone in the City. You are the one who should be helping us.'

'First, go to your embassies and report this to the concerned officials. Let them know that you might also end up in jail at this rate. Arrange to find refuge there, if there's an emergency.'

'Abdullah, what are you saying?' Vinod said. 'We have done nothing wrong.'

'Oh, do you think poor Riyaz did anything wrong? Rest assured, whatever crime he has committed is pretty much what you have committed as well. If they have arrested him, then you too deserve to be arrested. Because you all did the exact same work.'

That made us nervous. Though we had imagined this exact situation and had discussed it with each other, hearing it from someone else's mouth made it much more real. The police trying to arrest us, taking refuge in the embassy, our countries fighting for us, an international incident . . . were things serious after all?

Encounters

'Abdullah, you still believe in Riyaz, even though you know how bad our situation is. Nobody, not even our embassies, can help us as much as you can.' I went up to him.

'Me? What can I possibly do? I am just an ordinary citizen. The Sunnis hate me for having been born a Shia and the Shias hate me for becoming a Sunni.' He tried to manoeuvre his way out of what I was asking him.

'You avoided this question once before. But now you have to tell me, who was that Sameera who worked in your radio station? What is her relationship with Riyaz?'

'Pratap, I have nothing more to tell you than what I already told you that day. I am not the kind of guy who hangs out with young women. Riyaz also asked me about her one day and told me to introduce him to Rajeevan sir.'

'Did you?'

'It was not necessary. A few days later, Riyaz told me they met.'

'What else did Riyaz ask you for?'

'He wanted me to introduce him to my old radio station friends, but I couldn't.'

'Did you ever ask him why he was so interested in the radio people?' Vinod asked.

'Let me ask you a question – why are all of you constantly asking me about Sameera? Who is *she*?'

'She was your radio station colleague Ali's girlfriend. Do you know why he is in jail?'

'They put thousands of young men in jail in connection with the protests. Ali is just one of them. No idea what they charged him with. I lost my job during the protests. So I lost touch with all of them. No one stood up for me though they all knew I was innocent. They went right back to playing games on their cell phones. When times are good, there will be plenty of people to kiss you on both cheeks. When times are bad, all the kissers will disappear. Anyway, forget all that. You need to go to the embassies right away.'

After what Abdullah had told us about the jails, even the last straw of our confidence had floated away. The three of us drove to the embassies. We dropped Vinod off at the Indian embassy and then went to the British and Canadian embassies.

'Shall we talk to that radio director once more?' Edwin asked on the way.

'What would be the point of that?'

'I don't know. I just have this feeling he might be useful.'

I got the number from Bijumon and called Mr Rajeevan. He was free and told us to come over to his place. Luckily, his villa was on our way. It was a beautifully decorated house in a very posh neighbourhood. Mr Rajeevan, who had just finished his breakfast, met us at the door.

We reminded him of our previous encounters. I had talked to him once before from Bijumon's phone and Edwin had met him at the foreign minister's reception. His polite coolness towards us changed to warmth.

'Come on in. I am usually late getting to work because I spend the evenings there,' he said.

'Radio is one of the many things you do, right?' I asked.

'Yes, I have a few other things going on. It's a bad time for investments, so it's best to diversify. I have my hands in a pipe factory, a flower shop, a hospital, interiors . . . and a bunch of other things. In fact, radio was just a hobby. I fancied myself a bit of a culture vulture. You know, did some theatre in college, wrote some poetry. Well, after radio sank some of my savings, at least I am cured of all that. Anyhow, what is your assignment here?'

We told him about the market study.

'What a beautiful country this used to be. Truly a traveller's paradise. An Eden for investors. Of course, foreign powers developed vested interests in a country like that. All these protests were a drama they directed and produced. The script was written somewhere else, far away from the City, but the City was the stage. The West thought they could use the instability here to blackmail the oil-rich country next door. But it didn't work. All that moaning and groaning by Western countries about democracy and human rights, but our oil-rich neighbour knew exactly what to do, and they did it. They sent their army to us and thwarted those protests. God knows how the entire region would have suffered if they hadn't acted so intelligently, so boldly.'

'Did you ever wonder the protesters might take over, Mr Rajeevan?'

'Never. Lord Krishna said you need three things to win a battle: intelligence, weapons, money. The insurgents had none of these. They were fated to lose. But they did succeed in two other matters. They divided the society along communal lines and disrupted the financial stability of the country. So whatever they are getting now, they deserve it.'

'In other words, you justify the brutal repression of the protests?'

'Look, let me tell you something. There is no point in making a fuss about a problem that has nothing to do with us. All kinds of horrible injustices are happening around the world. Are we going to stop living because of them? Then why stop for something just because it is happening in our neighbourhood? What is the difference between an injustice that is just outside the walls of our house and an injustice that is thousands of miles away? Religion is at the bottom of all the troubles here. It is up to them to fix that themselves. All these protesters harping on justice – if they came to power, they would simply create another dictatorship. It's not going to fix anything; in fact, the situation will get worse. So yes, I am aligned with the establishment, which is the better of the two evils.'

'It must have been quite a tough time at the radio in those days.' I slowly steered the conversation towards what we had come in search of.

'Tough is an understatement. The government insisted on absolutely no bad press. I was at the studio twenty-four hours. Who knows what my employees would do if my back was turned. So that is just what I had to do for survival.'

'Wasn't there a Sameera in your radio those days?'

'Yes, maybe. Wait, now I remember. We hired her when Meera Maskan went on leave.'

'I'll be frank with you. We would like to know more about

her. In fact, we need to know more about her. Otherwise we might end up in serious trouble ourselves,' Edwin said.

Rajeevan stared blankly at us.

The day's newspaper was lying on the coffee table. I showed him the news item on the fourth page.

'This Riyaz is one of us. He was arrested by the police, but we don't believe their charges. There are other reasons behind all this. We think that he came to this country in search of the Sameera who worked in your radio station. We have to find out more about her so we can find out more about Riyaz. Please help us, Mr Rajeevan.'

As he read the news about Riyaz, Rajeevan's face became as colourful as the newspaper he was holding. 'This is a major criminal case,' he spluttered finally. 'You are not going to get him out. The best thing you can do is to take care of yourself.'

'We can't even do that if we don't find Sameera.'

'I don't know if you know, but she was the victim of a huge tragedy. Her father was killed here. She was not around the radio very much after that. She resigned before her contract ended.'

'Then why did Riyaz come here in search of her?' Edwin asked. 'We heard she wrote a book. Is that true?'

'Yes, there was a rumour going around, but I heard nothing about it afterwards. Frankly, I don't believe it. She was not capable of it. She was just a chatterbox radio jockey.'

'Do you think you could use your influence to talk to your contacts in the police or the government for us? Not about all this, just about why Riyaz has been jailed,' I asked.

'My influence would be useless. The government here

knows how to maintain secrecy around matters like this. In fact, asking about it will draw unnecessary attention to me. You know what my business is like.' A kind of pathetic awkwardness had crept into Rajeevan's voice.

'No, no need to take any risks like that,' Edwin said.

'Well, let me make some inquiries. Anyway, I should get going.'

We walked out feeling empty.

Hope Springs Eternal

When the car arrived at the British embassy, Edwin did not get out. 'The embassy is our last refuge. Before that, let's meet a few more people,' he said, heading the car towards the medical college. 'Let's go see Doctor Mamu. As far as I can tell, he sounds like a genuinely good human.'

It was my job now to lead him through the labyrinthine corridors of the medical college. But when we finally hunted down his office, he was not there. We pleaded high and low and got his number. When we called, he invited us home. This was better for us. It would have been hard to get his full attention amid his hospital duties.

'Hello, Canadawala, I thought you must have left by now. What's new? My visa is getting processed. It should be ready any moment. Maybe I'll get to Canada before you!' He greeted us happily. It was as if he were a different person at home, far from the pressures of the hospital and patients and medicine.

After some small talk, we presented our problem.

'Oh, is that the case? I too had read the news. I can't believe it is one of you. He is a Pakistani, right? I believe he came to see me one day.'

'Yes, we came together, along with Jahangir,' I reminded him.

'No, no, he came by himself after that. But now I don't remember why . . .'

'Doctor, you are so influential here. Can't you make some calls? I am certain he is innocent.'

'That certainty of yours is what scares me,' he replied slowly. 'If he is innocent, then why was he caught? That means the police suspect him of something much worse than what they are charging him with.'

'All we want is to know what that something is. We know it will be difficult to get him released.'

'But why don't you just ask your friend Jahu?'

'Why?' Edwin and I asked at the same time.

'He works in the CID. He would know everything,' Doctor Mamu said casually.

'CID? But he told me he runs a cable company,' I said.

'Haha. So that was his story for you, was it? Sorry, I probably should not have mentioned it. Just forget I said anything.'

'No, he never said anything to us. That means he has no intention of helping us out with this. Doctor, will you please help us? We have no one to turn to,' I said sadly.

I could see that Doctor Mamu was touched. He picked up his phone and called someone.

'I have a friend high up in the police department. Ashraf Khan. He must know something. The phone is ringing but he is not picking it up. Maybe he's in some meeting. Why don't you go see him? I'll give you his number. He's a good man.'

'We will. The problem is he might not be as open with us as he might be with you.'

'Don't worry, I'll call him too.'

Half hopeful, half disappointed, we went back to our car.

'I have always thought there was something fishy about Jahangir. Didn't I say so even this morning?' I said.

'It's a good thing we didn't tell him anything. I am beginning to think he's the puppet master behind this theatre,' Edwin said.

'In other words, the enemy is very close. We must be careful.'

'I used to think that humans were essentially good. Now I realize I was wrong. Jahangir is evil. Pure evil. We have been fearing the wrong people. We were afraid of the police, the government. We should be more afraid of people like him who pretend to stand with us,' Edwin said.

We were driving aimlessly now, rapt in our conversation about Jahangir. Then we remembered the number Doctor Mamu had given us. Edwin dialled it. 'I have a hard time understanding the way people speak here,' he said, handing the phone to me.

But the person who picked up the phone at the other end spoke perfect English.

'Yes, Doctorji had called me. I am at home today and you can come see me. Park in front of the supermarket near the police headquarters. I'll send someone to guide you,' he told us after the greetings and introductions.

'I guess we might as well go meet him,' I said to Edwin. 'But he'll probably make the usual excuses – let me see, very complicated situation, best not to interfere, etc., etc. Anyway, at least we'll feel like we did everything we could.' By then I was feeling exhausted by these hopeful journeys and inevitable disappointments.

'Let's go. Journalism is all about undying hope. We may be clutching at straws, but at least we have something to clutch,' Edwin said.

'You are right, let's go.' We turned the car in the direction Ashraf Khan had given us.

Prisoners

A young man was waiting for us where Ashraf Khan had told us to wait. As we followed him, I realized why. We would have surely got lost if we had tried to find the way ourselves. He led us through tiny galis that twisted and turned. 'There's a highway on the other side. If you come by the highway, you'll never find parking. That's why we asked you to come this way,' he said as we stopped in front of a house and rang the bell.

He had spoken very little till then. In fact, his face had been marked by melancholy as we walked.

'What do you do?' I asked him.

'I am in the police. Got a holiday today, so I came to sahib's house.' His voice too, like his face, was sad.

'Are you related to sahib?'

'Yes, I am a distant relative. I got the job through him.'

Before we could continue the conversation, the door opened and we were in the presence of a distinguished-looking man, the kind who would play the role of a police officer in a Hindi movie. Proud, handsome, stately.

'Sergeant Ashraf Amjad Khan,' he introduced himself. We, too, introduced ourselves.

'I don't encourage people to visit me at home. But I couldn't refuse Doctorji. What can I do for you gentlemen?' He led us inside and invited us to sit.

Like a parrot in a cage, Edwin repeated our story yet again. When he was done, Ashraf Khan shook his head incredulously.

'We, too, were discussing this matter just now. How to believe and how not to believe. And that too a Pakistani. So many of us have been working in this country for years and years. What a blow to all of us. The entire community will come under suspicion now. The government will hesitate to give us positions of responsibility, or even work visas. I pray that the case will be dismissed. Allah, grant us your mercy.'

What could we say? We sat there eating our words.

'And the funny thing is, this boy Riyaz came to see me here once,' Ashraf Khan went on.

We both jumped. 'Here? Why?'

'That too was a call from Doctorji. That's why I didn't suspect anything. He told me a relative of his had been working in the police here for a year or two. That kid was ready to leave the job and return. Riyaz wanted me to help him.

But a three-year contract is a three-year contract. Impossible to leave in the middle. So I flatly refused. Do you know how much hard work it is to bring someone here? And after all that, when they get here, they are not in the mood for work.' Ashraf Khan's voice was authoritative. He pointed to the young policeman who had led us to the house. 'Look, here is another one. It's just been four months since he got here and he wants to go home. I just finished giving him a piece of my mind.'

'So did Riyaz come to the City for such a small thing?'

'Even after reading the newspaper today, you are still wondering about that rogue's intention?' Ashraf Khan shot back.

'It would be easy enough to believe that and close the case. But if you consider that he might be innocent, you will see there could be another interpretation.'

'The government and the police here think through things before they release news items like this one. They make sure what they tell the press is true. In fact, no other truth is possible here.'

His statement contained both judgement and threat. It was clearly meant to prevent further questions from us. But Edwin did not give up.

'It's up to you, of course, what you want to believe. Could we please see Riyaz?'

'No way. As soon as they finish questioning him, they will present him in court and the court will judge the case. There are no delays. But till then, his whereabouts will be a secret. Especially since it is a case of treason. Don't even think about seeing him. But look here, I'll do you a favour. I'll find out what date he is being presented in court. Stand outside the court that day. You can catch a glimpse of him when he is being brought into court.' He shrugged as if to say nothing more could be done.

As he was talking, something else was bothering me. The house. I felt as if I knew it from somewhere. As if I had visited it before. But, of course, that had never happened. Was this one of those déjà vu moments that psychologists talk of? Was this an illusion? How could I possibly know this house? And yet I did. Throughout our conversation, up until we said goodbye to him, a part of me was searching for something in that house. But I did not find it.

Could that be why Riyaz had come here? It seemed such a trivial reason – to get a policeman released from his job. Could that really be the reason for all his secret goings and comings, his meetings, the trouble he went through? And he tried to leave the City because it didn't work out? And that is why he got arrested? How could we believe this? But faced with Ashraf Khan's wall-like demeanour, we had nothing left to counter.

'So why are you trying to leave a decent job?' I asked the young man who was now accompanying us back to the car.

For a moment he was silent. Then he said, as if to no one, 'A policeman without weapons is like a one-armed wrestler.' I looked at him in surprise but he did not even look at me. 'What hopes we had when we came. We thought we were going to fight the evil powers that were attacking this Muslim country,' he continued. 'We had no idea. Only after we got here did we understand. We were merely the bait they wanted to throw in front of the hunters. In the morning they would drop two or three of us in some little inland village. Our job was to stand guard there, sometimes for three or four days. Everyone in that village would hate us. Women would curse us. People would spit on our faces. They would rain abuses on us, our mothers, our sisters. We would have to listen. If we reacted, they would throw stones or even knives at us. Petrol bombs. They would burn whatever they could find on the roads, including police jeeps. All we would have were four electric batons and two guns. But we would not be allowed to use those even to protect ourselves. They were just for show. Each day would be a day in hellfire. We would be lucky to get through the day and return to our camps at night. No holidays, no rest, no recreation. It would feel like we were waiting for death. Aren't we humans after all? Some of us went insane. Some of us tried to commit suicide. If only I could go home. But no, they won't let us go. We are basically prisoners in police uniform.'

We had reached our car by then, and like a tired little dog he turned around. We stood there watching him walk away.

Part Nine

Mera Jeevan

Ali Al Saad

'So looks like we have reached the end of our journey. And with nothing to show for it,' I said as we settled into the car, all hope shrivelled. We had not even visited our embassies.

'When I was in school and my friends would make fun of me for this or that, I would get the feeling that no matter what, I will show them. I had to win. That's how I feel now. So they are beating us right now, but let's show them we are tough. We won't be defeated,' Edwin said.

'But Edwin, what if we are wrong? We have been assuming that Riyaz is innocent. What if he's not?'

'I cannot be certain we are right. But these people who refuse to even consider the possibility of his innocence, they drive me crazy. Why are humans so afraid of life? I am going to consider Riyaz innocent until he is proven guilty. And I am going to pursue every avenue till then.' Edwin's voice was firm.

'But what avenues are even left at this point?'

'Let's talk more when we get to the flat.'

That's when I remembered Vinod. Was he still at his embassy? I called him.

'Where were you? I called you and waited for you forever. In the end, I got a ride back with Faisal.' He sounded annoyed.

'Okay, sorry about that. We are on our way to the flat. We need to talk,' I told him. When we got there, he wasn't around. Perhaps he had gone out to eat. A little later, Faisal came and gave us a piece of paper.

'This is from Vinod sahib,' he said. I opened it wondering what on earth it was.

Pratap and Edwin, I am getting out. Following my embassy's instructions. Your First World people have the safety net of your embassies and governments and legal rights. But a Third Worlder like me has to look out for himself. Anyway, I am not interested in gambling with my life. Perhaps our paths will cross again. Till then, goodbye.

Yours,

Vinod

What a blow, and this one from within our own team. I handed Edwin the note. He crumpled it and flung it on the floor.

'If anybody else wants to run for their lives, feel free. I don't need any of you,' he said. I didn't even bother to respond. I knew he was simply venting his anger.

'So where is he now?' I asked Faisal.

'I dropped him off at the airport. He told me you knew.'

I went to Vinod's bedroom, maybe to make myself believe he was really gone. It was empty, except for a couple of briefs in the corner. He had planned this. Clearly this was not a last-minute decision based on what his embassy had told him.

Edwin raised his hand when I approached him to talk about Vinod. 'That chapter is closed. Let's not waste any more time on him.'

'Here's what I am thinking,' he continued. 'Everyone we saw today was clearly pro-government. We should talk to someone on the anti-government side. I want to see how they would interpret this news.'

'Do you mean Ahmed Al Qaid? Or maybe Khalil? We don't know any other anti-government people.'

'No, neither of them will do. They are both moderates. Anyway, they don't have much sympathy for the problems here. We need to find someone who is firmly involved in the opposition, maybe even a front-line leader.'

Then Faisal spoke, 'I have a friend, a poet. His name is Ali Al Saad and he was pretty much in the thick of all the protests here. He just got out of jail.'

'Yes, that's a good start. Call him right away.'

Faisal got in touch with him then and there. 'He can see you at four o'clock today. Does that work?'

'Yes, where should we meet him?'

'I'll take you.'

He returned as soon as we were done with lunch to take us to a small flat full of books. The windows were wide and looked out on to the sea. The tall, lean, young man who met us there looked only slightly older than Faisal. With the jeans and T-shirt he was wearing and his long sideburns, he seemed more like a magician or a football player.

'This is my writing office.' He welcomed us inside. 'I come here every day to sit and write. Just like any other office job.' His voice brimmed with a confidence that awed me. It was clear he believed in his work.

'I have heard of novelists who do that. Can poets write through the day?'

'I write poems only occasionally, mostly for literary festivals. Right now I am in the middle of another important project. An alternative history of this country. It will have seventeen volumes and will be narrated by people from the margins. And the police know what I am doing, so whenever there is a problem, they make an appearance here. It's as if I am in the mafia. And now even I feel a bit homesick when I am not in jail.'

'So Ali, you were in the front line of the protests here?'

'Yes, but not as long as I wanted to. They put me inside early on and only released me recently,' he said with a kind of comic indifference.

'You may have read this news item in yesterday's newspaper – a foreign terrorist who was arrested for helping plant bombs in the City . . .'

'What nonsense! The police must think we are idiots. The City certainly does not need to import foreign terrorists. I know for a fact that there are hundreds of young men ready to commit suicide bombings. The only reason they are not going up in flames is that they have been told to hold back.

After all, we shouldn't use the same tactics as the people we are protesting against.'

'I don't understand. Please explain,' Edwin said.

'Sunni terrorist organizations like al-Qaeda are always talking big talk about how much they hate the West and Israel and other religions . . . but we know all too well that their real targets are the Shias, people of their own religion. We could turn to terrorism too, but then what would be the difference between them and us?'

'But Shias also have terrorist groups of their own?'

'Yes, like Quds in Iran and Hizbollah in Lebanon. I, too, have attended their trainings. But then I learned better and distanced myself.'

'How do they manage to train so many human bombs?'

Ali switched on his computer and clicked on a video. It showed Israeli soldiers torturing Muslim prisoners. 'You don't need eloquent speeches or brainwashing,' he said. 'Simply show an ordinary young man a twenty-minute video like this one.'

'So is it purely revenge?'

'Imagine someone with no relationship to art or literature. Religion is often all they have. It becomes a home for their worst instincts. Tell someone like that there is a special place in heaven for martyrs – why would they not want that? Khomeini gave each person who fought in the Iran–Iraq war a key to wear around his neck. He told them it was the key to heaven's door. The Christian soldiers who fought in the Crusades wore clothes branded with the cross. People in power have always known how to trick the poorest.

'Then, of course, the virgins. Seventy-two beautiful virgins waiting in heaven for each martyr. And this to young men who have never had the opportunity or freedom to talk to a woman face to face. Who wouldn't want to die and get to heaven as soon as possible?

'Once, in Karbala, I narrowly escaped a bomb explosion. I was walking slowly with hundreds of thousands of pilgrims. Suddenly, the earth shook. A sound loud enough to stop hearts passed through me. For five minutes or so I had no idea what was going on. When I opened my eyes, I was lying on the ground. Smoke and screaming everywhere. Then my vision cleared and I saw a street burned to the ground. Bodies in pieces. Vehicles in flames. When I finally came to my senses, I joined the rescue efforts as a volunteer. We eventually found what we believe to be the body of the suicide bomber. Right beside that shattered corpse, we found a strange object. A carefully wrapped penis. Yes, a penis. He knew that he was going to explode into pieces. But nothing must happen to his penis! Because what would be the point of reaching heaven without his penis? Do not laugh. This is how a man's lust can lead him directly to jihad. What amazes me is the innocence of it.'

'So are you saying that there is no basis to yesterday's news?' I asked yet again to confirm.

'Absolutely no basis. That poor guy is caught in a police trap. Look, if you still want confirmation, I'll introduce you to someone. Dr Tahir Rajab. He is the head of the Hizbollah in the City.'

'How . . . when?' Edwin almost fell off his chair. 'We have been very eager to meet someone like him.'

'First, calm down! Obviously, it won't be easy. You are both on the police radar. They know that you are here meeting me. They will be following you wherever you go from here.'

'How can the police know all this?' I asked.

'The masterminds in the police department here are retired from Scotland Yard and the CIA. They inherited the good and bad of those organizations. Let me see if we can arrange a meeting with Tahir.'

'We don't just want to meet him; we want to see his headquarters. Please help us, Ali,' Edwin said.

Ali made a few calls. We could make out arguments and counterarguments and explanations and elaborations. Finally, his face brightened in hope.

'It's going to happen. Go back to your flat now. You will be informed where, when and how.'

He offered us his hand. We were ready to leave, happy and hopeful after a long time. Riyaz was innocent and we were going to meet the head of the Hizbollah!

However, right at the door, Edwin turned to Ali again. 'We haven't spent much time with you, but you still believe in us? How do you know we won't betray you?'

Ali laughed. 'You haven't spent much time with me? Is that what you think? Do you think I would give you a single name just like that? You think you arranged this meeting with me? No, we organized this meeting. From the day you landed in the City, we have had our eyes on you. For now all you need to know is that we have a larger network of spies than the police here.'

Ground Zero

At eight o'clock that evening, a restaurant delivery guy rang our doorbell. 'We haven't ordered anything,' I said, ready to close the door in his face. But he stopped me. 'I am here for you. Here's the message. Fifteen minutes from now, leave your cell phones behind and walk into the street. A car will stop next to you. Ask the driver if it is a taxi or a rent-a-car. If the answer is rent-a-taxi, then and only then get into the car. You will receive the next set of instructions then.' He handed us a parcel of food and walked away as if nothing strange had happened.

We stood there gaping for a minute. Only then did we realize this was what Ali Al Saad had told us to wait for. We got excited. Fifteen minutes later, we were on the street walking helter-skelter. Taxi after taxi passed us by but nothing stopped for us. We had walked roughly a kilometre when a car came to a halt next to us. 'Taxi or rent-a-car?' we asked. 'Rent-a-taxi' came the answer. We got in.

The driver confirmed with us that our phones were at home and that we were not carrying any electronics that could be traced. He drove for a while and finally stopped in front of a shopping mall. 'Go to the theatre on the second floor. Join the line for buying movie tickets. Someone will come and ask you if you want to see *Titanic*. Say no to him. Then he will say, in that case, let's go eat some ice cream. Follow him.'

I couldn't help smiling as I walked into the mall. It was a bit too much like the detective novels I enjoyed reading. Even in this digital age, they used these old-fashioned techniques. Only later did I realize that these cloak-and-dagger moves were used deliberately to avoid the omniscient gaze of technological surveillance.

Eventually we found ourselves following a young man 'for ice cream'. As we stood next to him in the elevator, he said, 'Parking Level 2, Zone B. There's a silver Toyota Yaris waiting for you. The door will be open.' He got off at the next floor.

The car was indeed waiting. The moment we stepped into it, it took off. Beside the driver, on the passenger seat, was a young man. It seemed the entire team was made up of young men in their twenties. The car left the highway and drove in the dark, speeding through different roads and galis. Finally, we arrived at a house and once we got into the car porch, the shutters behind us came down immediately. There was a van there. As soon as we got out of the car, two men came and inspected our bodies. This was not one of those examinations at the airport. They even checked the insides of our underwear and fingered our anuses. Of course, they found my little pen camera, which I had hidden deep inside my pocket. Without a single word, they threw it on the floor and stamped on it, breaking it into tiny pieces. What I lost in that moment was not just ninety-nine dollars and several pictures; it was an old trusted friend. After the inspection, they gave us blindfolds and sunglasses that would cover those blindfolds. 'The next part of our journey will be more dangerous,' they told us. 'I will give you a signal if the police stop us for any checking. You should pretend to be drunk and passed out on the back seat. Do not talk to the police. I will deal with them. And until you finish this encounter and return home, do not try any of the usual smartness shown by journalists. The consequences won't be pretty.'

We were herded into the van. By then I had lost all sense of direction, so I had no idea which way we were driving. When they made us get out and took off our blindfolds, we were standing inside a massive warehouse. Two young men led us through aisles full of boxes and pipes and chains and cement wiring. In the middle of an aisle, they removed some wooden planks from the floor and we descended downstairs into a narrow, dark corridor. We walked through the dark and reached a cellar. It was decked out like a plush multinational corporate office, with every technological convenience you could imagine. Next to the main door I saw the numbers 58:22 inscribed on a metal plaque.

The walls were full of pictures – young men, old men, young women, children. I had seen some of those pictures before on street posters and I guessed they were protesters who had died. After we had waited a while, a man in a dark suit emerged. He was not wearing a tie. It was a typical Iranian outfit. 'Are you Dr Tahir Rajab?' Edwin asked. The answer was no. We were led through a couple more rooms till we reached a small interior room. A man in simple clothes was sitting on the floor reading. He stopped reading and made us sit next to him.

'I am Tahir Rajab. I hear you have been searching for me. What can I do for you?' he asked softly.

This man was a terrorist leader? I was taken aback. I had been expecting a long-haired, turbaned, bearded man, armed with at least one gun.

'A friend of ours was arrested a few days ago. According to the police, he was arranging human bombs for you. We want to know if there's any truth to all this.'

Silently, he got up. We followed him. He showed us around that cellar. It was not just a secret office, it was a training centre. 'We call this our ground zero. This is where the best and smartest of our youth polish their skills after training in Iran and Syria,' Dr Tahir told us.

It was incredible that such a place existed in the City where the police roamed all over and the CID seemed to be at every corner. Three men were practising firing at a target shaped like the human body at the shooting range. There was a section for physical training and another for weapon training. Dr Tahir called one of them and said something. The man placed the palm of his hand on a table. Another man stabbed him with a knife. A bouquet of blood spouted out of the wounded man's palm. But he did not make a single sound, much less cry in pain. Dr Tahir told the men to dress the wound with medicine.

Then Dr Tahir called another man, took his gun from him and gave him an order. He raised his hands in the air and stood in front of Dr Tahir, who pointed the gun at him and commanded him to turn around. 'Allahu Akbar,' Dr

Tahir said and pulled the trigger, but aimed in the opposite direction. The man responded, 'Allahu Akbar,' but did not even flinch at the sound of the gunshot. Dr Tahir returned the gun to the man and took us back inside his room.

I finally realized what kind of people these were. And with that realization came fear.

'These are my students. My wish is their command. And we have hundreds of young men like these. They are waiting for a word from us, ready to die in whatever way we choose. Do you know why I allowed you to see them? To prove that neither I nor my organization need to buy human bombs from other countries. Now do you realize that everything the police are saying about your beloved Riyaz is a lie? Or do you still prefer to believe the police?'

Our eyes had seen what they had seen and there was nothing left to say. As we walked back through the cellar, I noticed the numbers 58:22 again. I wanted to ask what they meant, but didn't.

'So by now you must have figured out that we arranged this meeting with you; you didn't arrange this meeting with us.' Dr Tahir Rajib took us back to his room.

'Yes,' Edwin said in a chastened voice.

'But have you figured out why?'

'I thought about it, but I can't figure it out,' I said.

'Because we have a responsibility to save this innocent man who has been arrested in our name. We attack governments and we will destroy enemies and we will betray anyone who betrays us, but we have nothing against innocents. We believe Riyaz to be innocent.'

'Why are the police hunting him? What did he do to this country?'

'Smart reporters like you should be finding that out, instead of asking an old terrorist like me!' Dr Tahir laughed.

'We know now that you are more informed than us journalists or the police. And I believe that you want to do good.'

'Tell that to the world.'

'How did you become who you are?' I asked, eager to hear all about his life.

'My story is not relevant here. But there is one thing you should know. I did not get to this point out of a desire for revenge. What inspires me is nothing but political dissent. I dissent against the way this world is run. Do you understand me?'

'Yes,' Edwin said.

'Then listen carefully. Your problems are the consequences of this administration's efforts to destroy a book. That book was written by a girl called Sameera. And Riyaz's arrest is also one of those consequences. Sameera didn't write the novel to take revenge on anyone or out of hostility to this administration. She was simply expressing her dissent. But the administration does not understand that. That is why they are intent on destroying it. Is a world without dissent ever possible, friends?'

'But aren't you doing the same thing as the administration, except through violence?'

'No. Our violence is only a smoke signal. The point is to simply show that we exist. We are here. I have read Sameera's book. It is not by any means a book that shows us as good guys. But we believe in her freedom to write that book.'

'But Dr Tahir, you may be alone in having such a progressive perspective. Terrorist organizations around the world are religious fundamentalists. Aren't you whitewashing yourself? I will not hesitate to say this even though we are sitting in your lap. If the administration had not tried to destroy that book, you would have, I am certain,' Edwin said.

'My friend, when has any freedom movement, or to use your mocking words, "terrorist organization", ever issued a fatwa against a book? And we do not follow fatwas issued by governments. That is why Salman Rushdie is still alive, not because he was good at hiding.'

'Dr Tahir, how easily you wash your hands off this. It is true that Rushdie continues to live, thanks to the Western powers that gave him refuge. But what about the hundreds of thousands of lives that are lost because of the religious fundamentalism that people like you encourage?' I asked.

'I will acknowledge that you make a valid point about religious fundamentalism. But know that many of us hold on to religion and become fundamentalists as a last-ditch attempt to hold on to identities that are in danger of being destroyed. Unfortunately, we don't have another identity. The Kurds in Iraq, the Tamils of Sri Lanka, black people in America – they all have their own identity around which they consolidated their struggle. Perhaps if we chose to identify ourselves as Arabs, the world would have accepted us more willingly. But our own internal conflicts prevented us from doing that.' Dr Tahir's voice sounded a bit sad, a bit tired when he said that.

Easy enough to come up with these rationalizations, I thought to myself. What would we even gain by responding to such statements?

'What happened to Riyaz?' I asked.

Double Agent

'Sometimes it feels like you are chasing hares. Things don't make sense. Mysterious incidents take place. There are no explanations. But once you figure out the underlying causes, it all seems so simple. Sameera's novel was not just hers. She didn't even think she was writing a novel. She was simply writing to her friend Javed, sharing her memories and her thoughts. But that novel was not received the way she had hoped it would be. It never saw the light of day as a book. By the time the proofs came out, the thugs in our administration had sniffed their way to it. They went all out to destroy it. They bribed the editors in Pakistan where the book was being published. The book was withdrawn halfway to publication. The remaining proofs were burned. Not even a summary of the book was available. Everyone who could be influenced was influenced. But luckily a handful of books had already gone out as advance copies to reviewers. So they started hunting down each of those copies. We are in the middle of that hunt,' Dr Tahir Rajab paused.

'Where does Riyaz come into this? Did he meet Sameera? Did he get hold of a proof copy?'

'No. Javed, to whom Sameera addresses the letters in the novel, is Riyaz's brother. Javed arrived in the City in the middle of the book's publication. We don't know exactly why, especially since he probably realized that he was putting himself in danger. He went missing as soon as he got here. Riyaz came to the City so he could find Javed and rescue him.'

'And did he?'

'Sadly, no. Instead of rescuing his brother, he simply walked into the trap the police had set for him. He was betrayed by one of his own friends.'

'Vinod?' Edwin and I spoke at the same time.

'No. Jahangir. He came to see you often, didn't he? You couldn't figure out he was from the CID.'

'Please, please tell us how we can rescue Riyaz. We cannot abandon him to the prisons here.' I was close to crying.

'It is not impossible. But it will take some sacrifices.'

'We are ready. Just tell us what to do.'

'If you had gone to the embassy today, one of you would have been arrested. We made arrangements for that, via Abdullah Janahi. But you didn't fall into that trap. That's why we organized this meeting in a hurry.'

'So . . . Abdullah Janahi . . . ?'

'He's a double agent. He works for us and the government, whereas your Faisal works only for us. Since the day you landed, we have been keeping track of your movements through both of them. We know you are not here for any market study. We know you are here on behalf of a novelist.'

'Is there anyone in this city who is not a double agent or a spy?' Edwin asked, annoyed.

'Doubtful. Each and every person in the City is part of a complex network of surveillance. We are all traitors and preys.'

'What were you hoping to accomplish by getting one of us arrested?'

'The world wakes up when a First World citizen gets arrested outside his country. No one cares for a Third World citizen like Riyaz. His fate is to rot in prison. His own government will not give him a second glance. But your arrest will be different. It will become a headline for the international media. We'll take care of the rest. It's a good thing people use social media more than they read newspapers. Even the most ruthless government cannot ignore social media.'

'What do you want from us?'

'Go to your embassies tomorrow. Tell them your lives are in danger and ask them to get involved if anything goes wrong. They will agree because you are journalists. Call a press conference about Riyaz's arrest. There is nothing to worry about. You will be arrested before the conference. We'll operate the rest of the plan, from here and abroad. I promise you won't be in jail very long. And rest assured, you can trust a terrorist's promise. It is not like a government's promise.'

Dr Tahir Rajab rose. So did we.

'What is the significance of 58:22? I have been wondering since we came here,' I asked as we walked out.

'Oh, you don't know? I thought journalists had more general knowledge,' Dr Tahir teased us. 'It refers to the twenty-second verse in the fifty-eighth chapter of the holy Qur'an, Al-Mujadila. The last part of the verse says, "Then surely the party of Allah are they that shall be triumphant."

That is the Hizbollah's motto as well. It is inscribed on our flag.'

'With this underground universe that you have here, you have not been able to shake the government even once. Do you still hope to do that?'

'We have big dreams. Until you dream the impossible, how can you make it possible? Could anyone in the eighteenth century have imagined a France without kings and queens? Fifty years ago, if someone had told you about the European Union or a united Germany, you would have laughed. Someone in 1960 must have dreamed a dream about the dissolution of the Soviet Union. Who could have imagined that Saddam would fall? Or Gaddafi? Someone imagined it though. Entire peoples imagined, dreamed, hoped. No one knew they were imagining or what they were imagining. And thus, we, too, dream dreams, and we have to move towards those dreams. I fear there will be heavy prices to pay on that path. However, we have no option but to go forward.'

We were back in the warehouse by then. Once again I tried to calculate where we might be, but it was impossible.

'You know how they say everything happens for the best? I hope this encounter is also for the best,' I said as we parted from Dr Tahir.

'Everything does not always happen for the best. But what happens at the right time happens for the best. This encounter is indeed one of those. Goodbye. We may not meet again,' he replied.

And then we began our return from those moments of beautiful terror.

Prison Days

The next morning, we went to our embassies and informed them that our lives were in danger. My embassy advised me to leave immediately. It was best not to interfere in the internal affairs of another government, they warned. But I told them I was determined to carry out my duty as a journalist. Finally and unwillingly, they agreed to look out for me if there were any problems. Edwin, too, had a similar experience at his embassy. With the embassies standing behind us, howsoever reluctantly, we declared a press conference, inviting the media to meet us at 4 p.m. at Cafe Radwa. We sent faxes to the newspapers, called television studios, and posted far and wide on Facebook. Then we waited for the police.

They did not come.

Some journalists who had gathered early at Cafe Radwa called us to confirm we were coming. Eventually we had no option but to go to the press conference. Well, then, we decided, let's have a press conference. I wondered if Dr Tahir Rajab had pranked us handsomely. On the way to Cafe Radwa, we called Abdullah Janahi. What concern he had had for us yesterday, how he had exhorted us to be safe. But today, not even a phone call. I could imagine how embarrassed he was – we now knew everything. 'We are going to the press conference. Will the police come there?' I asked him directly. 'I have reported it to the right places,' he responded shortly.

We arrived at Cafe Radwa. The media stakeout we were expecting was not there. Four or five reporters and one measly camera crew – that's all. And clearly, they were all trainees and interns. The kind of junior journalists who get sent out to cover stuff because they have been sitting around too long in the office. We waited for a few more minutes and then began the press conference. We talked about Riyaz's arrest and declared his innocence. We demanded an inquiry and asked for the truth to be revealed. The baby journalists wrote down what we said and didn't ask any questions. Then they drank the coffee we paid for and went back. The two cameramen hung around, slowly putting away their equipment. They stepped out with us. We walked together, making small talk and sharing cigarettes. When we reached our car, they took out their identity cards. 'Do not make any noise. Please get into your own cars. You are now in CID custody,' they informed us in soft voices.

Even though we had expected it, even wanted it, I was paralysed for a minute. God and the CID could take any shape, I realized then. We got into the car as if nothing had happened. They took us to their office where we were questioned by multiple investigators. What had motivated us to hold the press conference? What proof did we have that Riyaz was innocent? Where had we gone yesterday? Who did we meet? We told them about meeting the poet Ali but did not mention Dr Tahir. Where did you go in the evening when you left the flat at 4 p.m.? We stuck to a story about going to the movies and then eating out. It was clear how thoroughly they had been following us. We thought they would let us go after the questioning, but instead they fed us and put us in jail. They refused to let us call our embassies or friends, and we were not allowed to share a cell.

I shared a cell with three locals. Two of them were regular hooligans. They harassed me throughout the night, elbowing me and pinching me and kicking me. The third was an old man. He scolded them in the local language, but they ignored him. The old man spoke excellent Hindi. He told me he had been to Mumbai and Pune and Bengaluru.

Soon I was fed up. What was the point of this imprisonment, what would it achieve? How anxious Shanti and the children would be when they heard of it. I comforted myself by remembering that this was for Riyaz. The hooligans showed some more of their colours. When a policeman came for the routine night check, they hid in one corner. The minute the policeman put his head inside the cell to flash a light around, they pounced on his neck like a wolf catching a hen. He struggled and writhed and pleaded with them, but they wouldn't let go. The old man begged them to stop, but to no avail. Some other policemen came running when they heard the screams. But the hooligans were strong. Finally the policemen negotiated with them. One policeman went out and came back and handed them something; only then did they let go. It was two cigarettes. Later the old man told me it was weed. The hooligans spent that night getting high and harassing me physically.

In the morning, we were taken out for a walk. We were given our daily quota of four cigarettes. Since I did not smoke, I gave mine to the hooligans. They were so happy it was as if they had found a treasure. In all the days that I spent in the jail, that became our agreement. I would give them my cigarettes and they would not harass me. And not only that, they scolded me, 'Surely gentlemen like you should know better than to get imprisoned.'

The old man and I soon became fast friends. One day we were resting under a tree in the prison yard. Out of the blue, he started reminiscing about his life. 'In my childhood and early youth, I never imagined that this country would see such inequality of wealth,' he said. 'A small country. People had more or less the same amount of money. No one was particularly rich or desperately poor. Luxury in those days meant a cycle or a radio or, if you were very lucky, a donkey cart. Even the palace had nothing more than a couple of cars and three or four horse carriages. His Majesty would often visit the markets, talk to us ordinary people, often sitting down to drink kahva with us. Then the world changed, almost overnight, like daylight taking the place of darkness. It was the early 1990s. Till then, this country was like one big village. And that goodness was in every corner of the country. But in the 1990s, some men became rich before our very eyes. We couldn't figure out how they got hold of so much money. Our farmlands suddenly emptied out. We abandoned our date orchards. Huge buildings came up in their place. Our clear streams full of fresh water made way for roads. Our community wells disappeared. You might be wondering – did this tiny Arab nation really have fresh water and community wells? Yes, it did. We did. But as some people became rich, our land became expensive. Real estate became a thing. Where in the old days all the houses used to be similar, now huge mansions started rising in some neighbourhoods. In the other neighbourhoods, the houses stayed the same, while the number of children in those houses grew. Everything in shops was too expensive for ordinary people to even touch. Huge families, two or three generations, crowded together into small houses. With that kind of inequality comes jealousy and resentment and anger. That is what is happening now. It may look like religious conflict and sectarianism and racism. But it's all about money.' He trailed off.

'What brought you to jail?' I asked.

'You know Pune?' he asked.

'Yes, I have been there once.'

'I have been there several times. My son used to study there. Not just my son, almost all the children of ordinary people here go to India for their higher education – either Pune or Bengaluru. He was in his third year of engineering studies when he got into an accident. He was in no shape to be brought here. So he was in hospital there for a long time. We spent a lot of money, went into debt. But the poor boy was unlucky. After three months in the hospital, he died. We had a huge hospital bill to pay before we could even bring his body back here. And I had no more money. You find this hard to believe, don't you? People think Arabs are rich, all they have to do is pump some oil from the well in front of their house and they'll have all the money they need. But this Arab did not even have the money to bring his son's corpse home. I used to be a gardener. Whatever small savings I had from that job, I used to send to him for his studies. And with the accident and hospitalization, I had borrowed from everyone I could ask. But I asked again. Didn't get much out of that. What could I do? I couldn't just abandon my son's body in another country. One day, driven to desperation, my younger son and I walked into a shop, pulled out knives, and asked them to give us money. I flew to Pune with that money. Before we were captured ten days later, I was able to bring his body here for a decent burial. Now I am at peace. I will happily spend the rest of my life in jail. I have fulfilled my duty.'

He stopped there. All the resentment and anxiety I felt about my imprisonment melted, turned into steam, and evaporated out of my spirit. Every day that I would spend with this man was a day to be treasured. I hugged him tightly. He was made of salt and sorrow, and as I hugged him, I felt my own humanity.

The Rescue

In the meantime, the world outside was not standing still. The first news item was published on an online news portal. Under the headline 'Three foreign journalists said to be arrested', it provided precise information about our imprisonment while leaving out our names and details to identify us. Clearly it was inside information. But the mainstream media said nothing. On the other hand, the news spread like wildfire on social media networks, giving rise to fierce guessing games about who was imprisoned and why. All foreign journalists in the City were tagged in the comments. The newspapers began to stir. Even then, they only noted that there seemed to be social media rumours about imprisoned journalists but that it was not possible to confirm these rumours.

Then *Toronto Sunday* called up the embassies and brought it to their attention that three of their representatives were suddenly missing. The embassies sent the complaint over to the foreign ministry and asked for an investigation.

Amnesty International got involved after some anonymous person complained to them. The complaint also stated that there was widespread abuse of human rights all over the country. It was not just these three, several other foreign journalists were trapped in the jail system, the complainant alleged. We are almost certain that the anonymous complainant was Dr Tahir Rajab. I believe that the news portal that published the first news item about us was also under his control.

Finally the police had to abandon the silent treatment and respond. 'We have not arrested anyone,' they tried to explain. 'We have taken a few concerned parties into custody for questioning and they will be released as soon as due process is completed.'

The next day our photos were published online, along with the news that we were not in custody for questioning but detained in secret prisons. 'A forbidden book about the country, several journalists under arrest' ran the headline which clarified that a book, *A Spring Without Fragrance* by a Pakistani woman called Sameera Parvin, was at the centre of the issue. The article also hinted at the government's attempts to destroy the book and voiced the suspicion that the book's editor Javed Ahmed had been detained without due process in the City for more than a year.

Thus it was that the world got to hear about Sameera's

book. The controversy then became about the book. No one had any idea what the book was about and everyone was curious. What did the book contain, they wondered. Could the author please publish the book in some other country, they asked. For a moment it seemed like someone who had read the book would at least offer a two-line summary, but that did not happen. Then the news cycle turned towards other controversies, and the discussion about the book died out. But our imprisonment continued to be in the headlines, because by then some international newspapers had written us up as a scoop. They celebrated their journalistic virtuosity without letting on that the news was first published by an online portal. Amnesty asked the country to respond immediately to the allegations. The government got a little anxious. The home minister asked the police chief to make the problem go away. That too was reported on the news portal. Our ambassadors met with the foreign minister.

We got the news minute by minute, thanks to one of the policemen who was posted to guard us. He was clearly part of the resistance. In fact, he was especially adept at sourcing weed for the two hooligans in my cell.

The authorities succumbed to the pressure. Though they tried to mumble something about court appearances, eventually they simply released us. But owing to a piece of advice by Dr Tahir brought to us by our policeman friend, we were not ready to leave the jail without Riyaz and his brother. The discussions continued. Our embassy officials came to negotiate and they assured us that Riyaz and Javed would be presented in court. That was a huge victory in itself because it was the first time the police acknowledged that Javed was in their custody. On the strength of that promise, we agreed to leave the prison.

They put forward three conditions. We were not to hold any more press conferences in the country. We were not to write anything that maligned the country, even after leaving it. Journalism was not allowed on a tourist visa, so the visas were being cancelled and we were to leave immediately.

We agreed to the first two conditions, but we refused to accept the third till Riyaz and Javed were also released. The truth is that by then we were emboldened. Around the world, we had become media celebrities. We knew how helpless the police in the City were now. They had to accept our counter-offer.

Thus, after three long weeks, we walked out of jail. 'Thanks to your First World passports,' Abdullah Janahi snarked on our heroics. Even while I disagreed with his philosophy, I couldn't help admiring the tactical thinking of Dr Tahir Rajab who had figured out exactly how to take advantage of those passports.

Some of my post-jail experiences were funny. Shanti, of course, called and cried a lot. She wanted to know if they had beaten us up. I told her they had put us up in a three-star hotel suite. 'Well done, boys,' James Hogan said. 'You have done *Toronto Sunday* proud. I want to hug you!'

'Did they ask you about your friends?' That was Bijumon. 'How did you get into all this? You didn't mention me, did you?' I assured him that I had in no way endangered him. 'I might not see you before you leave. Surely you can understand the situation of someone who has to continue living here,' he told me openly. I could not feel sad. Self-preservation is an animal instinct. Who was I to expect more?

An unexpected phone call came from Shahjahan. During my Delhi days, we used to meet regularly at a chai shop and talk politics. I had known that he lived in the City and had meant to call him and renew our friendship. But somehow it did not happen. But when he saw the news and figured out it was me, he managed to find me. He had given up his job at the American embassy and was working in the City as executive editor of a lifestyle magazine. A good life, he told me.

'I called you several times but did not get through,' I lied. Luckily, even some blind shots hit the target. 'I was in India for two months. I just returned,' he told me. 'Take this imprisonment with a sportsman spirit,' he tried to console me. 'This is all part of life. No need to feel sad or suicidal about this stuff.'

'Oh, of course. This is my fourth imprisonment, so I am used to it.' I, too, rose to the occasion. A journalist has to think of his reputation at all times.

But the most surprising call came from Daisy. 'Where were you these last few weeks?' she wanted to know. 'I kept calling and you did not pick up. I was beginning to worry that you left the country without telling me. You heartless man, you could have called me at least once,' she went on and on. How wonderful, I thought, that it was possible to live like that. No, we must all live like her – without seeing anything or hearing anything or knowing anything. 'I went to Hawaii with some friends; it was great. Sorry I couldn't call,' I told her and she swallowed it all.

But she was shocked when I told her I would be leaving in a few days. 'So soon?' she wailed.

'Did you think I was going to spend the rest of my life here?' I asked.

'No, but still . . . Before you go, I need to see you.'

'I am super busy. I'll try.'

'No tries, you have to come.'

I gave in.

There were more surprises in store for me.

Guest

A young man appeared at our apartment door the next day. A stranger. He looked as if he had been wandering the streets, homeless. Jeans and kurta and a small bag on his shoulder. Long unkempt hair and beard. Dazed eyes. I would not have been surprised if we were in Paris or London or New York or Mumbai or Delhi. But in this city, lazy anarchist characters were not allowed. When he assured me that he was here to see us, I invited him in and offered him some coffee. I got him some bread to eat. Some soap to take a shower. A room to rest in. But without so much as introducing himself, he collapsed on the bed and fell asleep.

I called Edwin. He was surprised and, more than that, annoyed. 'Don't we have enough headaches, Pratap?' he asked.

I had no answer to that. Caught in the middle of right and wrong, all I could do was wait for him to wake up and provide an explanation. Unable to pack up our office and arrange our return tickets, Edwin and I sat guard over him, cursing him. We speculated about who he could be, but none of our guesses seemed plausible.

He woke up around four in the afternoon. Ignoring his eager hosts, he walked into the kitchen wondering aloud what there was to eat. He opened the fridge and started helping himself to a fruit. It was like a movie scene.

'Listen, mister, we are tired of this drama of yours. We don't have time to humour you any more. It is high time you told us who you are and what your business with us is,' Edwin exploded.

'Today is a good day. For you and for me. A happy day. Is there a guitar around? I would make beautiful music today. Or a couple of beers? Let's get drunk!' he replied as if he had not heard Edwin.

'Yeah, no, we don't keep this apartment for strangers to come and sing and dance. Get out right now.' Edwin's rage had spilled over to me.

'I'll get out. Today, if possible. Will you get me a ticket to Lahore?' he asked as casually as if he were asking us to call him a taxi. 'Here's my passport.' He held it out.

I took it so that we could at least figure out his name and identity. His name was Yasin Malik. At this point, I did not even have any speculations left.

'Look, you don't understand. We are in the middle of

serious trouble and in no position to enjoy whatever prank you are pulling on us,' I told him.

He laughed. 'So if you are fed up of pranks after three weeks in jail, what must it be like for someone who spent seven months in the insane asylum here? I was joking around to get that insanity out of my head. But I scared you, didn't I?'

'Yasin, who are you?' I asked, fear and amazement fighting within me.

'I am Riyaz's brother.' When he finally introduced himself, I rose without knowing. Not even in my dreams had I expected this visitor.

'I never anticipated this outrage from them,' he went on. 'After shutting me up for months in a hospital room with three guards outside, today they kicked me out as if I were a little puppy. They told me, go, just leave. But where was I to go? I started yelling and screaming. They threw me into a vehicle and brought me to the gate of this building. I kept arguing with them – where are your laws? If someone has overstayed his visa, shouldn't you deport him at least? They laughed at me. Our laws adjust to the person and his status, they told me. What kind of country is this?'

'Was it you that Riyaz came to the City for?' I asked.

'Yes, but Bhai couldn't find me. How could he, looking in jail for someone in the insane asylum?'

'How did you hear that Riyaz was here?'

'Oh, these policemen here are such jokers. They told me everything that was going on. They enjoyed seeing the anxiety I felt when I heard all that.'

'So Sameera's novel was written for you?'

'Yes, that was a twist in my fate.'

'But we thought the novel was written for someone called Javed. So how did Yasin get into all this?' Edwin asked.

'Oh, that's a really funny story.' Yasin smiled. And though he was enjoying narrating it to us, it was not a happy story, the story of how Yasin became Javed.

Fake ID

'One day long ago, I was so bored out of my wits that I came up with a silly prank. Have you noticed how you get several emails every day from strangers? So many of them are forwarded emails, often forwarded multiple times, perhaps by people in office jobs sitting at their computers without too much work to occupy them. Often these emails contain quotes from famous people or random greetings or Sufi verses, you know the kind I mean. Or maybe they are some promotions or discount offers. The kind of emails that get forwarded only to disappear with the help of your delete button. But that day, I decided to have some fun. Who are these people forwarding emails? Are they connected to each other or did they just happen to end up in the chain because of the "select all" option in our online address books? People don't realize that they are not just forwarding random emails, but also the email addresses of their friends and acquaintances. I decided to try out an experiment.

'I chose a forwarded email which contained a beautiful

Sufi poem. The mail was originally sent by someone called Javed Gulum. Between him and me, there were three or four friends who had forwarded his email.

'I made a new email id for myself with the name Javed Gulum. Then I looked at the original email he had sent and chose about fifteen addresses, all seemingly belonging to women. "Hi, how are you?" I wrote to those fifteen addresses. "Long time, no news at all. Hope you are doing fine. May God bless you. Javed." That was it. An ordinary email. And to make it seem like the email was truly coming from the other Javed, I made sure my fake email address was similar to his real email address. There was only one letter different between the two email addresses. His was javed.ak101@hotmail.com and mine was javed.ek101@hotmail.com. One would have to look closely to notice the difference.

'I hit send. It was like flinging thousands of fishing lines into the ocean. I did not hope to achieve much. It was a prank! I just wanted to know if anyone would bite. The first few days I would check that inbox daily, but no one wrote back, and I lost interest. Then one day long after, I checked and found an email there. It looked like it was from a former girlfriend or at least someone very close to him. Clearly she had mistaken me to be her beloved friend. I could not help but respond as Javed. That was the beginning. She replied to me, I mean to Javed. And I replied to her. Soon we were corresponding regularly. From her first few emails, it was obvious she was writing from the City. I became curious about her life and I started enjoying this strange, sideways glimpse into the City. Only later did I realize how grave things had become.

Her words pulsed with life, a life no one knew much about. I couldn't bear to have them die in my inbox. So I collected them and gave them to my brother. Riyaz bhai works for a newspaper and he was the one who got the idea of developing it into a book. When I told Sameera about it, she was hesitant. But I pressured her and finally she agreed. Then her writing became deeper.

'Of course, I wanted to tell her on various occasions that I was not Javed. But by then I also knew that I had become a drowning woman's straw. By then we were far gone in our publication journey as well. Bhai prepared a proof and we sent her a copy.

'The next message from her said that she was under house arrest. I was terrified. I wondered if I had pushed her into this danger. I wrote to her that I was coming to the City to help her. She wrote forbidding me from coming. That was the last message I ever got from her.

'Around then I heard that a band in Lahore was coming to the City for a concert. I decided to join them. I am not a bad singer and luckily they were looking for a vocalist. Thus, disguised as a musician, I arrived in the City in search of Sameera.'

'And?' I couldn't control my eagerness.

'The news that greeted me was that Sameera had left the City. But I didn't believe it for a minute. She would have told me if she had. I knew she was somewhere here. So I asked a friend of my brother's, a man called Jahangir, for help. By then it was time for the band to return. But I couldn't think of leaving without seeing Sameera. I had no option but to ask the band to leave without me. One day I even went to her house, but no one there would tell me anything. But I made a mistake along the way. I trusted Jahangir. I told him about the novel. Little did I know that snake was a government spy. Within three days, I was in jail. Then came the interrogation. All day and all night. I couldn't withstand it, I admit freely. It was from me that the police here heard about the novel and its publisher. Sameera herself probably didn't know all the details I gave them. And after I had told them everything, they did not deport me or put me in jail. They admitted me in the insane asylum. I didn't understand why. It was another inmate, an Indian man called Basheer, who told me the reason. They wanted to destroy my memory and muddy my brain. He told me how to resist it too. I followed his instructions, and from day one, I pretended to have gone insane. They gave me electric treatments, injections, medicines every day. I was able to withstand it only by holding on to my strong spirit. Otherwise by now I would have been fully insane. As it is, they succeeded. I don't remember a single sentence from Sameera's novel. The memory of the novel is like a fog in my brain. Do not for a moment think they released me because you went to jail or because Amnesty demanded reports. They released me because they knew that the novel had finally disappeared completely, not just from printed pages but from human memory itself.'

'So Yasin, do you think every copy of the book has been completely eradicated from the surface of the earth?'

'Yes. Otherwise they would not have delivered me to you. They know now that I can give you nothing. But what I am

really worried about is what they are doing to Riyaz bhai. We
have to get him out before they destroy him the way they
destroyed me.'

'And Sameera?'

'Sameera is still a sad riddle for me. Is she in jail or is she
free? Is she in the City or abroad? I don't know. But I will find
out. Even if she is underground, I will track her down. For
you, she is a character in a story. For me, she is my beloved.
A beloved I found from far away. I cannot lose her. As my
name is Yasin, I pledge this – I will find her.'

Surprise Gift

Though it was Jahangir who brought us the news and we
didn't know whether to trust it or not, what we got to know
that evening brought some peace to our hearts.

'Our Riyaz was presented in court today. The judge ordered
him to be deported. If you can get his flight ticket, they will
release him tomorrow. I have already informed Abdullah
Janahi, so now I am letting you know as well. Do the needful.'

I marvelled. Not that it was he who called to tell us Riyaz
was free. I marvelled at the way he said 'our Riyaz'. By now
Jahangir was aware that we knew how he had stabbed us in
the back. Yet how blithely he had called us up. Or was this
business as usual for him? All in a day's work. I did mine,
now you do yours.

We called Abdullah Janahi right away. 'I am on it,' he said.
'The ticket is already with the jail authorities. The flight is at

three in the morning tomorrow. They will take him directly from the jail to immigration and only then will they unlock the handcuffs. There is no need for you to come and see that.'

'Would it be possible to get one more ticket on that flight?' I asked and explained Yasin's situation.

'This is nothing compared to what goes on here,' Abdullah Janahi said. 'Okay, ask him to get ready. I'll arrange the ticket.'

We worried that with every passing minute, the authorities might change their minds and come for Yasin. But nothing happened. Abdullah arrived at the right time with the ticket in hand. We took Yasin to the airport and paid a small fine at the immigration counter. That was all. They sent Yasin through immigration and into the airport as if he were a tourist leaving after a nice vacation. Abdullah confirmed that Riyaz too had cleared immigration. The moment we heard that, our shoulders relaxed, our backs straightened, our heads cleared. Now we, too, could leave. We had done our duty. We celebrated that night by bar-hopping and getting drunk and finally falling into delicious, deep sleep after a long time.

Perumal's call woke me up in the morning. 'Pratap, if you are not busy, I would like to come and pick you up this morning. Daisy is very eager to see you and I don't want to disappoint her.'

Before I could respond, he disconnected, like Daisy. I had no option but to go with them. I was getting ready half-heartedly when Edwin came over, joy radiating from him.

'I just got my ticket home, Pratap,' he said. 'I will leave tonight. And Abdullah Janahi said your flight is tomorrow night.'

'So you will just abandon me and I'll have to spend the entire day alone in the City,' I said glumly.

'Look who is talking!' Edwin said. 'Think of this as an opportunity to catch up with your many friends here.'

'I'll manage somehow.' I smiled. 'It must be my fate to arrive first and leave last.' Deep inside, I felt sad. Edwin would leave with this assortment of facts and histories and interviews and anecdotes we had gathered. They would be reinvented as a novel. Perhaps some day I would read it. Would I ever meet Edwin again? The time we had spent together was indeed brief and our friendship was destined to be brief. Yet, we had shared so many joys and sorrows in that brief time and this brief friendship had grown deep roots in my heart. I felt afraid of my day of loneliness in the City.

By then Perumal was downstairs. Now it was Edwin's turn to be annoyed that I would not be around on his last day, but I assured him that I would return soon.

'Forgive me, Pratap,' Perumal said as he drove. 'I know what you have been going through. But I didn't have the courage to call you or find out more. I worried about falling into a police trap. So I didn't tell Daisy about it either. Not because she would worry, but because it would increase her admiration and love for you. So please don't tell her anything. Just make up some excuse for leaving the City. That is the safest thing. Trust me, no one will be happier than me when you leave.'

'If you are so suspicious, why did you come and get me? Why are you taking me to Daisy? Didn't we decide not to see each other again?' I asked without mincing words.

'Me suspicious of you? Not at all. Once you gave me your word that day, I had no more suspicions. I know you are a gentleman. I am taking you to Daisy because she desires it so intensely. I want her to see how I fulfil her every desire. There's only one way to chain a woman to you and that is by giving her the impression that you will fulfil her every desire, her every whim. I will do anything to keep Daisy.'

'You are something else, Perumal. I don't know anyone more devious than you,' I said, not caring if it hurt him.

'No, you don't know anyone more honest than me. That's what you mean. While the rest of you live inside half-truths, I live a life of realism.' He would not give up.

I was a surprise gift from Perumal to Daisy. She had no idea I was coming. The moment she saw me, her mouth fell open in amazement.

'Today is Daisy's birthday. What better gift can I give her than the company of a good friend like you?' Perumal said, holding Daisy close.

'Perumal, you truly love me.' She kissed him while I watched.

'Well, why don't you old friends catch up while I make a brief appearance at work. I'll return for lunch and we'll eat together and then part ways. What do you think, Pratap? Isn't this the best way to celebrate Daisy on her birthday?' Perumal asked with a mischievous glint in his eyes.

'Yes, yes, but today is Edwin's last day. I need to go back sooner than that,' I said.

'Well, in that case, leave whenever Daisy is done with you. So this is goodbye then. We might not see each other ever again.'

And Perumal walked out of my life. I watched him go thinking about all the little mysteries and complexities of that strange man.

Daisy brought some noolappam and chicken stew for me to eat and force-fed it all to me. She sat next to me chatting away, eating from my plate, finishing off my leftover tea. We remembered the old days. She was a bottomless vessel of old memories and could have talked all day, but I insisted on leaving soon.

'Let me get ready,' she said, going to her bedroom. I stepped into Perumal's library and browsed through his books, reading titles, smelling pages.

Daisy reappeared looking exactly the same. She had not changed. Her hair was loose, and her eyes were wild. I felt afraid of them. She came and stood behind me and I felt her breath on my shoulder. Then she embraced me.

'Pratap ... I have always loved you. I could not love anyone else the way I love you. All these years, you were always with me, in every moment, in every breath. I never thought we would meet again or that I would be able to share my feelings with you. Only God knew how intensely I desired that. Now I realize that even the most impossible dream can come true if one wants it badly enough.'

I did not reply. I knew it would wound her if I moved out of her embrace, so I stood there silently.

'Pratap, you are leaving tomorrow. We might never see each other again. In fact, it might be best if we don't. But I want to fill these few sweet moments of our togetherness and live on their memories. Can I ask you for a gift before you leave?'

She waited for me to respond. And then waited some more. Minutes passed. The wait continued. When the coldness of my response finally penetrated her, her arms around me loosened. She disentangled herself from the embrace.

Then she left the room to get ready quickly. 'Let's go,' she called out to me.

In the car, she turned into the old Daisy. She talked non-stop about our Delhi days, our college life, about the friendships and romances of those times. But the conversation was like the final twitch of a lizard's tail – there was no life left in it. Her heart was broken and my mind was numb.

We said goodbye mechanically. She drove off without seeing me wave.

Forgive me, Daisy. It's not that I don't understand you. But my love knows it has to wait for Jasmine.

Revelation

I was standing in the check-in line at the airport counter when I saw Doctor Mamu standing in front of me.

'Oh Canadawala, what a surprise.' His eyes bloomed like flowers. 'Everything worked out. We are migrating to your country.' He introduced his wife.

I, too, was surprised. I had not actually believed that he would leave this country and migrate to Canada.

We got seats next to each other so we could talk more.

After we cleared security and were waiting for the boarding announcement, I said to him, 'I am pretty sure you never told us the real reason you wanted to leave this country. Is this a good time to tell me the truth?'

For a moment, he considered it, softly wringing his hands. 'Wait till we are in the air. Right now, we are still on His Majesty's soil.'

I didn't insist. I knew that before this trip ended, he would tell me. It was on the second leg of our journey, on the flight from Istanbul to Toronto, that he finally revealed all.

'All the reasons I told you before – they are all valid. But there is something else, an incident that haunts me beyond anything. It was the last day of the protests. They brought to the hospital a policeman who had been wounded in Pearl Square. He, too, was a Pakistani like me. Someone had driven a car over him, but his wounds were not fatal. I could have saved him. But I was not allowed to treat him. There was a lot of pressure from our top executives to let him die. When they saw that I was resistant, they locked me up in a room in the hospital.

'On that day, eight protesters had been shot to death. That is, eight martyrs for the protest movement. The government needed at least one martyr to counter that. So they deliberately sent that poor policeman to his death. And I was ruthlessly prevented from fulfilling my duty of attending to a wounded man. My soul has never recovered from that. That one incident made a mockery of the integrity with which I had led my life till then. How could I continue to live in such a damned place? That is why I am leaving.'

I had nothing to say to that. I closed my eyes and sat still for a long time.

Doctor Mamu tapped me on the shoulder. I opened my eyes. He took a book out of his bag and gave it to me.

I stopped breathing for a few seconds. The book was *A Spring Without Fragrance*.

'Doctor Mamu, where did you get this book from?'

'A policeman gave it to me secretly. He said it was a banned book or a secret book or something. I wasn't very interested. But you are a journalist. Maybe you'll find it useful.'

He spread his blanket around him and fell asleep peacefully. I opened the book and turned to the last section.

Epilogue

The path to this book was a strange one. I never dreamed of writing a novel like this. Our internationally bestselling writer abandoned the novel project; perhaps our research did not inspire him. When Edwin told me about it over email, I felt bitter for days. We had given so much of our life to that novel. All that for nothing. But then I remembered something Daisy had said. It was just a foolish dream of hers, but like an oracle from beyond the mountains, her words returned a sense of possibility to me. I started dreaming about writing my own novel. When I told Edwin, he supported it fully. I planned to write it in English. But there was one problem. According to the contract between *Toronto Sunday* and the writer, we were not allowed to use any of the material we collected in the City for the next five years. Since we had been paid regularly as per contract, I could not break it. Edwin suggested a way. 'Why don't you write it in your regional language? That won't bother our writer in any way.' But then there was another problem. It had been many years since I had left Kerala. I could not rely on my Malayalam.

Around that time, my sister introduced me to a writer she had gone to university with. I sought his help as a ghostwriter. He had to say no because he was in the middle of writing his own novel. So he introduced me to a writer friend of his. And miracle of miracles, it was none other than the writer I had met in Jasmine's city, the one whose book I had thrown in the trash because I had immediately disliked him. We met again and again; we couldn't see eye to eye. I was so furious with him that I gave him Sameera's book and told him mockingly, 'This is the book you could have written.'

But that turned out to be a good move. Sameera's book touched his heart. Perhaps it was his guilty conscience. He asked me for permission to translate it. I had secured translation rights to that book from Riyaz. So I told the writer that if he was willing to ghost-write my novel, he could translate *A Spring Without Fragrance*. There were long negotiations. We shared our dreams and ideas. Slowly the ice between us thawed. I agreed that he would write his own novel using my ideas and material. It was a small tribute to Daisy who had loved me and longed for me. In return, I gave him the right to translate Sameera's novel.

He set forth three conditions. First, it would be a liberal translation. Secondly, the novel would have a different name from Sameera's book. And thirdly, if the novel was published, I would arrange for him to see the Niagara Falls.

I let Riyaz know about the first two conditions and he was willing to go with them. And I agreed to fulfil the third condition. Thus it was that Sameera's book was published in Malayalam as *Mullappoo Niramulla Pakalukal*.

Words cannot convey the affection and gratitude I now feel for that writer who not only helped me write this novel but also translated Sameera's novel beautifully. And I offer you, dear reader, Sameera's novel which tantalized me and turned upside down my life in Jasmine's city.

juggernaut

THE APP
FOR INDIAN
READERS

*Fresh, original books tailored for
mobile and for India. Starting at ₹10.*

juggernaut.in

1

CRAFTED
FOR MOBILE
READING

*Thought you would never read a book
on mobile? Let us prove you wrong.*

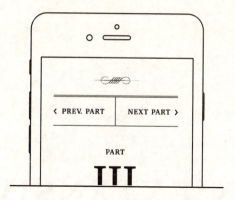

Beautiful Typography

The quality of print transferred
to your mobile. Forget ugly PDFs.

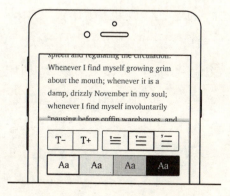

Customizable Reading

Read in the font size, spacing
and background of your liking.

AN EXTENSIVE LIBRARY

Including fresh, new, original Juggernaut books from the likes of Sunny Leone, Praveen Swami, Husain Haqqani, Umera Ahmed, Rujuta Diwekar and lots more. Plus, books from partner publishers and loads of free classics. Whichever genre you like, there's a book waiting for you.

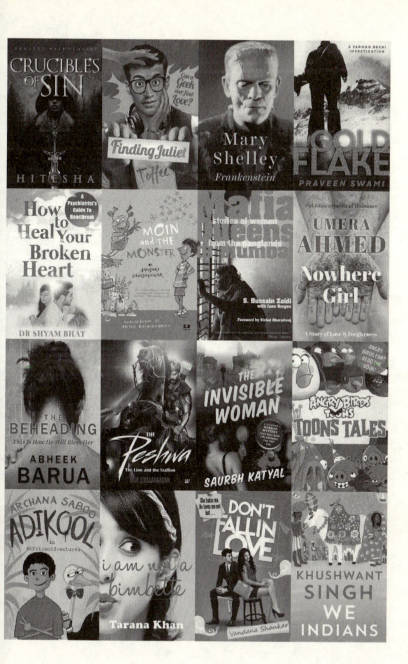

DON'T JUST READ; INTERACT

We're changing the reading experience from passive to active.

Ask authors questions

Get all your answers from the horse's mouth.
Juggernaut authors actually reply to every
question they can.

Rate and review

Let everyone know of your favourite reads or
critique the finer points of a book – you will be
heard in a community of like-minded readers.

Gift books to friends

For a book-lover, there's no nicer gift than
a book personally picked. You can even
do it anonymously if you like.

Enjoy new book formats

Discover serials released in parts over
time, picture books including comics,
and story-bundles at discounted rates.
And coming soon, audiobooks.

4

LOWEST PRICES & ONE-TAP BUYING

Books start at ₹10 with regular discounts and free previews.

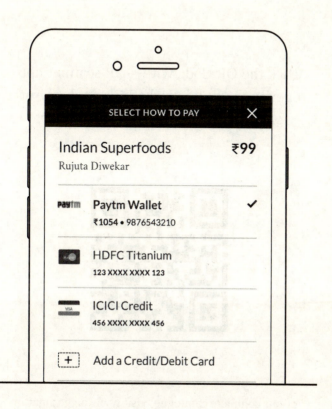

Paytm Wallet, Cards & Apple Payments

On Android, just add a Paytm Wallet once and buy any book with one tap. On iOS, pay with one tap with your iTunes-linked debit/credit card.

Click the QR Code with a QR scanner app or type the link into the Internet browser on your phone to download the app.

For our complete catalogue, visit www.juggernaut.in
To submit your book, send a synopsis and two
sample chapters to books@juggernaut.in
For all other queries, write to contact@juggernaut.in